Cracked!

A Magic iPhone Story

Janine A. Southard

Cover Design by James, GoOnWrite.com
Editing by Jen Levine
Copyediting by Rachel Lynn Solomon

ISBN: 978-1-63327-018-3

Morena's new iPhone double-buzzed on the bathroom counter, perilously close to the washbasin.

"I didn't know you'd decided to use this one exclusively," Suzyn said, hoping Morena would donate the older Samsung to her. Unfortunately for Suzyn, that would never happen. Not only did Morena prefer her familiar old phone for work purposes, but she hadn't actually noticed she'd transitioned to the new iPhone.

The iPhone was just so handy. Somehow, it was always there, as though it were tethered to Morena's subconscious. Why, it was almost like it had followed her to the bathroom.

Morena shrugged and thumbed the unlock with her left hand while her right fished for the liquid eyeliner she knew was somewhere in her makeup kit. Why was it that the thing she wanted always shifted to the bottom? "I'm just gonna check Mãe's location..."

There might have been an end to that sentence, but she was distracted by the hunt for the all-important eyeliner.

...and by the bright green heart that filled the screen. That was not the regular dashboard, nor was it the friend-finding app.

Suzyn giggled and knocked their elbows together over the laminate counter showing water stains from the '80s, '90s, and today. "If you can't handle an iPhone, maybe you should just give your oversized thumbs a rest."

For my husband,
who plays a part I like to call,
"cheerleader with a whip."

Acknowledgements

I owe so many thanks for making this book everything it could be. In chronological order, I thank my parents for listening to me ramble about the previous iterations of this story, starting in 2006, I think. I thank my spouse, who supported and soothed me whenever I got despondent because the book wasn't working (and who later helped me figure out the solutions to plot problems, suggested Luiza's operations research difficulties, and was my very first reader). Shout-out to Alex Cook who suggested that Morena should work at Starbucks HQ instead of Amazon/Microsoft, and then explained why. After the book was in its later drafts, I have to acknowledge all my wonderful beta readers (in alphabetical order), some from my mailing list and others because they love me: Taryn Albright, Ian Brown, Jess Downs, Chuck Howerton, Rachel Lynn Solomon, Tiffany Lutnick-Coleman (who hated it the first time), and Sarah Mendonca (who still doesn't like it much).

I would be lost without my Kickstarter backers. Those wonderful people made this book possible (so that I could pay my editor, cover designer, and all the other people whose work went into making this a high-quality book). In particular, I'd like to thank the following backers for their contributions:

Gretchen Bauman
Mike Kenyon
Melissa Pagonis
Alan S.
Astrid Utrata
Anonymous

Oh, and I can't forget: huge thanks go out to the mysterious gentleman who heard me struggling and kindly imparted all of his knowledge about purchasing cocaine in the city of Seattle. (Sometimes, being a writer means you need to know the mundane aspects of illegal things, and there's rarely a good place to get your answers. This time, there was a good place. So, thank you, anonymous man with the gauge earrings and friendly demeanor!)

Chapter One
Hello, Moto. Errr. Hello, Apple?

This is the story of a girl and her iPhone. No, that's not quite right. This is the story of a middle-aged statistician and her best friend. Though she didn't consider herself middle-aged. And the best friend was more of a roommate-with-whom-she'd-developed-a-friendship.

And this description completely ignores the 6,000-year-old elf with whom the woman and her best friend enjoyed story gaming.

So let's try this again.

This is the story of a woman who wished to find love, but who would rather play story games than actively look for it. Especially in the wake of a horrid break-up six months before from a man had who never sent her a single gift.

Until now.

That man, who is otherwise unimportant to this narrative, had no sense of timing.

He had, foolishly perhaps, expected something different from their three-year relationship. He'd been after crazy spontaneity and over-sexualized Carnivale stereotypes from his Brazilian-American girlfriend, whereas she'd merely expected companionship and a proposal.

So when the breakup arrived instead of a ring box, it came as quite a shock to Morena (for that was the woman's name). And on *this* day, when she saw a package on her kitchen table sporting his return address (likely carried inside the night before by her staggeringly drunk roommate), she almost took it down, unopened, to the recycling bin in her apartment building's garage.

But she didn't.

In a fit of whimsy disguised as righteous fury, she wielded a utility knife and tore into the obviously reused box with *Amazon.com* emblazoned on the side. She slashed at the cardboard and threw packing peanuts all over her matted beige carpet, which had witnessed many a discarded packing peanut before.

The carpet didn't mind, but it would have worried about usually sensible Morena's mental state if it had the kind of mind that knew how to worry. But it was a carpet, so it didn't.

If this book were a movie, the non-trash-bound contents of the box would now be surrounded in a soft yellow glow. There would be swelling music whose pulsing undertone would let the viewer know that this, *THIS*, was a significant moment. But since this is a book (and, for Morena, this was real life), these things did not happen. Instead, she got a paper cut from the crumpled newsprint that cushioned a very ordinary-looking iPhone.

It is perhaps sacrilegious in this day and age to refer to an iPhone as *ordinary*. For Morena lived, as many do, in Seattle, Washington, USA, Earth, Milky Way Galaxy during the first half of the 21st century. And during this time period, new iPhones were referred to by such words as "sexy" and "groundbreaking" and "indispensable." Mostly "sexy." To call one ordinary would be like calling Mata Hari or James Bond or Cleopatra *some old dead person.*

For someone who was usually connected to trends, from her Louboutin shoes to her barely there diamond necklaces, Morena had managed until this moment to avoid the sexy iPhone revolution. Now, though, Apple could claim one more household in its quest for 100 percent market domination.

She plucked her prize from its newspapery confines and turned on the sexy, ordinary-looking iPhone. If she hadn't turned it on, she might have managed to avoid the unpleasant moments upcoming in this novel. She might have repackaged it in another, less damaged, box and scribbled RETURN TO SENDER all over.

But she did turn it on. And she saw that the home screen had only one icon, and that glossy, round-cornered, green icon sat dead center.

This was very strange for an iPhone, or for an iDevice of any kind. They usually overflowed with too many apps for a sensible person to use, forcing the owner to create ever-more-ridiculous categories until finally giving up and purging a few, only to realize those apps would have come in handy for leveling a friend's DIY table or translating the back of a packet of potato chips in the grocery store's international foods aisle.

The glossy green icon sported a large, beveled heart. It practically screamed *romance.* Or perhaps *bizarre panic button.*

Morena pressed it, and the app opened with a kitschy chime, expanding to fill the screen with its green branding. A slot machine slid in from the left as though the app had been designed by a C-list executive new to PowerPoint in the early '90s.

As a background process, and unbeknownst to Morena, the device synced itself to her life. It swiped her passwords and added all her contacts. For this was a magical iPhone, and it attached itself to our heroine like facial hair to a male hipster in Movember.

She rotated the phone to landscape mode in order to better see the user interface. The slot machine had five columns, as follows:

The leftmost column offered spinning choices of number ranges: 12–15, 16–17, 18–20, 21–26, 27–35, 36–46, 47–55, 56–65, 66–75, 76–90, 91–201, 202–364, 365–572, 573–700, 701–1500, 1501–4000, 4001+. Morena had to scroll to see them all.

The second column offered financial situations: Broke, Hand-to-mouth, Comfortable enough, Comfortable, Lucky, Crazy rich.

The center column only had one option: a bright green heart. Some people, like Morena, might have called it *pond-scum green*, but it was really more the color of antifreeze that has eaten through the radiator hoses and then puddled beneath a 1982 Toyota Corolla (hatchback) on a light gray garage floor, a description very few people can easily picture, so this book will allow *pond-scum green* as an acceptable, mainstream substitute.

The fourth column suggested: Male, Female, Both, Neither, It's complicated.

The fifth, and final, column offered: Single, Dating, In a relationship, Engaged, Married, Polyamorous.

Beneath each column was a picture of a lock. Not a modern lock, like the locker-style ones used in the Urbanspoon app, though it did feel very like Urbanspoon (not that Morena would know, since she had yet to explore other iPhone apps), but more rounded on the bottom, suggesting something antiquated that would never belong on the bike storage boxes for Park & Ride commuters.

The maker of this mysterious slot-machine app had clearly realized that *antique* translated to *romantic* among people searching for love. Readers will agree that this is a ridiculous conceit because *love conquers all* is a recent invention. To marry for love, prior to the 1800s and even during much of that century, was lucky but unlikely. To fall in love at all, before then, was actually an unfortunate event because odds were good the couple would be ripped apart once a more sensible match was established by parents or necessity.

But the app maker prized his target market more than he believed in historical accuracy.

A line of text below the slot machine told Morena to *Shake to find your perfect mate.* Below the line of text was a button that just said *Randomize.*

Though she may have been new to iPhone culture, Morena knew that affecting one's iPhone by shaking it in one's hand was The Best Feature. So she shook, and the slot-machine's rollers spun until they shuddered to a stop with a loud *ding ding DING!*

Across the top of the screen scrolled: *Rest easy! Your perfect mate is on their way to you.*

Whatever. Morena knew finding love wasn't that easy. It

hadn't even told her who this mystery mate might be.

Back in their shared single bedroom, Morena's roommate made a vaguely unhappy noise and slammed a pillow over her kink-curled head. Suzyn, the roommate, was NYC-raised and therefore familiar with city noise, but not inside her own apartment at this time of morning (where "this time of morning" was any time before she was ready to get up, in the tradition of recent college grads everywhere). It wouldn't have bothered Suzyn at all if Morena cursed in three languages or drove a backfiring car beneath her window. But a *ding*-ing iPhone was just not acceptable.

As Morena had suspected, Suzyn had indeed been drunk the night before when she'd tripped over the package in the hallway. She'd been more than just drunk. She had shot up a drug cocktail between songs at karaoke before somehow getting home to their one-bedroom apartment in Lower Queen Anne, a trip that necessitated at least one bus transfer or some very shady ridesharing because, as Morena knew full well, Suzyn certainly did not have the kind of money a taxi would require. If she had had that kind of cash, she wouldn't be sharing a one-bedroom apartment.

But if Suzyn was attempting to convey her irritation at the iPhone's noise via the dramatic pillow over her head, then the gesture went unnoticed; for Morena was in the main room and could neither see nor hear Suzyn's protests at the loud *dings*. No, Morena just laughed at the silly scrolling message until she noticed the time, at which point she slipped into her wool (Prada) pea coat and red-soled shoes, grabbed her tote bag and ORCA card, and speed-walked to the downtown-bound bus stop where she could catch the RapidRide D with both the new iPhone and her regular Samsung in her pockets.

The morning bus was standing room only, as commuter buses usually are no matter whether one rides them in Seattle or New York, Tokyo or Los Angeles. The only difference is that no one *wants* to ride a bus in Los Angeles, largely because the buses don't run on time and have a disproportionate number of knife-wielders; plus, they often truncate in complete violation of their posted schedules.

Since this story takes place in Seattle, however, the buses were reliable and often full of affluent commuters like Morena who, in fact, owned a car and rented a parking space for it next to her apartment building but preferred the speed of the RapidRide (even if she told acquaintances she cared more about the environmental repercussions than about the convenience; all good Seattleites cared about the environment, so finding a reason to tell people about conservational efforts was a badge of honor. This was how plastic bags, desirable for storage and trash removal, found themselves pushed out of supermarkets in favor of less sanitary canvas bags that everyone already owned too many of and nearly always forgot at home, at which point they needed to buy new ones, thus adding to their never-ending piles of forgotten canvas bags).

On this particular trip, more people than usual jostled Morena's body. By the time the RapidRide D had turned into the downtown RapidRide C, Morena had been fallen on, bumped into, nudged, and stumbled over no less than seventeen times by a mishmash of passengers wearing everything from torn jeans to suits and all sporting the ubiquitous ear buds. Each touch had been preceded by a muffled *ding* from Morena's coat pocket, which, of course, no one could hear over their podcasts and MP3s.

Only slightly rattled (for she was used to *some* touching during her daily commute but still appreciated the personal-space bubble inherently understood by commuters), Morena disembarked and walked southward through Pioneer Square, a place much less dangerous in the early morning light than people gave it credit for.

As she passed the south end of CenturyLink Field, she was joined by a tall aging hippie whose gray hair clumped greasily below his shoulders. He wore a tie-dye t-shirt underneath his ratty Army/Navy Surplus jacket.

"Hey there, pretty lady," he said as he fell in step beside her.

While the man in question *did* enjoy making conversation with strangers, he wasn't prone to walking heavens-knew-where with them. And yet, something about this one caught his attention. Her right pocket, in particular, sang the siren song of socialism and SUVs.

Morena shied away, walking dangerously close to the curb in an effort to create distance between them, and ignored him. Even if she hadn't been conditioned to ignore creepy men on the street who called her *pretty lady* and demanded her attention, even if she didn't have places to be, she still wouldn't have talked to him. His hair was vile, and she had never felt comfortable talking to new people anyway. (This had been a problem when she was eleven and her mother had shipped her off to visit her grandparents in São Paulo, whom she'd never met before stepping off the plane.)

The aging hopeful tried again. "Aww, c'mon, sweetheart. Talk to an old man for a minute."

He didn't really think of himself as an "old man," but she was walking much faster than a person in spiked heels should be able to move. (At least, so experience told him. The one time he'd tried drag back in '85 had been a disaster as far as footwear was concerned, and he hadn't cared to practice again, swearing that he could feel the blisters forming on his pinky toes after only two minutes.) If he wanted to chat, he needed her to slow down.

Morena had been raised to respect her elders, so she sighed and slowed. "Can I help you, sir?" She ran a nervous hand through her dark brown hair with its subtle golden highlights.

Shrugging, he shoved his hands into his pockets. "Just wanted to get to know you better," he mumbled.

Morena thought that was a pretty weak reason to stop a stranger on the street at morning-commute hour. However, she *could* believe he was simply lonely. Who knew why this stranger spent time in SoDo at the start of the workday? His clothing betrayed his unemployed status, so he had to have an alternate motivation, and maybe it was loneliness. If he'd been across the lake in Redmond, she'd have pegged him for a computer programmer. SoDo, however, was for service, industry, or super-corporate jobs. There was no room for a messy hippie.

"I need to get to work," she said.

Acting as though she hadn't tried to extricate herself, he ignored her words and used his favorite pick-up line. It was so philosophical, so deep and engaging. It always attracted the right sort of woman. Morena wasn't his usual type, but he couldn't let that keep him from trying. That would be *discrimination*. "We should shower together," he declared.

Not if it was the last shower on Earth. Morena rooted around in her bag for any relevant prop. "I need to take this call."

He sped up to match her steps. He'd met a woman like this at a concert once, uptight until he showed her that a good friend and a good joint could relax anyone. "When two people want to know each other better, they should always shower together. It's the perfect start to a friendship." He bounced on holey-sneakered feet, warming to his topic. "It lets you see everything a person usually hides, gives you perspective about a person's true self."

They were closing increasingly quickly on the Starbucks at the corner of 1st and Walker, Morena's usual morning caffeination station. "Excuse me," she said and ducked in the door so fast that he would have to double back if he wanted to join her.

Worried he might try to follow, she slipped past the customers waiting in line, trying her best not to jostle or upset them. Gracefully, she wended her way to the pick-up counter where a barista was slinging and steaming away.

The barista looked up and greeted her. "Hi, Morena."

"Hi, Violet." Violet's hair was as purple as her name suggested. "Can I hang out here for a minute while I avoid this creepy guy on the street?"

Outside, said creepy guy was deep in conversation with a man dressed all in green. The Green Man wore an emerald wool coat, a forest green slouchy knit hat, and Kelly green gloves. (People frequently asked him whether he bought coordinating contact lenses, or whether his eyes were naturally green.) It had to be concluded that the man enjoyed wearing the color green.

The aging hippie who'd wished to shower with Morena was not, in fact, asking about the Green Man's contact lenses, though that was at least half because he believed it was none of his business. Instead, he was explaining how he'd seen the most amazing woman and had to pursue her; yes, all the way into that Starbucks, vile purveyor of burnt coffee and corporate consumerism that it was. The Green Man, in response, tried to dissuade him from this course of action. After all, no one wants to be That Guy. And so Morena was saved from further discomfort by a man she'd never even seen. Eventually, her pursuer-to-be gave up, partially thanks to the Green Man's persuasion and partially to inertia.

And partially because the iPhone in Morena's pocket made another *ding*, which no one could hear over the shrieks of milk held just short of boiling.

Inside the café, Violet shrugged her reply to Morena's desperate request. "Sure. Oh, hey. You can talk to this customer, Vadim. Keep him company while I—"

The milk steamer fired up, providing a perfect example of what Violet was doing that kept her from entertaining customers.

"Hello," said Vadim over the roar of frothing non-fat liquids.

"Hello," said Morena.

"Are you from around here?"

To the casual reader, this sounds analogous to *D'you come here often?*, a phrase that Morena would rightly be wary of in the best of situations. But Morena was not the casual reader. She was actually there. And she heard his delectable Slavic accent, a clear sign that English was not his first language and that this was not, then, his attempt at a stilted pick-up line.

No, it was small talk. And given a choice between small talk with a tall, neatly groomed, dark-haired, polite man and going outside to brave the possibility of re-meeting the man who wanted to shower with her, her choice was obvious.

For his part, Vadim *would* have been willing to jump into a shower with Morena. But he wasn't going to ask. He knew better. He also knew that he'd be leaving the country for his native Ukraine in under two weeks. Some men might use this as an excuse to be boorish because *what chances would it hurt?*, but Vadim was not that sort of man. He was the kind of man a woman hoped to meet, whether it was in a crowded bar (for fun) or a deserted alleyway at midnight (for safety).

In this particular crowded bar, Vadim felt a sort of pull toward Morena that his childhood physics professors called gravitic attraction. So he stepped closer. To facilitate conversation.

She was saying, "Yeah, I live a few miles north. Over in Queen Anne." Morena might have been familiar with small talk, but that didn't mean she was any good at it. Her answer did not invite further discussion.

She ducked her head and ran a hand through her hair, twirling the ends. She looked up at Vadim through her lashes, fearing she was failing at the whole flirting thing. She had long preferred new numbers to new people.

Vadim's breath paused in his lungs when Morena's eyes met his. He counted to three while internally rhapsodizing over her dewy lashes, her skin the color of his sugar-free-hazelnut-vanilla-caramel mocha, and her subtly sparkling necklace. His internal rhapsodizing went something like this:

> *She stands in licorice;*
> *The cancerous black framing her orbs*
> *Spikes into my soul.*
> *She shivers my pancreas*
> *When the dog dies on the side of the road.*

It was better in the original Ukrainian.

Vadim yipped, "Then you must tell me all the best places!" He reached for her hands and pumped them up and down, up and down.

Contrary to what any onlookers probably believed, he intended this purely as an expression of enthusiasm, not as an excuse to touch a beautiful woman. It thrilled him, of course, that her warm hands rasped against his own (an excuse to share his hand lotion!) and that she seemed amenable to his touch. But that hadn't been the *intention*.

Morena also enjoyed the feeling of another person's skin on her own. Growing up in her mother's household and sporadically in Brazil, she often found herself missing casual touch when among the culturally American. And since she'd broken up with her boyfriend six months ago, she hadn't experienced much deliberate touch, either.

She gripped his fingers in return and laughed, showing off straight white teeth. "What do you want to know? Have you been to the Space Needle yet?"

"Yes, yes." Vadim was not interested in the Space Needle. "You must tell me something that is purely of Morena, yes?"

Luckily for Vadim, Morena was more than familiar with second-language acquisition and the way a person had to talk around what he or she wanted to say. She'd had to do it with her Portuguese-speaking grandparents, and her mother still occasionally needed the trick to get by in English even after forty years in Washington state. "I don't have a lot of favorites. Maybe some restaurants..." She trailed off, wondering where she could send him.

"Restaurants!" crowed Vadim. "Yes, yes! We go to restaurant together. Tonight at nine. It is, how you say, a date." Vadim, of course, knew exactly how to say *it's a date*. He could say it in English, in Russian, in Ukrainian, in Spanish, in German, in French, in Breton, in Latin, in Egyptian Arabic, and in Cantonese. But not in Afrikaans. Never in Afrikaans.

"I, ah, um." Morena pushed her hair back again. She turned away from Vadim to rifle through her shoulder bag, looking for nothing other than an excuse to compose herself. "Right. A date. But not tonight. I have plans. How about the day after tomorrow?"

Her mother would be so pleased: her little Morena jumping back into the dating scene and not growing old alone.

Morena worried that she might be a bit too old for him. Vadim looked perhaps in his early thirties, and she was nearly forty, but statistics showed that women aged slower than men all over the world. This disparity put them on even footing.

"The day after tomorrow is perfect. It is a date," he reiterated. Then he kissed her hand, on the palm side, and felt the twitch in her fingertips against his clean-shaven chin. It tickled.

And so they arranged to meet two nights later, Saturday evening, at 9 p.m. for dinner at a location she'd choose and text to him. Nine p.m. A nice, non-American dinner hour.

Morena had always eaten later than the majority of her friends, and that only got worse when her friend group got older. Many things, in fact, had gotten worse for Morena as her friend-group aged. She tended to lose them to children or marriage or disinterest, as their lives changed and hers did not.

This, then, explained how she ended up with a twenty-two-year-old roommate whom she'd met while story gaming in Capitol Hill a few weeks after breaking up with her boyfriend.

After moving out of his apartment, she'd first gone to stay at her mother's townhouse in Issaquah. But she couldn't live there indefinitely. She needed a place closer to work. Still, she'd waited on getting a place of her own, hoping to find a roommate to defray the loneliness. When Suzyn had arrived at a story gaming meetup in all her sprawling, dusky glory, mentioning that she'd just moved to Seattle and was looking for a roommate if anyone knew a person who needed one, Morena was ecstatic.

Morena had dragged Suzyn to her mother's after a vicious game of Fiasco, because although the young woman might not have minded sleeping wherever (intimated: with any hottie who picked her up in a club after story gaming), Morena didn't let potential friends put themselves in such dangerous situations. Suzyn and Morena's mother (Luiza) had chatted about Harlem and the New York art scene, and then Suzyn had tried to turn Morena off being her roommate.

"I'm a super-geeky story gamer," warned Suzyn. But so was Morena.

"And I love watching the SyFy channel, especially on Friday nights," she continued. But so did Morena.

"...after which I like to go dancing, where I will probably get drunk or high." Well, Morena wasn't into getting wasted, but she loved dancing. During the periods when her age-appropriate friends outgrew clubbing, she'd taken her mother along. Having a less-embarrassing dance-mate would be glorious.

"And I can only afford five hundred dollars a month," said Suzyn, "so you're not going to do much better than living with your mom. Even if you've got the same amount available, that's only a thousand-dollar apartment."

But Suzyn was still thinking in terms of NYC rent prices. In Seattle, $1,000 could get you 800 square feet and a parking space with a convenient location to cafés, clubs, and bus lines. Plus, Morena would only be responsible for $500 a month—which was, like, half a pair of shoes for her—while getting to live with a fellow gamer who appreciated SyFy and could share cabs. Score!

And that is the story of how Morena and Suzyn came to live together.

But this scene was not about Morena and Suzyn. It was about Morena and Vadim making plans for their first date. Before this six-month flashback, the potential couple had decided on a 9 p.m. Saturday dinner at a location of Morena's choosing.

Still holding her hand, Vadim played with her fingers, taking special care with the fourth finger. "This is the start of a beautiful relationship," he misquoted *Casablanca*, jewel of English-speaking cinema. "We should get married some day in this very café. We will live together forever."

Morena laughed, unaware that this was only *half* a joke and, therefore, half serious. "Sure," she agreed. She'd believe a proposal when she saw it. None of this nebulous *should* or *maybe* or other finagling. She'd waited three whole years for her jerk of an ex to propose. She'd thought she'd found someone who'd care for her when she was sick, whom she could support and be supported by, who'd be her lifelong companion.

And after three years, all she had to show for that relationship was a new iPhone.

Leaving on a high note, Morena waved goodbye to Violet and headed out. As Morena walked the last few blocks to her office at Starbucks Corporate Headquarters, she unlocked her new iPhone. The screen lit up and the silly app started to spin, but she needed to send a text, so she hit the button at the bottom to get back to the home screen—the only actual button on the phone—and closed out of it.

Then she laughed at herself, a mix of rue and general elation at having a date. She couldn't text from this phone, she remembered. She didn't have a phone plan for it yet, and her

SIM card was still in her other one. How strange that she'd pulled it from her pocket instead of her Samsung. She couldn't even recall putting it there...

A practical woman, she'd believed her old Samsung had worked just fine. Moreover, it had synced with her work computer years before the iPhone could. The Samsung was truly viable as a work phone, a feature that was deeply important to Morena who spent even more time at work than she did on shoe shopping and story gaming combined. This, then, explained how she could afford Louboutins not only now but also back in her second year in the workforce.

So why had her ex-boyfriend thought she'd need the phone?

Morena's mother's voice in her head suggested, "Maybe he wants to get back together with you, *minha filha*. I do wish you'd get married. I don't want you to grow old alone."

And hells no to that, thought Morena. Because there was no way she was getting back with the jerk who'd led her on for three years and broke it off like their relationship was nothing. In retrospect, she understood that he fetishized women from South America. He got upset when she wasn't all warm and loving. And he always wanted her to speak Spanish, when the second language she knew (ish) was Portuguese. No matter how many times she'd told him, the jerk couldn't seem to remember that they didn't speak Spanish in Brazil.

She decided that as soon as she reached her office, she'd email Suzyn and her mother. They had to know as soon as possible: Morena had a date!

(It never occurred to her to use the other phone, the normal phone, waiting in her bag.)

Chapter Two
Let You Tell Me a Story

It is a peculiarity of our modern world that a coffee shop with free Wi-Fi and numerous power outlets is full of patrons, each possessing only *one* coffee and *one* pastry in order to rationalize five hours' rent on one little table. This was nowhere more true than in Seattle, which purposely catered to such patrons by offering games (e.g., Wayward Coffeehouse in Ravenna), books (e.g., Bauhaus in Ballard), or spare computers with InDesign installed (e.g., Online Café in Capitol Hill).

On the night following the day wherein Morena met Vadim, she and her roommate drove their obnoxiously cute Smart Car to that evening's story game meetup. An astute reader would recall that Morena had earlier been in possession of an ORCA card and, therefore, didn't need a car to get around the city despite having plenty of money for such luxuries (and the accompanying parking spot).

But a Seattleite would know that crossing diagonally from one end of Lake Union, such as Lower Queen Anne where our heroines lived, to the other end was a bus rider's nightmare. There were no direct routes either coming or going, and a hopeful mass transit user might wait an hour at some unfortunate transfer location where another poor soul may or may not have been attacked the week before. It was, oddly, even more difficult to get from the uber-artsy neighborhood of Fremont to the uber-hip neighborhood of Capitol Hill, but this did not concern Morena and Suzyn, who, as noted above, were using a Smart Car.

They were the first of their group to arrive at Wayward Coffeehouse, and Morena bought their mochas while Suzyn established their group's presence at the reserved table. Story gaming had taken on a certain cachet in Seattle. The gaming part counted as a respectably nerdy pursuit, and the story part counted as creative. Together, they blended into a Frankenstein-esque symbol of fun, appropriate for Microsoft employees and multi-hair-colored rebels alike. It was also a microcosm of Seattle life: a chance to interact with other people but still not have to be friends with them.

The guide books and blogs called the city's propensity for surface acquaintanceship the "Seattle Freeze." The system worked well for locals (the only people who understood it): people seemed friendly enough for smooth civil interaction, smiled and made vague plans to get together, but no one ever formed deep personal connections. Newcomers, however, were often bewildered by potential friendships that sizzled and fizzled in short order.

One newcomer who was *not* confused by this non-interactive interaction was Magic Guy. Technically, his name wasn't Magic Guy, but he'd gone by many names over the 6,000 years of his life. He believed that any one was as good as any other. Ashton, Bing, Cecil, Doan, John, Jacob, Jingleheimer Smith. They all served their function as far as Magic Guy was concerned. Since he will later in this story be given the name Magic Guy, he shall (for ease of reading) be called such, even now when he is currently answering to a different, irrelevant moniker. When characters refer to him as "Magic Guy" for the first few chapters of his involvement, then, readers should understand that those characters are really saying [Ashton, Bing, Cecil, Doan, John, Jacob]. For now.

Magic Guy was only slightly taller than Morena, certainly shorter than Suzyn, and was possessed of winter-pale white skin that he sometimes drew moles or pockmarks onto à la Marilyn Monroe so that he wouldn't stand out as *too* perfect. He was slender, sported a fashionably bland medium-length hairstyle that could be swept back, and was entirely unremarkable for the time and place.

Just as he liked it.

When Magic Guy entered Wayward Coffeehouse that night, he sauntered past the *Serenity* silkscreen to order from the barista on duty.

Said barista gestured to his trendy hoodie and blue knit hat. She asked, "Aren't you bored of this?"

What she really meant was *I was enjoying my solitude from the supernatural world before you came here to shatter it. You've been here five times in the last two weeks. Don't you dare become a regular.*

But she didn't say that out loud because, while she and Magic Guy both knew that magic was real and some people could live forever, most patrons of Wayward Coffeehouse did not. Of course, this was a ridiculous silence to keep, since most patrons of Wayward Coffeehouse would happily believe any sensible excuse for discussing topics such as immortality. It was a place for story gamers, fantasy writers, and *Firefly* Browncoats.

After a few minutes, Magic Guy collected his green store-branded mug, not having purchased any of the vegan pastries on offer. He inhaled the cayenne-and-coffee scent of his Minbari Mocha and replied, "Whatevs." Magic Guy had clearly been working on his insouciant millennial slang, not that he'd become proficient in it quite yet.

He wended his way to the table where Morena and Suzyn already sat. "Ladies," he greeted them.

But they paid him no attention, not even when he set his mug onto the wooden table top with an uneven *thu-thunk* that caused its contents to slosh out of their ceramic confines. With the women's focus elsewhere, Magic Guy used his strength of will to capture the liquid and return it to the drinking vessel. With. His. Mind.

Yes, although Magic Guy looked like a modern human and had taught himself to act like one as well, he was—at his core—a 6,000-year-old elf on a centuries-long break from the supernatural world (ever since a giant falling out with his best friend in the early 1800s). Life among mortals provided a fast-paced and, so far, emotion-free way to get some distance from his natural society.

Again he went unremarked, as neither woman noticed his feat of magic. Instead, the pair was deeply embroiled in a discussion of how men are super creepy.

"Ugh," said Morena. "Men are super creepy."

"Preach it, sister," said Suzyn. Suzyn was lounging at an

almost-impossible angle in her chair, her bottom perched on the very end of her seat, batik-clad leg anchored on the broken wicker of the next chair over, and left arm torqueing her body so that she could drape it over the backrest. This position was terribly uncomfortable, but it looked so athletically effortless that Suzyn enjoyed cultivating it.

"Like, after Shower Guy, there was Please Enter My Pickup Guy. Then there was Flash Me Your Tits Guy. Oh, and let us not forget I'll Share My Heroin With You Guy." Morena shivered dramatically. The first two men had freaked her out something fierce. Who slows down and invites a woman, walking alone, to jump into his truck? And what kind of moron passes a woman while driving on the freeway with a sign that says *Flash Me Your Tits*? Even if a lady were so inclined, she'd be busy driving. And even if she were willing to take her hands off the wheel at 50 miles per hour on the 520 bridge, she'd still have to undo her seatbelt and wrestle with her shirt in order to make it work.

It is beyond the scope of this story to discover what prompts some men to hope for success with actions like these. It is an exercise left to the reader.

Morena thought that I'll Share My Heroin With You Guy was kind of sweet in his own way. He had happily offered to give a gift of the most important thing in his world. And he wasn't at all pushy about it, which was how she knew she'd reached Belltown: home of the friendly drug addicts. (While Seattle has a large number of drug-loving denizens, none were more polite than the ones in Belltown.)

Suzyn, unlike Morena, would have been thrilled by an I'll Share My Heroin With You Guy. Not for the pick-up line, but for the heroin itself, though "yay" was usually her drug of choice. Later this evening, she would sneak out for a quick break "to get some fresh air" and end up with a hit of cocaine (hand-delivered by her regular dealer), which she would proceed to take in the café's bathroom.

"Why do the inappropriate men all cluster around me?" Morena moaned.

Suzyn shrugged, her chair tilting precariously. "It's your aura."

"Well, *I'm* not an inappropriate man," said Magic Guy, "and I'm around you right now."

Suzyn collapsed forward to slump against the table. "You don't count," she said. "We already know you." And it was true. To an extent. They knew him as well as anyone knew any other stranger at a story game event, a place where players took on a slew of false personalities for fun.

For his part, Magic Guy often played as himself, or rather as a personality he'd lived in previous centuries. He delighted in the freedom of being himself without outing himself (or his people), since no one believed his characters were anything more than that: characters.

"Besides," said Morena, "you've never tried to pick me up."

Magic Guy laughed. "I wouldn't. I'm asexual and aromantic, so it seems horribly unlikely."

"Of course," said Morena, oh-so-put-upon. "All the good ones are taken, gay, or ace."

Suzyn patted her shoulder in mock-consolation. "Finding true love isn't magic, you know. It takes hard work."

"Easy for you to say. You're only twenty-two." Morena choked down bitterness like burnt coffee beans about being seventeen years older than her roommate. Not that she hadn't come to adore Suzyn, but she'd somehow been unable to hold onto her previous, more age-appropriate, friends. While the rest of her social circle from ten or twenty years ago had moved on with their lives—gotten married, stopped drinking and dancing, had children, and/or otherwise grown apart from her way of life—Morena still did all the same things she'd enjoyed when she was twenty. Just with a larger bankroll.

She shopped, she ate at classy restaurants, she did pub quizzes in dive bars, she visited friends in other cities... and she had no steady companions her own age. She missed the times they used to have, the people who "knew her when." And she hated the cycle: make a new friend, form a close friendship, watch it wither and die when the friend abandoned her for something else. Always for something that Morena didn't understand, but that the friend inevitably thought was better than the life they'd been living. They wanted to do home-y things, or needed to watch their children, or wearied of dancing until two in the morning at Chop Suey's Bollywood night.

"Let's talk games," said Magic Guy, in an attempt to get the others back on track. "What're we playing tonight?"

One would think that a meetup group would be more organized, with an activity planned in advance, but this particular cadre reveled in their slapdash methodology. Sometimes it made their meetings run especially late since they spent time figuring out what to play before spending yet more time figuring out their characters, but that was just more chance to pseudo-socialize.

"Is this everyone?" asked Morena, because so far only the three of them had sat at the table and it was already fifteen minutes after the scheduled meeting time.

"Fiasco?" suggested Magic Guy. "Monsterhearts?"

Suzyn sighed. She was getting sick of Monsterhearts, a

game where players acted like teenagers at a supernatural high school, complete with teenage drama. As the youngest of the crowd, she was still quite close enough to that sort of thing, thank you very much. Maybe the thirty-, forty-, and fifty-somethings wanted to relive those glory days, but she recalled the horrors. She knew the hot-faced feeling and the tightening in the throat when asking for something as innocuous as a bathroom key. Her heart still sped with shrieking embarrassment from accidentally bumping into a crush on the street, something that wouldn't remotely disturb her now. She didn't want to relive those times. She couldn't gloss over the bad memories for the fun and the good. Not yet.

"Let's see if anyone else shows up," Morena suggested.

It was twenty after the hour. No one else was showing up. And even if they did, the reader has to agree that people *that* tardy probably didn't deserve to vote on the night's game. This group was, however, nothing if not fair to the point of unfairness.

"Excuse me," Suzyn said. She flowed to her feet, sprawl translating to tall. She cultivated the height rather than hiding it, going so far as to style her tight black curls into upward-reaching flames, spiraling toward the sky. "I'm going to go look at the drinks board if we're waiting longer."

She was not, in fact, going to look at the drinks board. Not only had she memorized it, but this was her moment! She sailed outside and scored the foreshadowed bag of cocaine, which she then snorted in the bathroom.

Suzyn's love affair with cocaine had started in ninth grade when her parents and her test scores had earned her *entre* to the very snobby, very rich Stuyvesant High School. (No relation to the poor, mostly African-American neighborhood of

Bedford-Stuyvesant, where her family had coincidentally lived for three generations.) It took her no time at all to fall madly into addiction with the drug. She loved the focus it gave her when she worked on art projects. Plus the high was great, and she got to meet her new classmates when in her role as a buyer, a noteworthy benefit since none of them lived anywhere near her home address. Sure, she only met the kids who were doing or dealing, but powder was a preppy drug, and they were still useful people. She'd been starting over at a new school, and here was a whole subculture of smart kids and artists and people who were going far.

"Oh, good," said Morena when Suzyn returned from her nose powdering. "You're back. I saved you the Werewolf sheet."

Monsterhearts, of course.

Morena's high school years had been nothing like the overwrought emo version in the game, and she liked the movie-industry quality of playing. As for Magic Guy, he had never attended high school and needed to study his soon-to-be peers. No, he wasn't planning on attending one soon, but he *didn't age*. Soon enough, current high school students would be in the same apparent generation as he pretended membership. The better he understood them, the more equipped he'd be to interact in the future. If he couldn't adapt, he'd be on the wrong end of a pitchfork brigade, or whatever was fashionable for death and ostracism when the time came.

Hence, Morena and Magic Guy had chosen Suzyn's least favorite game in her absence. She resigned herself to following their lead.

Suzyn pulled a whiskey flask from her Timbuk2 messenger bag and took a swig. "Are you guys going to the story gaming convention in Oregon?" It was more an attempt to procrastinate on character creation than an honest desire to know the answer. She could only afford it if Morena went. And, as far as she was concerned at this point in the story, Magic Guy's answer didn't really matter. Just like points on *Whose Line Is It Anyway?*

Morena shrugged. "I vote Magic Guy runs the game today."

Magic Guy wished she had suggested someone else. He had so few chances to learn about the modern high school experience as it was. Playing the teacher and Game Master was fine, but it was nothing compared to actual teenage role-play. In about twenty years, he'd have to convince his new peers that he'd grown up with them, and that took a deeper understanding. He envied Suzyn her boredom. Oh, he could tell she was bored; he simply counted his level of caring on one finger. But he said, "Sure," the better to make himself agreeably indispensable to the group overall.

Suzyn took another hit from her flask, drowning in the euphoria until she didn't care that Morena's character had two sex-based strings on her own. She was going down the destructive path—for her character, that is. She took a sip as she discussed her character's plans to skip a class. Drank deeply as she brought her character into violent sync with her animal nature.

She swapped her flask for a fresh one from her bag, wrapped in pink leather, and attempted to murder their economics teacher for giving her a failing grade. How Suzyn hated Monsterhearts. It made her feel like a character in a Hemingway novel, always saying "I need a drink." She giggled at the thought. Old Papa Hemingway would approve of a creative artist sitting in a café and drinking. If only she lived in Paris! No, she'd miss Morena if she lived in Paris. Suzyn tilted in her chair, spilling whiskey onto the table and soaking the character sheet printouts.

Magic Guy leapt from his seat. "I'll get napkins."

While he was gone, Morena leaned over to subtly support Suzyn's listing form with her own. "Wanna get out of here?"

Suzyn giggled. The light was so pretty in Wayward. It shone from the buttery bulbs to reflect off the metal cuts of Boba Fett, et al. She said, "Buttery bulbs," and collapsed heavily onto Morena's shoulder. Twirling a lock of her roommate's highlighted hair, she whispered, "You're my best friend."

Morena's chest puffed, expanding to accommodate the competing rue and love that bounced off her ribs while they fought for dominance. She heaved Suzyn to her feet and gathered both their bags with one hand. All that corporate-sponsored gym time paid off.

"I'm taking her home," she said to Magic Guy as they passed him beside the espresso machines, barely whirring at this point in the evening because the patrons had already bought their coffees and considered their obligations fulfilled.

"Of course." He shook the napkins. "I'll just..."

"Thank you."

"I'll see you next week?" Maybe next time, he could play a student.

"We need to go."

Morena was glad she'd driven. Suzyn would have been a nightmare on the bus. As it was, she and Suzyn were both quite familiar with wrestling Suzyn's long limbs into the Smart, even while her arms flailed energetically as she expounded on photography principles.

"I hope you vomit soon," Morena said. "Because I have work tomorrow morning and can't stay up with you all night."

Suzyn told her about the importance of proper lighting techniques.

Chapter Three
Gas Works Gadflies

Saturday morning (two days after Thursday's story game meetup) dawned cloudy and cold. Long-term locals who were awake and wanted to walk mostly chose their closed-toe, closed-heel boots and donned their favorite North Face zip-ups.

Short-term locals were largely optimistic, California transplants who decided that (since rain had yet to fall) they could wear sandals. This would prove to be a foolish choice on their part, because sandals in thirty-odd degrees is never a good idea. Moreover, any iPhone weather app could have told them it was slated to rain later in the day, and their feet were doomed to squish about.

Those who were awake and wanted to *drive*, however, courted more than discomfort: this lot flirted with death. An inordinate number of Saturday morning drivers believed that fewer cars on the road meant they didn't need to waste time defrosting their rear windows. Consequently, no one could see anything behind them, and most couldn't see anyone coming up on the sides, either. They'd all have been well served by a $10 ice scraper from Target, but they only pulled those out for actual snow.

In our heroines' apartment, Suzyn wore her Stuyvesant High School sweat pants and a stained Pixar t-shirt. These would be terrible choices for going out in the cold and rain but better, at least, than her sleeping roommate's silk pajamas. It was a good thing, then, that she was still inside.

Suzyn's often-impeccable hair flames had fizzled in the night, but she would restyle them before leaving the building. Her mission for the morning was to wake Morena, who took about a zillion hours to get ready.

Morena found dressing in Seattle to be extraordinarily difficult. When she'd gone to college in Boston, it had been much simpler. There, she could dress up or down without drawing comment; a student in a power suit could sit beside another in bunny slippers. There, she could experiment with thick liquid eyeliners and not be asked what costume party she planned to attend later.

Seattle, however, had a hate-hate relationship with women's beauty regimens. It wasn't the French maxim of *no one should be able to tell you're wearing makeup*, which really meant *wear makeup, for God's sake, and no one will comment unless you've chosen outlandish colors*. No, it was a distaste for makeup altogether. Makeup was for teenagers, bankers, and marketing consultants, with the possible exception of funky hipsters, though they'd be better off skipping everything except shimmery blue eye shadow. And clothes? If people wore suits, they were trying too hard and probably terrible at their jobs (again excepting financial professionals).

Unfortunately for Morena, she liked to feel beautiful, and she couldn't just pick one vector. She couldn't say, "I'll dress nicely and skip makeup," as her mother would, because American culture outside Seattle emphasized hair and makeup over clothing. And she couldn't say, "I'll get out the blow dryer and mascara but wear wrinkled cargo pants," because her mother's voice would ring accusingly in her ears the next time Morena went to visit for the weekend.

Luiza, Morena's mother, probably wouldn't comment at all, being both a long-term Seattle resident and a staunch supporter of whatever made her daughter happy. Morena's internal editor, however, often used her mother's voice. As far as Morena was concerned, there was no worse mistake than disappointing her mother.

This dilemma led to Morena's taking upwards of two hours to *look* like she'd picked the first shirt out of her closet and like she had a beauty routine that consisted of running a brush through her hair. It took effort to make her wavy locks fall in mostly straight layers. She painstakingly enhanced her eyes with golden crayons and super-fine pencils. She ironed black, Prada button-down shirts and rolled the cuffs below her elbows, showing off her grandfather's Patek Philippe watch. It made for a practical, but very classy, bangle bracelet, and most people didn't notice just how glamorous she was being.

But Morena noticed, which was the important thing. And her mother noticed, which was also important. And Suzyn had learned to notice, mostly because Morena would silently mope if Suzyn didn't compliment a part of the day's outfit.

Knowing all of this, Suzyn shook her roommate into a bleary, almost-wakeful state at eight in the morning on a Saturday. Morena shook back until Suzyn's hand vibrated off the bed, leaving space for Morena to tug the 2,000-thread-count Egyptian cotton comforter (purchased the same day as Suzyn's matching one, both on Morena's credit card over Suzyn's weak protestations) more securely into place.

Suzyn poked and prodded and made a nuisance of herself until finally Morena flipped over and sat straight up. "WHAT?" she said. Morena's tangled hair fell in frizzy clumps over her shoulders, and her cream sleep shirt slipped down one bronze arm. "What could you possibly want? The sun is still voting against daylight."

Suzyn bounced into the space Morena's movement had made on the mattress. "It's not raining! We have to go out."

Morena slumped backward, but that only brought her into sharp contact with Suzyn's bony shoulder. "What are you *on* this morning?"

For most people, this would be a rhetorical question, but... well... Suzyn. Morena was more than familiar with taking double showers at one or two or three in the morning, hoping to get vomit off everyone's body parts before attempting to get some pre-work-hours sleep. Today, with no professional obligations, she'd hoped for a bit more.

But this particular morning, Suzyn was not (yet) pharmaceutically conditioned, nor was she planning to let Morena laze in bed as they usually did on the weekends. Not when the weather was perfect for creating art! If she was ever going to become the famous photographer she knew she could be, she had to take advantage of the opportunities Seattle provided. Like her parents before her, she had to work *hard*. Otherwise, why had she left New York?

Suzyn was blazing her own path, and on some Saturdays that meant waking up early to drag her favorite, live-in, free model out to pose.

"Come on." Suzyn tugged on her roommate's moisturized arm, and the two of them lurched to standing. "It's not raining yet today. We're going to Gas Works Park for a photo shoot."

Morena stumbled forward. "I have to do my hair."

"I know." Suzyn propelled the older woman into the bathroom.

Three hours later, the pair had finished dressing, bought their Starbucks lattes to-go (on Morena's card), and set up Suzyn's photography equipment under the curve of some rusted metal at the park. The grass sloshed around Morena's wedge-heel boots, but the sky was momentarily clear. The winter sun sparkled on Lake Union.

Suzyn looked up at the gray-blue, contemplating where to put her reflectors. "Maybe it'll snow."

"You sound far too happy about that." Morena dug her fingers into the depths of her coat's cashmere-wool-blend pockets, seeking out the littlest extra warmth. Her right hand curled around a Stila lip gloss, and her left clanked against unforgiving plastic. *Oh, right. The iPhone.* "While you change your mind a million times, I'm going to be over here with my new toy."

Suzyn left her reflector where it was and dashed over to pull the phone from Morena's icy clutches. "Oooh, I've been wanting this model." She tilted her head curiously. "But I thought you liked your Samsung?"

"It was a gift." Morena paused but then realized that if she couldn't tell her roommate-cum-best-friend about it, she was more alone than she was prepared to be. "Would you believe my ex sent it to me?"

"He didn't! And on *Valentine's Day.*" Suzyn remembered the package she'd brought in.

Sure, it was a jerk move to send presents that proved your financial solvency to an ex, especially if you were pretty sure they were single on a romantic holiday, but Suzyn still wished *her* exes would give string-free gifts. Thinking about strings on people reminded her of Monsterhearts, and she frowned.

Morena borrowed the mantra of all Seattle twenty-somethings to express her amazement: "I know, right?" She took the phone back and unlocked the screen. "I'm totally keeping it. He sends me a phone, he's out a phone. I'm not calling him with it."

"Do you have a minutes or a data plan for it?"

At that very moment, it began vibrating, keeping Morena from thinking too deeply about how easily the phone had slunk into her life. Because, no, she'd never gotten a plan or activated a card or whatever it was she'd have had to do. The iPhone had done that all on its own.

Morena glanced at the display. "My mother. Probably to confirm that we're still on for brunch tomorrow." She hit the button on top to ignore the call. "She won't expect me to be awake to answer it. Besides, I don't need to chat about work, that she doesn't understand, or my dismal love life right now. Not when we're out taking photos in the cold." She rubbed her runny nose. "Let's hurry this up, yeah?"

"You can't hurry art." But Suzyn went back to her reflectors anyway.

Morena sniffed again, probably inhaling hazardous

chemicals from the rusting gasworks, and poked at the single green icon in the center of her phone's screen. She needed to kill some time, and the sexy new phone was so appealing. Besides, she could use some help with finding love. Her single upcoming date wouldn't do much for providing permanent companionship.

She'd been content with her ex-boyfriend, had never felt more for anyone else. Why hadn't he proposed?

When one's only fear is being alone, one is pleased by any acceptable candidate who promises to stick around forever.

The app opened, unfolding into its slot machine with the same five rolls as before. She scrolled the first number column to *27-35* and pressed the antique padlock, ensuring that choice. The next slider she set to *comfortable enough*. Suzyn was still fussing with a stand, so Morena shook the phone and waited for the *ding ding DING!* to tell her the identity of her true online dating love.

It made the sound, all right, but it didn't give her any names or contact information, just like it hadn't the times before. Clearly it wasn't that kind of online dating app. It was, in fact, utterly useless, purely about spinning wheels and loud noises. At least it was cheaper than Vegas.

She locked the screen with a sigh and put the phone away. Her shoulders hunched up and she chased the coat's warmth, pushing her hands deeper into the pockets.

Suzyn, meanwhile, had finished her tweaks and level-setting... and sent a quick text to her favorite dealer out in Bellevue because if she was going to make something beautiful, then she needed the right amount of focus.

"Get your gorgeous self over here!" Suzyn positioned her glamorous roommate-cum-model half in the shadow of a giant pipe and half in the softened wintry light. "Lean on that," she ordered.

"That" was a pipe with decades of rust and a season's worth of rain-slick mud on it. "Hells no," Morena called back.

"Just for a minute?"

The pleading tone melted the grossed-out ice around Morena's fastidious heart. "Ugh." Gingerly, she reached out a finger and poked the metal. It was frosty, and her skin came back with a coating of gray-black sludge. It was probably cancerous. "I hate you," she yelled. But she lifted her arm above her head, all the same, and put her whole bare hand against the slippery structure.

Suzyn grinned behind her camera. "You love me," she corrected. "Take your jacket off!"

"Are you kidding me?" Morena's jacket came off anyway. This was the price for having an artistic best friend.

Suzyn had only snapped two pictures, framed against the old gasworks with Morena's perfect hair flowing in the breeze, when some guy stepped into her viewfinder. He was the opposite of glamorous, in stained cargo pants, a hoodie with holes in it, and (horror of horrors) a baby spitting up on his shoulder. Like a cabbie from her native New York City, Suzyn railed against the injustice. "Get out of my way, moron."

The unglamorous guy ignored her, making straight for Morena. A few yards away, the man's wife and older child floated plastic boats on the lake water. Even if his wife had been watching more closely, she wouldn't have worried about his approaching a beautiful model. Not only was she secure in her ten-year relationship, which had weathered two children and a major move, but she would have been sure that some-one like Morena wouldn't give someone like her husband any sort of encouragement. Beautiful, confident women just weren't interested in cheating slobs, and he'd certainly be a cheater if he was trying to start something.

The slob part could be detected by any neutral observer. For instance, a man wearing all green and reading his Kindle on a park bench looked up to observe the commotion. Yes, this was the same Green Man from Chapter One who stepped in with the shower-hippie guy.

He lived in the city too, okay? It wasn't *that* big a coincidence that he ended up in similar places as our heroines.

On this occasion, he regarded the parental slob forcing attention on two women and decided to step in if the ladies needed backup. He would have sworn he'd seen the modeling woman before.... Since the pair were not yet in distress, however, he tapped a touch-screen-friendly, forest green glove-tip against his e-reader screen, thereby flipping the page forward.

The slob in question reached Morena and leaned his shoulder against the pipe, uncaring of what might come off on his clothing. "What's a pretty girl like you doing in a place like this?"

Is this guy for real? Morena still politely answered him. "Freezing for photos. Please move out of the way."

The guy noticed Suzyn for the first time. He took in her furrowed brows, her puckered mouth, her hands on her hips, the furious sweat beading on her mahogany-dark skin even in the inclement weather. And then he dismissed her. Morena was far more interesting. "My name is...."

He told Morena his name, but it wasn't important to the story or to her, so it shall remain absent from this narrative. No need for anyone to remember it.

Morena didn't reply, and the guy might have tried another

avenue of conversation, but his baby vomited on his shoulder and he was immediately distracted by cooing and spittle-cleaning.

"I'll be back," the guy said. His kept his gaze on Morena even as he backed toward the lake shore where his wife had a bag of baby supplies.

Suzyn glared after him. Morena readjusted her position against the pipe. The green-clad man on the park bench looked up from his Kindle to assess the situation, found everyone safe and content, and went back to Sidorova's *The Age of Ice*, which he'd once heard the author read from.

"Move a bit to the left," said Suzyn. "The light's shifted."

Obediently, Morena pulled her boot from the sucking mud and sank it down a few inches over.

"No, no!" Suzyn stalked up to her, sneakered feet less bothered by the grassy glue. "Your other left." As soon as she was close enough to prevent eavesdroppers, she leaned in, all excitement. "Oh my god. What was that guy about?"

"I don't even know. I think he was trying to chat me up." They'd been watching BBC shows on Netflix for the past month—*Sherlock, Doctor Who, Being Human*, etc.—and random Briticisms like *chat me up* kept creeping into their speech.

"Weird." Suzyn fussed with Morena's shoulder seams, pretending not to notice the goose bumps on her roommate's neck. She'd been blessed with such a good model.

Right then, back in Brooklyn, the girl who would have been Suzyn's roommate (had she stayed and taken that soul-sucking internship with the outdated *New York Times* instead of moving west to try her luck at freelance photography and design in Seattle) was lazing around in a '70s housedress and refusing to leave her fifth-floor walk-up, not even for the chance to talk to her building's superintendent in person.

"What's weirder," said Morena through teeth she would not allow to chatter, "is that I'd just set my dating app to find me a guy who was about that age, I think, and financially comfortable."

"You think your iPhone tried to set you up with that loser?"

"He's not a loser!" Morena found herself in the strange position of defending a married guy who'd tried to pick up a stranger in the park while carrying his baby. "Okay, maybe he is, but he fits the criteria I gave the app."

"I could use an app like that," said Suzyn, but she didn't really mean it. Single people were meant to always be on the prowl, and she liked the way she could use her slyest vocal tones on sexual topics. Still, she didn't have trouble meeting potential partners, and she was young enough to wait for effort-free methods like partying to pan out. She didn't need help.

Morena, however, did need help. She was practically forty! All the good men were taken, gay, ace, or divorced. And *divorced* was just another word for *failed at marriage the first time.* Sure, some divorcees could be good people, great people, but she wasn't sure her mother would see it that way. And her mother was half the reason Morena wanted to find herself a worthy man and settle down.

Maybe seventy-five percent of the reason. Her mother worried that Morena would grow old and die alone, and she worried vociferously.

Suzyn peered around, looking for the device. "Where's your phone?" It couldn't be in any of Morena's remaining pockets. The lines of her casual wear smoothed down her body. Suzyn wondered if Morena bothered wearing under-wear with that particular pair of tight jeans. "Show me! Try it again. I want to see if it really works."

Morena plucked her jacket from their pile of belongings and extracted the phone from it with cold-clumsy fingers that could barely clutch well enough. "I was playing with it the other day." She gasped, realizing: "When I met Vadim!"

"The hot guy with the Slavic accent that you're taking to Toulouse Petit tonight?"

"You know I'm addicted to the seasoning on their fries." Both women took a moment to remember the texture, the crunch, of Toulouse Petit's amazing fries. But they weren't discussing dinner options for an ideal date, they were trying to talk about the iPhone app and about when Morena met Vadim, so they observed their moment of silence and then picked back up with the thread of conversation. "Before I ran into him at that Starbucks, I'd been messing with the phone."

"You think the app found him for you? But you said he knew the barista." Suzyn was jealous of how many baristas Morena knew. Of course, they were all *Starbucks* baristas (none from the little local shops), and it was only because Morena's job was to send the right amount of pastry and coffee to every store in the region, but everyone knew that baristas rivaled brain surgeons as the smartest, kindest, awesomest people in the city. Not to mention, they got to pierce and tattoo whatever they wanted without career repercussions.

They also hooked people up with the local dealers near their stores, if need be. Not that Suzyn needed that anymore, but she had when she'd first moved.

Morena gusted out a heavy sigh, her breath visible and white in the misting air. "You're right. Besides, how much can a phone app really influence a person?"

While Morena was busy reassuring herself of the app's ethical non-consequences, if it truly worked, a man drifted off the footpath in their direction. He bumped into Suzyn, surreptitiously dropping a bag of blow into her pocket. She shoved money behind her back, which he snapped up.

"Sorry to run into you, miss," he said, overplaying it wildly. When Suzyn had called him earlier and scheduled the transaction, she'd impressed upon him that she was out with a straight-edge girlfriend who couldn't know, and he wanted to make sure he did everything right. Suzyn was one of his best customers.

Luckily for both of them, Morena's dilemma occupied her mind during the handoff. The dealer was already gone by the time she refocused. "Well, a date can't hurt, no matter what."

"Let's go get you ready for it," Suzyn said. "Put your coat on, and we can get a coffee and go home." And Suzyn could take her powder.

Chapter Four
Translated Bodily
from the Original Hindi

Morena's brilliant plan to take Vadim to Toulouse Petit was foiled by her uncharacteristic lack of preparedness. Admittedly, she had never attempted to get a table there for 9 p.m. on a Saturday night, but she really should have thought ahead. As it was, she tried to make an OpenTable reservation two hours in advance, only to find there were no available bookings.

She hated to disappoint her hot Slavic coffeeshop man, so she and Suzyn quickly brainstormed a list of activities Morena might do on a night when she *didn't* have a date. The list was fairly short.

- Catch up on her DVR. (Not the best choice for a first date where she was supposed to be showing someone around her city. So, no.)

- Go clubbing at the Tiki Room and cart home Suzyn's drunken body. (Clubbing on a first date seemed to negate the point. How could she learn more about her potential mate if they were mostly yelling into the beat-pounding void? So, no.)
- Prep a soundtrack for the next time she got to GM Monsterhearts. (Suzyn vetoed this one, more out of a desire to avoid the dreaded MH than because sitting around the apartment listening to music was a lame Saturday night date plan. So, no.)
- See a movie at the Hindi theater in Kirkland.

The Hindi theater in Kirkland was a favorite mostly of Indian ex-pats. The owners inevitably chose the worst films. They wanted "serious" titles AKA "nothing too Bollywood," but since super-serious titles didn't bring in as much audience they had to compromise. Half the stock were song-and-dance options that didn't have the adorable heart of a classic Bollywood flick. The other half were depressing, but not deep enough to count as "important cinema." (One movie had been so awful that the reel operator hadn't even bothered to stop for intermission. He'd known that stopping would lose the audience to the parking lot, never to return.)

Still. It stayed in business because it catered to those with no other options: ex-pats, Silicon Valley transplants, and Morena's mother. Morena's mother had attended the theater's first showing, reveling in viewing a movie where she wasn't expected to automatically understand the dialogue or the culture.

The films were slightly off the modern American norm, just like her. Sure, a Brazilian movie theater would have been more comfortable, but the Hindi theater reminded Luiza that her current location wasn't everything, and that she was pretty darned good at keeping up.

And so, the little theater was a slice of home for Morena, who otherwise had no ties to India at all.

As a date, there was nothing obviously wrong with seeing a movie in Hindi and foreign-accented English, so Morena texted Vadim with the change of plan. He immediately hit the Internet in hopes of finding a second late-night activity for *after* the movie so as to extend their time together.

Cradled by her passenger seat, he was still finalizing plans on his smartphone when Morena parked her Smart Car in the theater's dark, mostly empty parking lot. She was a little miffed that he'd spent their entire ride tooling around with his phone instead of speaking with her, but when he turned a giant, crooked-toothed smile her way and announced, "Triumph! I have our after-movie plans!" she forgave him.

A little.

Mostly.

The movie theater's lobby smelled of popcorn, like every American movie theater, but its dingy floors and unlit concession stand didn't project an air of welcoming confidence. The couple skipped the dark bank of candies and headed straight for auditorium number two.

The run-down theater had Vadim a bit worried. Morena was beautiful and clearly successful, and something about her drew him in like no other woman before, but maybe she wasn't entirely there in the head. "This movie," said Vadim. "I have not seen trailers for it?"

Morena ran a nervous hand through her perfectly blown-out layers. Perhaps taking him to a non-American film had been unwise. Well, it was too late now. "No, no. It's not an

American movie. It's Hindi. Indian." She twisted an ombre-dyed end. "This was a terrible idea. I'm sure they're playing some blockbuster smash hit over at Lincoln Square."

He couldn't bear her nervous unhappiness, so Vadim pressed his warm hand over Morena's. Slowing her, shushing her. "It will be wonderful."

The couple's boots stuck to the slightly cola'ed floor, but that didn't matter. They chose a pair of seats from the multitude of empties, a few rows ahead of some teenagers giggling over a recent Snapchat and well clear of the sixty-something ladies dressed in jewelry and saris.

From Vadim's point of view, it was marvelous. From the moment the screen lit, he got the one thing he wanted: a chance to be near the object of his sudden affections. With his difficulties reading English fast enough, he had Morena read the subtitles to him. All the way from the trailers through the intermission, she leaned over and pressed herself against his side.

Her warm breath transmitted the translated dialogue into his ears. Her cotton-covered breasts pressed against his arm as she pushed closer, the better to whisper so quietly that even the biddies couldn't complain. Vadim thought she was wonderful and that this horrible movie (with its pointlessly layered-in romance plot) was the best date he'd ever been on.

When the intermission finally came, the house lights went abruptly from off to on. Morena squinted at his handsome profile. She'd been half watching the film and half wondering if she should have taken him to Lincoln Square after all. She didn't think he could possibly be interested in a movie haltingly narrated by another theater-goer.

"You can't be having fun," she said. "We could just leave

now. Skip the second half." Also, the plot left a lot to be desired, as anyone might expect of a piece with Superstar Whatshisname in it. Why the actor in question insisted on being billed as *Superstar* in every flick was beyond her comprehension. (The author would like to inform the curious that the actor's name is Rajnikanth, but his name is not what's important when contemplating his peculiarities, and Morena hadn't remembered it.)

"No, no!" Vadim hastened to reassure her. There was no way he would miss another hour or more of this intimacy. He could still smell her perfume's amber notes. "It is very charming."

"Next time, I'll take you somewhere that doesn't have subtitles." Which ruled out the opera, of course, but so few people cared about the opera these days, outside of *Les Miz.* "Assuming you want a next time." Even as she said the words, she knew he was required to respond in the positive. For politeness's sake. She'd forced him down a conversational one-way street. *I am such a bad date.*

"Ah, yes. Something active, maybe." Vadim thought this might be a good time to remind her that the movie wasn't the end of their outing. "Like we shall do later tonight."

"Hmmm." She tapped a finger exaggeratedly on her bottom lip. Vadim wanted to lick it but refrained. "It's only February, so Smash Putt isn't an option yet."

He'd never heard of such a thing. "What is this Smash Putt?" This was what he got for learning English from the Brits instead of the Americans.

"It's like mini-golf on spring break."

"What?" Vadim had heard of both golf and spring break, but the combination made little sense.

"I'll take you in March if they do it again this year," she said.

Vadim bit hard into his cheek, raising the flesh into jagged mountaintops around his molars. His nonrefundable return ticket to the Ukraine was dated for just under two weeks. February 28. He almost told this to Morena, but if she knew he had plans to leave so soon, she'd doubtless be uninterested in deepening their acquaintanceship. He didn't want to change the nature of their budding connection.

Unfortunately for Morena, he was right in this assumption. If she *had* known about his plane ticket, she wouldn't have let herself get so involved. But she didn't know. And she did get involved. And so things progressed.

The second half of the film went much the same as the first, and they walked to her Smart afterward, arm in arm, attempting to figure out what had happened after the giant plot shift that changed the movie from a dance film into something about artificial intelligences. Had the makers thought audiences wouldn't notice? Did the producers believe the intermission wiped a memory clean in the same way a week's break had for old *Doctor Who* audiences?

Morena didn't know much about the old *Doctor Who*, really, but Suzyn was a huge fan. (She liked to say Nyssa was her favorite companion, but it was really Adric with his tragic and meaningless death.)

After a quick dinner, complete with multiple margaritas, at Santa Fe—a sketchy-looking, but better-than-edible Mexican restaurant on car salesman row in Kirkland—Vadim announced: "And now: we dance!"

"Dance?" Morena would have admitted, had anyone asked, that dancing was close to her heart. She'd grown up dancing samba around the house while pushing her toy vacuum cleaner, graduated to awkward slow dancing in high school, taken classes for everything from ballet to hula, and now paid a willing Suzyn's cover charges at whatever clubs she could. She loved the beat, the sweat, the manic energy of it all. She even attended senior citizen ballroom events, though less often as she got older.

"Dance," agreed Vadim. And then he proceeded to give her such convoluted directions that they crossed the toll bridge three times and got turned around in the Highlands, where telephone GPS units stopped receiving signal. It took much map wrangling and near-hysterical laughter before they ended up at a dark church in southern Bellevue all the way down in Factoria.

The parking lot only had one lamp, and it had burned out, so only Morena's headlights illuminated the lot. Three cars, none parked near each other, had possibly been abandoned. Between the dark and the emptiness this scene could be ominous, but it was in *Bellevue*. Nothing in Bellevue could be ominous. It could be sad, perhaps, in a There Used To Be THINGS Here kind of way. But the city was a residential little cousin to Redmond, which gave it more of a Harmless And Trying Too Hard vibe than a truly dangerous one. No one would ever set a gothic novel in Bellevue, WA.

Well, maybe its downtown area counted as a small city in its own right, but the west-siders never took it seriously.

Morena parked but didn't turn off her Smart. "Are you sure this is the right place?"

Vadim had his doubts as well, but he would not be deterred by concrete and chain link! He would prove his ability to provide for his date. She would have fun if it killed him. So he laughed, the sound overloud in the tiny car. "Yes, yes! Is perfect."

Vadim's confident voice was so *dreamy*. Against her better judgment, hearing her mother's cautioning tones about deserted parking lots in the back of her head, Morena cut the engine and reached into the seat well for her camel-colored coat and bright red scarf. "Then let us be off."

The walk from their parking space to the church's door seemed to get ever longer, as if the lot unfolded with every step they took. Past the second car, Morena downloaded a flashlight app, the second non-factory app to grace her iPhone. She shone the light ahead of them on the ground, trying to keep them from tripping... and possibly to witness the pavement's stretching.

If the pavement really *had* been stretching, it didn't dare do so when people stared directly at it. And so the couple made it to the door, unimpeded by unlikely physics. Not that they'd been impeded before. Because metaphors don't come true. (At least not for Morena in this story. She's an utterly normal, very smart, geeky Seattle woman. If it had been Magic Guy on this date, things might have been different, but Magic Guy wouldn't have purposely gone on a date—being romantically disinterested in the world's mortal population— so the point is moot.)

Large wooden doors creaked open under Vadim's hand, and discordant notes crept along the air into his ears, the sound waves no longer hampered by a physical barrier. It sounded like nothing so much as a small chamber group getting into a brawl and involving their instruments in the scuffle.

Morena laced her arm through Vadim's, enjoying the warm presence of another human being against her side. "Live music, I take it?"

Pretending the clashing strings didn't bother him in the slightest, he escorted his date toward the stairwell from which the sounds emanated. The vile racket came from downstairs. "Are you sure?" he asked, forgetting for a moment that this was all his own idea.

She laughed, more at ease now that she could hear music... or something approximating it. She found it hard to believe anything bad could happen in a place where there was live music. Sure, there'd been that shooting at Café Racer a few months back, and the news article had quoted someone saying "But they play folk music there!" or something like that, but it was the aberration.

They stomped down the stairwell as loudly as possible, Vadim to increase his courage and Morena to warn the attendees of imminent arrivals. Morena's reasoning was clearly useful, since someone called out *"Tudo bem?"* before they'd even seen any other human beings.

This phrase is Brazilian Portuguese for something generic like "How's it going?" As such, Morena recognized it and caroled back, *"Tudo bom!"* before poking a furious finger into Vadim's arm. "You took me to a Brazilian church for dancing?" She wondered how he'd even found one. She'd attempted to go to BrasilFest at Seattle Center many summers in a row, and had never managed to find more than one booth and five soccer fans.

Vadim shrugged, unsure whether she was annoyed and how to fix it if so. Sadly for him, shrugging at someone who is annoyed with you only makes them actively angry. "You say your mother is from Brazil, yes? It seemed like a good idea." In the endless passageway to a basement that gave off creepy vibes to those who didn't know what it meant to be in Bellevue, he was rethinking the appropriateness of his dance plan. "We can turn around."

His offer came far too late.

"We can*not*. They already know we're here." It would be terribly rude to abandon this group now. And, what was worse, Morena probably knew some of them. So much for a date to learn more about her hot Slav.

In the end, it wasn't as bad as Morena expected. She didn't know anyone who would report this back to her mother. It turned out that Vadim couldn't dance or speak any Portuguese, and after he'd laughingly tripped over every dancer's feet three times each, no one took it amiss when he bade them all goodbye. Of course, Morena had to go with him, giving her the perfect excuse to leave the seven-person dance club, where "dance club" was like "chess club" but with more samba and frevo.

Out came the flashlight app again, and they stumbled back to the Smart on trembling legs that had worked hard to dance at ever-more-frenetic speeds. Morena propped her date against the car's cold metal nutshell while she fished in her clutch for her keys. Vadim was more than a little overheated from the strange dancing and surreptitiously pushed up his coat sleeves in order to press his bare skin against the chilly door.

"It could have been worse," said Morena. She went dancing all the time and could handle a mere two hours of well-lit samba drills, though she didn't usually have to hold up her partner as well. She found her keys and pushed the unlock button with steady hands.

Vadim slid into the passenger seat and stripped off his scarf, tossing it in the seat well behind him. "How so?" Up until she'd said something, he'd been sure she would never want to go out with him again. After all, he'd completely failed at setting up a suitable post-movie activity.

Most men can tell you that failing in a lighthearted and amusing way actually endears you to prospective love interests. However, though Vadim knew this in theory, his anxious heart felt differently.

Morena revved her little car's engine just to hear the sound. She felt daring and wild, even if they hadn't done anything particularly exciting. With a wicked smile, she explained, "They could have spoken Spanish."

Vadim exhaled, breath loud and white inside the still-cold car. At least he'd known that much. The label "Hispanic" did not include his beloved's Brazil. In this way, he was already far superior to Morena's ex-boyfriend.

"You must let me try again." He put all his conviction behind it. This was not the time to let shyness or cowardice get in the way of grand romance. "Next weekend. I will plan another."

She shrugged. He grinned.

They discussed his little sister's schooling plans for the rest of the ride back across I-90 and into Seattle. As first dates went, it wrapped up better than expected.

Chapter Five
Flowers Over Boys[1]

Sunday morning dawned late in Morena and Suzyn's apartment. This was often the case, since they were definitely a pair who stumbled home, together or separately, in the wee hours after a long night's dancing on those days when they hadn't stayed up watching DVDs or playing story games.

It was also true that February mornings dawned late for *everyone* at Seattle's northern latitude. It was the flipside of having summer days that lasted until 10 p.m. (not an

---

[1] The title of this chapter is a reference to the Japanese (and later, Korean) TV, movie, and anime franchise "Boys Over Flowers." Other than having a mention of flowers and a mention of romance in common, there's nothing else relevant to the show in this chapter. Unlike the other chapter titles in this novel, which, the author admits, are too clever and multi-layered for their own good, this one is just kind of cute. The author also recommends the mid-2000's live-action TV version of this show, if the reader is determined to watch it.

exaggeration for the sake of the narrative). Winter days enjoyed approximately eight hours between sunrise and sunset, and those hours did not start at 7 a.m. Only three of those eight hours on average, by the way, would have proper sunshine. This didn't help the slow-to-rise problem.

So it was around noon when Morena rolled out from her Egyptian cotton, swept her hair into a style she'd seen on an Australian beauty school's YouTube channel, and gently shook Suzyn's sleep-warm shoulder.

"Hey," Morena half-whispered. "You want to have brunch with me and my mom this week?"

Suzyn stretched, her forearms peeking out from her bedding and pebbling in the apartment's relative chill. "Fo' sho'!" She flung back her covers, baring her fading Grinch pajamas. Free food, the super-friendly Mrs. Blake, and *free food.*

Suzyn was neither far enough out of college nor possessed of enough freelance gigs to turn down free brunch offers. Especially at places that had been featured in *Sunset* magazine ("The Magazine of Western Living;" "Experience the West;" and so on).

"Where are we going this week?" Suzyn asked. Morena's mother tended to choose different locations in her "new" home city of Issaquah. She wanted to try them all, she'd said, and Suzyn was happy to go along, from the greasiest joint to the locavorest diner.

"I'll check in a minute." Morena's voice was muffled by the cashmere sweater dress partially over her head. The dress was gray, of course, and warm. It also smoothed perfectly over her hips, had a fun waffle-weave at the sleeve and skirt hems, and was practical enough as long as she didn't have to walk outdoors for long. One of the best things about meeting her mother in Issaquah? Morena drove the whole way. Skirts in rainy winter: safe!

Morena tugged on knee-high calf-leather boots and reached for her phone to text her mother about the location. The iPhone—*not* her regular Samsung, which made her pause for a moment before shrugging—was slick in her hand as she swiped to unlock the screen. When the home dash resolved itself, it showed spinning columns that framed a bright green heart. She must have left the app open.

She shrugged. Why not? Morena shook her phone (*to find your perfect mate*) and enjoyed the Las Vegas-y *ding ding DING!* when the rollers shuddered to a stop.

From the bathroom, Suzyn called back, "Damn, that's loud." She was tempted to storm into the bedroom and confiscate the thing. Morena didn't need cheesy iPhone apps, and she certainly didn't need to date strangers. Not when Suzyn was right here at home...

Suzyn should barely have been able to hear the ringing from that distance and through the walls.

"Mãe says we're going to—" Morena called back.

Morena said the name of the brunch location, but that wasn't important to this story. Nor was it important to Suzyn, who was briefly having a sexual crisis in the bathroom. Yes, Suzyn slept with a variety of interested parties when she was high, but she'd never been interested in Morena while sober. Well, not more than a person ever usually is in their roommate.

Many may not admit it, but almost everyone falls at least a little in love with a good roommate. It's easy to see all the best things about your roomie and to imagine your lives staying mingled like this forever. And that translates naturally into enjoying the person's physical beauty when you're sitting side by side in the glow of the television screen with a bottle of red wine between you.

Suzyn was more susceptible than most to glances in the near dark, her photographer's mind helping to soften the light or deepen the shadows. And, yeah, she was flexible with a lot of her day-to-day living.

But she'd never seriously thought about Morena as a love interest. They were too age-disparate. They wanted different things. Worse, Morena had found a lot of personal and career success, and Suzyn was still financially unstable.

Was Suzyn really changing her patterns and falling in love *now*?

Best-friendship had sprung up quickly between the two women, from the moment they'd decided to room together and Morena had brought Suzyn home to her mother's townhouse in Issaquah. But romantic love was another bucket altogether.

Morena tapped on the bathroom door and pushed it open when there was no resistance. "Scooch," she said. The older woman squatted down, gray sweater outlining her gym-defined quadriceps, to get her makeup kit from beneath the sink. The scent of baby powder and mouthwash filled the room, which were really face powder and astringent to clear away caked mascara.

Under the harsh yellow incandescents, Morena was *herself* incandescent. But the moment had passed, and Suzyn didn't have any further urges to kiss or strip or marry her roommate, only to photograph her and suggest a *Stargate: Atlantis* rewatch.

And thank God for that, thought Suzyn.

Morena's new iPhone double-buzzed on the counter, perilously close to the wash basin.

"I didn't know you'd decided to use this one exclusively," Suzyn said, hoping Morena would give her the cast-off Samsung. Unfortunately for Suzyn, that would never happen. Not only did Morena prefer her familiar old phone for work purposes, but she hadn't actually noticed she'd transitioned to the new iPhone.

The iPhone was just so handy. Somehow, it was always there, as though it were tethered to Morena's subconscious as her main device, though not by deliberate choice. Why, it was almost like it had followed her to the bathroom.

She shrugged and thumbed the unlock with her left hand while her right fished for the liquid eyeliner she knew was somewhere in her makeup kit. Why was it that the thing she wanted *always* shifted to the bottom? "I'm just gonna check Mãe's location with Amigos..."

There might have been an end to that sentence, but she was distracted by the hunt for the all-important eyeliner.

...and by the bright green heart that filled the screen. That was not the regular dashboard, nor was it Amigos.

Amigos, by the way, is the Brazilian Portuguese name for the Find My Friends app. (The magic iPhone had set itself to that language because Morena found Brazilian Portuguese to be both comforting and authoritative). Anyone who'd synced themselves with their friends could share their phone's GPS information. This was particularly useful for knowing how close a friend was to a meeting place, or how long it would take to walk and find them. It would be creepy if it didn't require opt-in.

Suzyn giggled and knocked their elbows together over the laminate counter showing water stains from the '80s, '90s, and today. "If you can't handle an iPhone, maybe you should just give your oversized thumbs a rest."

"There's nothing wrong with my thumbs!" Indeed, Morena's thumbs were normal-sized. And, even if they hadn't been, the app's opening was no fault of her own. It had just happened. Okay?

It was happening a lot lately.

"Then you must be super-old. Only, like, grandparents fail at iPhones. Apple products are so intuitive!"

Morena gasped and tapped Suzyn's nose with a powder brush, tickling the younger woman into recoil. "I'm not *old*!"

Morena would also have liked to point out that Apple products were most certainly *not* intuitive for everyone, especially for people who'd been firmly indoctrinated in non-Apple user-interface designs. If she hadn't had friends with iPhones, she'd never have known about the shaking thing. And the whole "just hold your finger over the icon until something happens" wouldn't occur to her until later in this novel when someone would do it in front of her and she'd copy their style.

Partially in apology, Suzyn offered, "You need any help with your eyeliner?"

Ready in under an hour, the pair piled into Morena's Smart and were soon possessed of drive-thru lattes courtesy of Morena's Starbucks card before they crossed Lake Washington.

There are many reasons a person might *not* yearn to drive a car across the toll bridge separating Seattle from "the Eastside." Among these are the journey's beginning at the Mercer Mess onramp, followed by paying a toll for the privilege of crossing the water, and then culminating with a spot of impromptu traffic in downtown Bellevue after the 405 junction.

The most common reason Seattleites tended not to cross the 520 bridge, however, was not traffic or money (neither of which were very relevant on a Sunday morning with Morena's budget). No, it was the prevailing attitude of why-on-Earth-would-anyone-want-to-go-east? Though the outside world saw Seattle/Kirkland/Redmond/Issaquah as the Seattle Metro Area, residents broke into two camps: east side and west side.

The west siders found the Eastside boring and uncultured, but possessing really good wine. The Eastsiders considered the west side to be a mess of horrible traffic, narrow streets, absent parking, and potential lawsuits that just weren't worth the effort.

The people from Spokane considered the two areas to be exactly the same: far away and citified.

The people from Tacoma were pleased by the east-west infighting because it meant no one was mentioning the Tacoma Aroma.

The people outside Washington just called it all Seattle. Except for the pockets of computer scientists who were more familiar with Redmond as a city name because that's where the Microsoft main campus was. Those people could also tell you more about Mountain View, CA (home of the Googleplex), than nearby San Francisco or Oakland.

But our intrepid heroes were local enough to know that they weren't supposed to enjoy going east unless it was to make fun of yuppies at wineries or to go hiking. However, Morena's love for her mother (and Suzyn's willingness to go along with whatever, even to the Seattle equivalent of New Jersey) made all that a moot point.

Besides: skirts and parking! Yay!

Soon enough Morena swung her leather-booted feet out of the car and onto the parking lot's pavement. *Glory be for suburban lifestyles.* Two empty spaces over, a water pool shimmered with someone's spilled gasoline, but she couldn't smell it over winter's green wetness.

Today's brunch choice was the in-house restaurant of a little hotel overlooking a park. Suzyn's sneakers squeaked on the hardwood floors as they dripped toward the dining room.

As they passed signs marked *Men* and *Women*, Suzyn pointed her intended destination. "I'm just gonna go powder my nose. I'll catch up with you in a minute."

"What?!" Morena's voice rose in a shriek, which Suzyn thought was excessive for wanting to go to the bathroom. "You can't do *that* when we're meeting my mom."

At which point Suzyn realized that "powder" had a few meanings. She was adult enough to admit that her own usage often trended toward the illegal kind. Still, it wasn't like she needed to relax in order to get through a free lunch with Morena's awesome mother or like she'd need the creative energy for some sort of artistic activity. It was *just lunch.*

"I would never!" Suzyn said.

Suzyn disappeared into the ladies' room, and Morena fished in her bag for a rattling mini bottle of Advil. She'd had a slight headache all morning, and the sudden rush of anxious blood had only made it worse. At least, that's what she told herself when she popped two pills into her mouth.

Without her roommate, Morena continued to the dining room and let the maître d direct her across the rose-carpeted floor to a table with a white polyester cloth hanging all the way to the ground and a woman with bra-length black hair already seated.

"Mãe!"

The seated woman stood. "Morena!"

They embraced as soon as Morena was close enough, pressing kisses to each other's right cheeks and grasping in a tight hug. It had only been a week since they'd had breakfast together last, but it had seemed longer. Morena couldn't wait to tell her mother about a new product Starbucks would be selling in local stores soon... and about meeting Vadim.

For her part, Morena's mother wanted to hear all about everything. Luiza had been a bit lonely, and she needed some mother-daughter time. She'd been exceedingly busy the past week, a problem that kept her from staying connected to her child.

"Do you think these tables need flowers?" Luiza asked before they'd even sat down.

"What?" In truth, the tables needed *more* than flowers if they wanted to be appealing. They needed something other than white polyester linens and the smell of greasy diner eggs. The rest of the hotel had looked organic and boutique-y, but this restaurant could have been in any Marriott in the world.

"These tables, they could use flowers." Luiza nodded agreement with herself since Morena was falling down on the job. "I think I'll talk to the manager before I leave."

Morena's mouth overflowed with saliva, and she swallowed hard. "What? No! Mãe. Why would you do that?" Sure, her mother was friendly and prone to chatting with managers everywhere, but usually it was to give thanks rather than to complain.

Luiza pasted a carefree expression on her face, even as her heart beat a furious samba. "So that I can offer to supply them, of course. I'm starting a florist business. I get my first shipment this Wednesday." This was the test. Would Morena approve? Would her daughter try to take over? "Here, let me give you a card."

She'd gotten a great deal with Vistaprint on the custom cards. It had taken her three days of nonstop studying and YouTube tutorials before she'd managed it, but she'd designed them herself using the GIMP (unwilling to spend money on Photoshop if she didn't have to). She'd chosen to do it all on her own instead of finding a designer for hire.

This DIY attitude is a common syndrome in entrepreneurial types, whether from Seattle or anywhere else in the world, but it was worse for Luiza. Luiza's very identity had become tangled in proving her self-worth. She *had* to be able to do things on her own, without a partner. When in Brazil, she'd lived with her parents; then she'd married Scott and moved to the United States with him. Now that she was alone for the first time, she was ready to show the world that she could do whatever she put her mind to. Hence: self-made cards.

Besides, if I got a designer, they'd just take over my project, right?

Morena took the card in numb fingers, her buffed nails tracing over the web address. "That's great! But... why didn't you ask me? You know I would have helped."

Luiza patted her daughter's hand. "Of course you would, sweetie. But I had to do this on my own."

"A whole business on your own? At least I can help you now."

No. Nope. Não. But Luiza knew how to deflect her child with the veneer of acceptance. "Of *course* you can. I'll make you drive things!" She laughed like it didn't matter at all, like Morena's help could somehow stay at the simple delivery level if only Luiza didn't acknowledge any further attempts. "I know it's hard for you to understand, but you're so independent. So used to doing everything alone. If you asked me for help, it'd just be help. But... since your father died, I've had to know. I need to prove to me that I can take care of me." So much for keeping her feelings under wraps. Hiding emotions just wasn't Luiza's way.

Morena's eyes crimped at the edges. "Oh, Mãe."

Luiza shook off her daughter's aborted hug. She didn't need sympathy. "Is Suzyn joining us?" Luiza enjoyed meeting Morena's friends. It was good to stay involved in her daughter's life. Plus, maybe the new friends would also become friends with *her*. Now that Morena was an adult, this had become a possibility.

"She should be here in a moment." Morena tucked the business card into her card case and resolved to look at the website later.

"From the moment I met her, I knew Suzyn would be good for you," Luiza said, thinking of the time six months ago when her daughter had shown up with a tired companion in tow and asked if they could both stay the night. "So, are the two of you, ah...?" She gave Morena the least subtle wink in the history of sexy winks.

It was more than worth it to watch her daughter splutter.

"Mãe! No! She's only twenty-two!" Also, Morena didn't have any sexual interest in women, and both of them knew it (because if Morena was ever to change, she'd talk it through with her mother first, obviously). But that wasn't a reasonable excuse somehow, not in the wake of same-sex marriage legality, so it went unspoken.

"That doesn't mean she's not a wonderful girl." Luiza's voice deepened, and her eyes focused on some spot of nothingness over Morena's shoulder. "You know, when I met your father, our relationship looked doomed. He was from another country. He wasn't Catholic. We didn't know his parents."

Luiza's gaze met her daughter's, willing her to understand that long-term relationships brought stability. "Compared to all that, what is Suzyn's age? You like the same things. You live in the same place. The two of you can get married and settle down together. It's perfect." Luiza's little girl wasn't going to miss out on happiness, not if she could help it.

Morena snorted. "I don't think Suzyn's anywhere near ready to settle down. Twenty-two, remember?"

It was, sadly, true. Luiza had to admit it. She blew out a breath full of hopes and dreams for Morena with Suzyn. She'd have to hope for another potential love match to come along. "But *you're* ready to settle down. Aren't you, *minha filha*?"

She really was. For a given value of settling down. Morena dropped her head and let her mother's fingers stroke through her carefully styled tresses.

That was how Suzyn found them, posed like penitent and priest among the lifeless polyester. "Umm," she said, unsure whether she should interrupt.

Luiza untangled herself and stood to pull Suzyn into a quick hug and cheek kiss. "Lovely to see you, my dear."

"Likewise, Mrs. Blake." Suzyn's parents had raised a polite child, even if she didn't often have a chance to pull out her manners.

"Mãe is opening a florist business," Morena said, voice heavy with a meaning that Suzyn couldn't decipher.

So she chose not to try. "Do you want me to take some photos for your website, ma'am?"

"No, thank you, Suzyn. I'm doing well enough on my own for now." And she doubted she could afford a professional photographer, not when her little camera-phone photos (touched up in the GIMP) served so well.

"I bet you'll be great at it," Suzyn said, paying no attention to Morena's ever-more-furious looks and negatory finger wags. "You're bilingual, right? That's got to open up a lot of markets."

Luiza grinned. This was something she could talk about. "Trilingual, actually. English, Portuguese, and Spanish. And I'm working on Hindi, but it's slow going."

Morena huffed and told Suzyn, "She's been working on Hindi for, oh, twenty years now."

Bored—well, annoyed, if she'd admit it which she wouldn't—Morena felt the iPhone's pull. *Use me, and I'll alleviate all your awkward feelings,* it cried. Metaphorically. She slid it from her bag and swiped to unlock it. Again, the bright green heart filled the screen.

Suzyn leaned into her, close enough to see what she was doing, and laughed. "Addicted much?"

"Are you checking your phone at the table? Has something gone wrong at work?" Luiza gasped, overplaying a little so that Morena couldn't possibly miss her disapproval. She slapped Morena's impolite, phone-using-when-in-company hands.

The phone went *ding ding DING!*

"Oh my gosh, you two." Morena pointedly turned the

screen black and put it in a purse pocket. "The evil phone is all gone now, okay?" She really needed some more Advil to get through this brunch.

Chapter Six
History Lessons

Wednesday was another story gaming night. Technically, every night was a story gaming night, just not always for Morena and Suzyn. Somewhere in the city, someone was playing a game. Somewhere else, another person was living life as though it were a game. And what is life but one long plot-less story? A James Joyce-esque stream of consciousness.

Of course, down in the city of Portland, there was even more story gaming on the schedule, and if one asked a Seattle story gamer they'd probably reminisce fondly about games played in Portland but be quick to reassure the listener that it was only a one-off, that Seattle groups were better across the board but that Portland was a quaint town to visit. Portland may have had more overt story games, more bicycles per capita, and more microbreweries (and a TV show named after it), but that just meant that its mustachioed and bird-appliqued populace didn't appreciate what it had. It ate lunch at gourmet food trucks without realizing non-gourmet was an option.

For all this intercity rivalry with Seattle's younger, hipper cousin, Morena never thought about Portland for any reason other than to take a weekend trip for a convention or to listen to a current roommate's friend's band.

So on this particular Wednesday, Morena and Suzyn were smushing two tables together at the Cupcake Royale on Pike between 11th and 12th. (They'd been able to ride the buses this time, a good thing since Capitol Hill's public parking was a disaster.) The tables in question were white-topped and lightweight, like confections from an *Alice in Wonderland* film. They were also round and intended for only two chairs, so pushing them together made a sort of infinity symbol with lots of opportunity for cards or tea mugs to fall through.

With such a seating and tabletop problem, a savvy meetup organizer might have suggested a different location for the night's activities, but Cupcake Royale had two things going for it. (1) Amazing cupcakes (including gluten-free options, meaning that anyone who showed up would be able to eat there, Seattle having more than its share of the celiac—or, it must be admitted, gluten-hypochondriac—population). (2) It was largely empty on Wednesday nights, in comparison to other public spaces.

Morena frowned at the two tables' messy mating. "Do you think we'll need a third one?"

"I'll be your third one!"

Suzyn jumped and screamed and assured herself that she could take something with calming properties later. God knew she needed it. "Damn it, Magic Guy. Do we need to get you a bell?"

The lame old cliché embarrassed her as soon as she said it, but Suzyn didn't blush. Since she considered both Morena and Magic Guy to be relatively lamer and older than she was, it wasn't the world's largest faux pas.

Magic Guy did the blushing for her, anyway. "I think we have two others tonight, and one of them's a newbie who might not show."

Suzyn rolled her eyes. "Flaky meetup members strike again." She ignored her own level of flakiness when disparaging others. It made things easier.

"We can pull up an extra chair and stick it on the end. Just in case." Magic Guy tossed his messenger bag beside theirs on the hard booth bench and reached for an empty chair at the table next to their makeshift one. "Excuse me," he said to the occupant.

Said occupant had headphones blasting, secure in the knowledge that no one could hear any evidence of his abysmally uncool musical choices. Little did he know that Magic Guy's uncommonly sensitive ears could make out each well-chosen lyric of Sugar Ray's "Every Morning."

Magic Guy waved his hand, and the audio connoisseur looked up from his MacBook to make a motion conveying "please take that chair; I'm not using it." Magic Guy nodded his thanks and slid the chair into its place at the end of the slapdash gaming space.

Suzyn asked, "Why didn't you take one from the other side?" The table beside them in the other direction had a number of empty seats.

Magic Guy shrugged. "Can I get you a cupcake?"

"I don't accept gifts from strange men," Suzyn said.

Morena giggled and sat on the bench, scanning the shop

for newcomers. "Since when?"

"Since that creepy guy on Saturday accosted you?" This was patently untrue, especially if a person considered the drug deal immediately following said event as involving a strange man. Paid drugs weren't a gift, per se, but Suzyn's dealer had thrown in an extra pinch for his favorite customer.

"What creepy guy?" Magic Guy settled into a seat instead of heading up to the counter, preferring to hear a juicy story than acquire a moist cupcake. He was particularly interested in learning what made a guy "creepy" so that he could avoid doing whatever it was.

"Just some guy at Gas Works." Morena shrugged, erroneously figuring that the nonstory wouldn't be of interest. "If you want to hear about my love life, though, it's way more exciting that I went on a date last weekend, and I'm seeing him again on Friday."

Standing back up, Magic Guy wormed the fingers of one hand into a tight back pocket to grab hold of his wallet. "What are you going to do?" He tugged at a vegan leather corner and got it halfway out before switching hands: the trials of skinny jeans.

"He says he's going to surprise me." She leaned her elbows on the table, the better to launch into a tale. "You should ask me about his last surprise."

Suzyn said, "He is so ridiculous. Perfect for you, really." Because, of course, Suzyn had heard all about everything that had happened, from the movie to the parking lot, in excruciating detail. She knew what Vadim had said, what he hadn't said, what he wore, what he ate for dinner, what his dancing was like, what languages he definitely couldn't speak, and what Morena wished he would have said but didn't.

Suzyn was more than ready to hear it all again, and possibly to interject some details of a date she hadn't been present for. She felt it was important to let Magic Guy know that she already had all of the information. It was like a sign proclaiming her as an expert, a warning that *she* was Morena's best friend and roommate—so he shouldn't try too hard to worm into her good graces without passing through Suzyn's gauntlet first.

Wisely, Magic Guy said, "I'd love to hear everything. But first: cupcakes! Or else they'll kick us out."

By the time he returned to the broken-infinity table, the night's two other players had arrived.

"Hi!!!" said the newbie. Everyone within a two-yard radius could hear the extra exclamation points. "I'm so excited to meet all of you! I didn't think I'd find a meetup that would combine my two interests of gaming and cupcakes!!!" The newbie had recently moved to Seattle from the Midwest, where there were, in fact, plenty of people who enjoyed both story games and baked goods. What really excited him was making friends in a new city. He'd always been terrible at making friends, ever since he was three years old and had attended a gymnastics class where the other kids (all female) shunned him, forcing him to wait at the end of every line for cross-mat drills. Luckily for him, "socially awkward" was a way of life for non-hipster geeks in his new home city. Hell, even for the hipster geeks.

"Take a seat." Morena gestured to the chair Magic Guy had acquired. "Now that we're all here, what shall we play tonight?"

"We're not starting another season of Monsterhearts," Suzyn said immediately. She was not getting stuck in that game again. No way, no how, no nothing.

The newbie suggested, "I brought my Chrononauts set!" He looked down at the table and gripped the edge. The tables were tougher than they looked and did not crack under the pressure. "You know, if you wanted it. Or needed it. Or, no, never mind." His hands fell to his lap, and his eyes followed them.

Having all had their own social issues, the other players felt for the poor n00b. Morena said, "We usually play story games..."

And Magic Guy picked up, "But since you *kind of* build a story with Chrononauts..."

Suzyn was sick of never getting to play what she wanted to play. Now that she'd asserted her will about Monsterhearts, she took it a step further. "No. Today we're playing Fiasco."

This startled a laugh out of the regulars and calmed the newbie, who felt much better now that memories had moved on from his misstep. At that moment, he fell a bit in love with Suzyn, with her artistic black-flame hair and her societally-admirable chutzpah. For the next few Wednesdays, he'd happily go along with whatever she said and gaze at her adoringly across his red velvet cupcakes... right up until the point where he saw her kissing one of her dealers in thanks and misinterpreted that as meaning she already had a boyfriend. He was smart enough to nip a crush on an unavailable girl.

The fourth regular, who had been heretofore silent because that was *her* brand of social awkwardness, tentatively raised her hand to head height, then snatched it back down because raising hands in social settings is kind of preposterous for a grown up. "Can we set it in the past, this time?"

"When in the past?" asked Magic Guy.

"Someone could get the time machine," suggested

Morena, who was familiar with Fiasco's time machine option.

"Oh my god! There's a time machine option?!!" enthused the newbie.

The shy woman chose to answer Magic Guy's question and ignore all else. She shrugged as though it didn't matter, which meant that it mattered a lot. "Maybe 1800s England? We could do something with the British East India Company?" Her voice trailed off into a whisper at the end.

Suzyn groaned. "I don't know anything about that period."

But Magic Guy did. He'd lived in that period. He had some fond memories of the early 1800s, back when he'd lived with his own best friend, a fellow elf named Chidiock (though he went by Charles in the post-Renaissance period when his real name went out of style). Magic Guy and Chidiock had met at the Italian court ballet in 1602 and become fast friends who bonded over their loves of dance, pranks, and horseback riding.

He had less-rosy memories of the mid-1800s, however. He and Chidiock had been sharing a townhouse in a somewhat-fashionable area of London from 1813. They had played at dissolute rakism in that country's decadence period, enjoying the relative peace and prosperity that came with being rich enough to get into all the card games (and fencing schools and scientific salons) but unimportant enough to be largely left alone. They were playing poker—a game Chidiock was winning by virtue of reading their opponents' minds—at White's one night in 1820 when a player made a snappy remark about the British East India Company's proclivity for encouraging good British citizens to intermarry and intermix with the natives.

The player had been William Henry Cavendish-Bentinck, later the CEO of the aforementioned Company and patron of the English Education Act of 1835 unfortunately for the Indians. At that moment in 1820, though, he was simply a bigoted duke with a pair of tens.

Chidiock had laughed along with the other men at the table. Not the gleeful laugh of a man about to take all the money from a group he didn't much care for, but the laugh of someone who agreed that perhaps the natives in question didn't deserve British patronage.

Magic Guy had tried to point out the flaws of this thinking. "It's been working well for the Company so far, Your Grace. They're tying smart young Englishmen to both ends of the major trade routes with marriage incentives. It's a brilliant plan for getting the best work out of a bright and virile population whilst keeping England's empire at the pinnacle of worldwide society."

Cavendish snorted and laid down four kings, prompting another laugh from Chidiock, who had seen the pair of tens. "Well, I'll put a stop to *that*, if I ever get the chance."

And he had, fifteen years later. Which was the worst thing. And the thing that had finalized Magic Guy's and Chidiock's falling out. Which had led to Magic Guy's determination to take a few centuries off from the ever-old (yet still somewhat short-sighted) culture he'd been born into, in order to live fully among the mortal humans.

Magic Guy gave the other Fiasco players a quick primer on Anglo-Indian education and the way the British East India Company initially took well-educated, but not necessarily well-heeled, members of society and elevated them to new levels of power and luxury if they moved to hot, remarkably civilized India. He kept his old accent from slipping in too much, catching all his drawling vowels and Oxbridge-dropped syllables before they could ooze from his mouth.

The newbie's jaw hung wide open, showing an unappetizing wet cavern of reddened teeth where cupcake crumbs had stuck to the enamel. The woman who'd suggested 1800s England was cleaning under her nails with the metal tip of a mechanical pencil, her shoulders hunched over and her hair falling forward to shield her sweaty brow. Morena and Suzyn, though, perched on the edge of their bench, enraptured with the level of information.

Suzyn's phone vibrated in her pocket over and over, but she didn't pay the device any attention, preferring to observe the movement of Magic Guy's mouth as he spoke—to watch his pale hands shape history with clashing forks. Unacknowledged, her dealer left messages begging her to come outside and take her yay already so that he could return to the comfort of his heated car.

When Magic Guy fell silent, the shy woman said, "Oh."

Newbie said, "Uh."

Morena sighed, frustrated as always with *some* players who couldn't handle the level of detail that verisimilitude required. "Maybe we'd better not."

Suzyn said, "Excuse me" and went outside to get her powder. But she didn't snort it yet. It seemed like a desecration, like she was mocking the hardship of the Indians post-1835 under British rule (which Magic Guy had touched on only briefly, as it clearly bothered him for some personal reason).

Five hours later, when the game wrapped and Cupcake Royale was closing for the night, Morena and Suzyn put on their coats and scarves, and each linked her arm through one of Magic Guy's. His heart sped—no one had touched him for *so long*—but he didn't shake them off. How they'd coordinated this move bewildered him. He hadn't seen them exchange any looks, nor heard them plan to keep him in their company, and he knew them both for standard-model humans who had no talents with telepathy, no matter what Suzyn's drugs tried to convince her.

The threesome emerged onto the cold sidewalk, made no warmer by the sheer volume of pedestrians. Walking three abreast became an exercise not unsimilar to dodgeball.

"I don't think we've ever asked, but—" Morena began.

Suzyn finished, "—what exactly is it you do?"

"Because that was an epic level of detail."

"And so interesting."

"Tell me you're a history professor," Morena begged, concluding the tag-teaming.

They hadn't planned to talk over each other in this actually understandable way, it just happened. It happened strangely often. And "strangely" was the right word because the two women had very little in common.

Yes, they were roommates, but they came from different ethnic backgrounds (half-Brazilian versus African-American), different cultures (Washingtonian versus New Yorker), different generations (nearly forty versus barely twenty). They had wildly dissimilar jobs, and only one of them had a self-destructive set of addictions. They only appeared to have two things in common: story gaming and an address. Yet, sometimes, their minds worked in perfect tandem, and it pleased them both to believe that this synergy made them family, though neither of them said as much to the other.

Magic Guy just grinned, very aware of the picture they made: a man with two good-looking ladies on his arms. Perhaps more worthy of envy outside of Capitol Hill, but still a picture of friendship that suggested a possible foray into lucky polyamory. "Not a history professor," he said.

Suzyn leaned into his shoulder. "Some kind of storyteller then. Novelist? Puppeteer? Political propagandist?"

"Silly child." Morena reached behind Magic Guy's back to swat at her roommate and winked at a pair of lesbians strolling behind them. *That's right*, she thought, *I'm still hot enough to snag these two young things*. "He's a *story gamer*. He always tells stories."

The lesbians behind them did not notice Morena's wink. Nor did they much care about the people in front of them. This was their six-year anniversary, and they were walking the two miles to dinner at Coastal Kitchen, just as they'd done on their first date.

"Still...." said Suzyn, not appreciating being called a child. "He must tell stories for money. And for enforced practice."

It is a sad truth that practicing improves a skill. Everyone knows this, but no one wants to do it. And so, paid practice—in the form of employment requirements— helps most people to become better at whatever it is they do, in ways that they wouldn't on their own. It made Hemingway more concise, made Morena even more programming-savvy, and made the author of this novel capable of concentrating on a manuscript for more than three hours at a time.

"Nope," said Magic Guy, because he didn't have a job as a storyteller in this lifetime. "I make accessible websites. You know, so that, like, blind people can still use the Internet even when there are mathematical equations and stuff." He might have been trying a bit too hard to speak like a modern twenty-something.

"Then we have to help you 'realize your potential,'" Suzyn said.

"My potential is really my own business."

"Your opinion doesn't count," said Morena, in full agreement with her roommate on this. "If you've been squandering talent, then you can't be trusted to manage it." She'd gone to a Starbucks management seminar the week before and had incorporated the pithiest slides into her daily life since. This phase would only last another few days, but it was relevant at this precise moment.

Suzyn nodded in utmost dramatic seriousness. She could spin this to her own advantage as well, if she approached it correctly. "We'll start small," she reassured Magic Guy. "Just a small project to get you started down the road to riches." Because, as far as she was concerned, talent ought to translate to patronage. "It'll have to be something we understand, so that we can help you along."

Morena took Suzyn's bait. "Making a story game!"

Suzyn nodded strongly and tugged them around a corner, past a storefront whose door opened with a wash of warm air. "And we've got to work in his accessibility thing. Maybe we could make it half-story game, half-boardgame?"

"Like The Resistance?" asked Magic Guy. He hadn't cared much for The Resistance. He didn't need that level of intrigue and falsity in his gaming life.

Suzyn hummed. "Maybe more like Bang!" She knew Magic Guy's distaste for The Resistance, even if she didn't know why.

"I love Bang!" said Morena. It was an elegant example of game theory in action, and she'd long held that economics professors should use it in college classes. Ever since she'd been told that perhaps she shouldn't write a paper on Colombian drug cartels in Econ 102, she'd searched for equally appropriate, but still somewhat edgy, economics paper topics. It didn't matter that she hadn't taken an econ class in more than fifteen years.

"We know," said Magic Guy.

Suzyn bit back a comment about how if Morena loved Bang! so much, why didn't they play it more often? Instead of Monsterhearts. This wasn't the time for that particular soap box. This was the birth of something new, something brilliant and shining.

Chapter Seven
Slow Up, Slow Down

"If we're going to discuss this more," Morena said, "can we get out of this cold?" Her words came out muffled through her cashmere, cable-knit scarf.

As they crossed under a blinking stoplight, Magic Guy demurred. "I really think it's time for me to head home. This has been lovely, but..."

Suzyn kept a firm grip on his arm, not knowing that he could break her hand if he so chose. Even if she had known, she probably would have done the same. The odds of someone breaking an acquaintance's hand *just because they can* is rather low. She rang a bell next to a nondescript door attached to a windowless room underneath a jutting, dilapidated second floor. The door was one of those 1970s plain wooden things, but painted blue at some point, and then white, then brown, and now a sort of dingy street camouflage.

Magic Guy wiggled his elbow in her grip, but didn't

reclaim his limb. "Where even *are* we?" he asked.

"Knee High Stocking Co.," said Suzyn.

The door opened onto a dark room with candlelit mahogany tables and warren-like offshoots. Behind the main parlor, squinting patrons could make out a bar, well polished and well stocked. The place styled itself a speakeasy, but there was nothing illicit about it. The city government knew it was there. The owners paid taxes. It had a Yelp score of four-and-a-half stars.

They waited a mere five minutes to get a table.

Seated, Suzyn drew senseless patterns with her finger on the smooth wooden table top. "So, what kind of game should we make? Something historical, obviously."

Magic Guy sighed but accepted a menu from the serving woman. "Are we *still* on this?"

Morena ordered lamb sliders and tater tots for them all to share (and whispered to the server that she'd be picking up the bill for the table, please, a gesture she often made when out with friends because she loved to take care of the people she liked, and this kind of money was easy enough to spend). "It needs a theme, though. Something catchy, but not too overdone. Like steampunk."

They all made lemon-faces at the idea of yet another steampunk game.

Morena brainstormed, "How about spies and counter-spies?" In her head, Morena envisioned something like the old *Mad Magazine* comic meshed with *Alias* and a world history textbook. Though how that would be a game was anyone's guess. "It should have a mechanic where you can sleep with other spies to get influence over them. Oh! We'll call the influence points honeypots."

Suzyn pulled a piece of paper from her messenger bag and stole a pen off the table next to them. Sketching quickly, she showed off a *Winnie-the-Pooh*-esque honeypot. "If you have more than four of these on another player, then they have to let you influence their actions."

Magic Guy, heretofore attempting to seem uninterested, leaned forward and fingered the paper with the game piece prototype on it. "And if you have six honeypots on another player, then your character has developed affection for them. So you aren't capable of killing them or whatever."

The waitress returned at this point, and all three of them ordered drinks with improbable names like *Hammock Between the Sugar Cane* and *The Cup of Awesome.*

"But where's the history angle?" Magic Guy poked Suzyn's shoulder, touching her on purpose for the first time. "You were so determined to use my history professor-ness."

Morena was the one who answered. "We'll use famous spies throughout history. Like Mata Hari."

"James Bond!" said Suzyn.

Magic Guy nodded slowly, not even bothering to point out that James Bond wasn't a real person. "Casanova."

Suzyn bumped her arm against him. "Casanova was a spy?"

"I'll tell you all about it some other time." Magic Guy was his own hoisting petard sometimes (and he knew what the expression meant from his years of living, not from the *Rocky and Bullwinkle* sketch, though Suzyn wouldn't be familiar with that, either). Always, he knew things that people his apparent age weren't supposed to know. The Beloit College Mindset List only helped so much.

"Well, you'll have plenty of chances," said Suzyn. She pulled out her scratched-up phone to check her calendar. It was mostly empty, but she pretended to scroll through the dates and hours all the same.

She, like most people, found it important to *look* busy, even when she wasn't. The rise of smartphones made this small deception easier, while also making it truer since anyone could schedule a get-together on the spur of the moment, making them much more likely to happen.

Assuming someone *wanted* those meetings to happen. The advent of easy scheduling also meant the advent of clearer social snubbing. If someone didn't want to see you again, they didn't have the excuse of going home to check their calendars; they simply didn't pull out their phone. (This level of passive-aggression was common discourtesy in the neighborhood.)

"We'll have to get together outside our regular gaming hours," Suzyn said.

Magic Guy flinched away but covered his physical lapse with a sip of vermouth and Benedictine. Spending time with people outside of his safe story gamer space was dangerous. He might forget his current persona, drawing attention to his oddness. They could uncover his magical ability and try to sell him to the government, or on eBay, or to an institution. Worst of all, though he didn't consciously realize this, spending creative time where he built a fun product with sweet people could lead to his *forming friendships*; he'd come to this city to avoid making friends, especially with the short-lived humans.

But since Magic Guy refused to admit that last possibility to himself—and he trusted his own discretion to maintain a consistent, non-magical façade—there was only one answer he could give. He pulled out his own phone and suggested, "I have tomorrow after six if you do. We're gaming on Thursday. But maybe Friday at seven?"

Suzyn tap-tap-tapped on her screen. "Friday is perfect. I'll sketch out some possible character cards and think about the board-and-story mechanic and learn about your Casanova." She danced on her bench. "We can totally make this happen! I'll be artistic, you'll be historical, Morena will be practical. We'll have a game and be selling it in no time. Oooh, we can make a Kickstarter for it!"

Magic Guy laughed at her excitement. He told himself it would be good for his future cover to spend more time with Suzyn, to learn her speech patterns and her mannerisms.

He believed he could protect himself from forming strong bonds with a relative child.

He was wrong. Even elves are wrong sometimes.

Morena raised her hand like an elementary school student. "Ummm... Friday's no good for me. I have another date with Vadim." She bounced a bit at the very thought of it. He was so fun! And different.

Even if she hadn't had a date planned, though, she would have made an effort to schedule one the moment Suzyn started talking about starting a small business (not that Suzyn realized that was what she'd suggested) and spending all their spare time on an involved project. Not only did Morena have no interest in being the practical, and therefore liable, third of a business partnership, but she didn't have the attention and hours for it. She had a job, a *real* job, at which she spent at least sixty hours a week.

Morena loved her job. She enjoyed the statistical modeling and the light friendships she'd formed with the managers of various Starbucks store locations. But it was still a *job*, and it was the one thing she held up to herself and to her mother as a measure of success. (Her mother's primary metric was romance, with a secondary allowance for workplace success as evidenced by financial security. And Morena had the latter, at least, with her $300,000 base salary and brilliant performance reviews.) She didn't have the energy to devote her spare time to some new project, nor the desire to cannibalize her work time.

"That's okay," said Suzyn. "Me and Magic Guy can start fleshing out the details while you go gallivanting about with your man-friend. Right, Magic Guy?"

"Right." He looked up at the ceiling with its ostentatious chandelier. "We should find a way to use some local settings, like this one. Seattle is so evocative."

Suzyn cocked her head to the side. "On the one hand, I could take some great photos for that. On the other hand, I was thinking maybe ancient Rome or something for setting. Like, why would Mata Hari be in modern Seattle?"

"Why would she be in Ancient Rome?" countered Magic Guy. "We could do expansion packs."

"Oh my god, yes," said Suzyn.

When they closed the Knee High Stocking Co. at 2 a.m., Magic Guy had joined in sketching on the paper. At no point had Suzyn snuck out to score some drugs. But Morena had grown ever quieter, going along with their planning, but not truly invested. Not yet.

Cynical people (often referred to as practical people) will see a product used in some visible way and ask, "But who's paying for that?" By this they mean to say, "Is someone feeding me advertising or propaganda?" Obvious sponsorships are one thing, but clandestine product placement is another.

In Seattle, for instance, everyone is required to love Microsoft, Amazon, and Starbucks. But, even knowing that, there is a moment when a Duck Tour passes a Starbucks and the driver gets all the tourists to make the *cha-ching* noise that a cynical person wonders: "Does Starbucks have a stake in Ride the Ducks?"

As Morena was passed by one such bus at 3 p.m. on the Friday following the previous scene, she waved to the passengers and went to join them in *cha-ching*ing. But right then, her phone—her Samsung—double-vibrated in her purse, and she paused in bolstering her personal corporate sponsor to check the message. This took some juggling of a white mocha, from another Starbucks of course, in one hand and her bag's straps with the other.

The text was from Vadim, and it read: *Excited to see you, pack a bag!*

Seeing as it was still firmly mid-afternoon and Morena was heading back to her office for a post-caffeination meeting, she wasn't sure when she'd get around to packing a bag, especially not if they planned to meet at seven. She had statistics to interpret and products to order before the weekend. Moreover, it seemed odd that someone she'd only been out with once would ask her to spend the night.

Since she was familiar with second-language accidents, she decided to clarify whether this was a vulgar sex request. She texted back, *What kind of bag?*

Prior to receiving this question, Vadim had thought this was rather self-explanatory. He scrunched up his nose and stuck his tongue out at his phone. He flopped back onto the borrowed futon in his brother's best friend's cousin's ex-roommate's apartment in Renton and slowly typed. *Everything you need for two days. We are adventuring!*

Back in SoDo, Morena bit her lip and didn't answer. She walked in a haze, not seeing the food trucks in her building's parking lot nor the man dressed all in green who dodged out of her way when she almost ran into him.

Behind her, the green devotee stopped at the I Love My GFF truck for a fortifying quinoa bowl after his near miss. "I think I need one of those vegan gluten-free chocolate chip cookies of deliciousness," he added to his order. "It's been that kind of day."

And it had been, because the poor Green Man had not only been trampled by the heroine of our story (and this only the third time he'd seen her!), but he'd also started out the morning doing voice over work for a company that had declared bankruptcy halfway through his session. Then his younger brother had called to ask for money. And then he'd nearly been run over when some jerk in a Tesla had decided that red lights were for other people. If anyone needed a non-inflammatory chocolate chip cookie, it was the Green Man.

But, its being the end of the lunch rush, the truck had run out of the amazing cookies. The green man was forced to eat his quinoa bowl in the cold, overcast parking lot with no dessert prize to look forward to.

Inside the building, much warmer and more chocofied, Morena felt ready to address the text message from Vadim. It raised more questions than it answered. She tried to pry further information from him: *Flashlights and bungee cord?* She hoped not.

The reply was immediate: *Formalwear.*

Morena did not have the time to acquire new formalwear, but she did have an asymmetric silk-crêpe dress that she'd only worn once so far and that Vadim, obviously, had never seen. After a moment of relief that she was indeed prepared for whatever eventuality, she glared at her phone. Formalwear! One night, maybe, but what was this about two days? She told herself she wasn't annoyed at his lack of detail and gave in to curiosity: *What are we going to do?*

Buzz-buzz. *It's a surprise. Let's meet at Westlake Station.*

Meeting anyone at Westlake Station tended to go very badly. It is easier now that it doesn't have an aboveground component and that its four bus-and-lightrail bays are clearly marked. Still, the point stands that in the two-story station with multiple entrances and exits—and with no landmarks other than the bay numbers, the Nordstrom/Macy's entrances, and the ORCA card machine—managing to find a friend in the crowd is highly unlikely. Moreover, by virtue of being underground, the station doesn't allow for cell phone reception or GPS tracking.

Worse than all that, though, was the conclusion Morena quickly jumped to, supported by the dual information "meet at Westlake" and "pack a bag": Vadim wanted to take the lightrail down to the airport and then fly somewhere else.

She shook her head. *No,* she thought, *that couldn't possibly be right.* It was only their second date, and she wasn't that kind of girl. Besides, a second-date trip around here? That wasn't airport material; that was an impromptu drive for skiing up at Mt. Baker.

She didn't want to let him know she doubted his planning, though, so she tried again to worm the information out of him. *I hate meeting people at Westlake. Somewhere else?*

He replied: *Southwest ticketing.*

She wrote: *No.* And then she put her phone away to go over the data for the Canadian border area's store inventories since she was already thinking about going north for skiing.

Inside Morena's bag, her phone double-buzzed four times in succession. After a two-minute pause, the vibrations started again. All eight times, the Samsung phone went ignored.

The phone would have found this particularly vexing and might have worried that it would soon be replaced in its mistress's affections, seeing as the woman had acquired another device recently and one with a slimmer form, but it wasn't really capable of feeling much of anything. Which might have led it to wonder whether an unwatched smartphone could ever be an artificial intelligence. But, again, it was only a phone. By virtue of not being sentient, it cared nothing for such philosophical debates on its own intelligent status.

Six o'clock rolled around, and people waved to Morena on their way out of the office. At 6:15, she admitted to herself that she'd need to leave if she wanted to get home in time for her seven o'clock date. The date that she'd mostly rejected. Even though she liked Vadim... or had liked him before he'd gotten weird about travel plans.

Heart beating a little too fast, she took out her phone to read the missed text messages. There were three from Vadim. And a fourth from Suzyn, reminding her that she was going out to plot with Magic Guy that night and that the apartment would be empty in case of a romantic emergency. As if Morena ever had romantic emergencies.

The messages from Vadim were less informative:
What for no?
Formalwear means suits, yes?

Where meatgrinder no Westlake?

Morena was pretty sure most of those texts were intentional, but that *meatgrinder* had to be an autocorrect version of *meet* and some other word she couldn't figure out. She sighed. If she wanted to go out with this guy—this guy who was hot and fun and tried so hard to impress her—then she had to reply.

She texted: *No to the airport. Yes to date. Let's do something else.*

His reply came in fewer than two seconds. *Morena! I worried!* This was followed by *Tickets purchased already. We go, yes? Adventure.*

She envisioned him as a giddy child, jumping up and down yelling "Adventure!" and brandishing a toy sword. This faux-movie in her mind looked a lot like the *Peter Pan* from the 1960s. Which she hadn't seen recently. It was unbelievable, the number of *Peter Pan* versions made. A quick IMDb search revealed eight obvious ones. That had nothing on *The Three Musketeers,* though, which appeared to be the most remade movie in the world. Suzyn was partial to the 1939 version with Don Ameche and the Ritz Brothers, which was almost a musical comedy, but this was a secret known only to the roommates.

Morena texted back: *We don't go, no. Netflix?* Then she hit control-alt-delete to lock her computer for the night. Workday over.

Vadim knew when he'd been beaten. She'd rejected this advance too many times for her to be unserious or politely declining because he'd paid for something she couldn't afford. Still... he tried one last time. *VEGAS!*

The reply: *HELLS NO.* Morena didn't usually use the

phrase *hells no* or its close cousin *hells to the no* in text message format, but she'd been so shocked that it had just come out of her fingertips. Because, well, hells no. They'd known each other barely a week. They'd gone on one—count it, *one*—date. She had plans on Saturday. No.

So she offered, *John Cusack movie marathon?*

Which was how they ended up cuddling on her microsuede couch with takeout from Chef Liao strewn across the coffee table while learning all about Rob's top five breakups. Since this activity does not make for interesting reading, the author will end the scene here and now switch to a different plot line.

Chapter Eight
Friendships Begun
and Friendship's Ending

While Morena and Vadim were figuring out their plans for the evening, Suzyn and Magic Guy did the same. At four in the afternoon, Suzyn lounged around the apartment in Grinch pajamas that had been her favorites since Christmas. What was the point of getting dressed earlier? Maybe she could just stay in her comfy house clothes indefinitely. It wasn't like she needed to impress her so-not-a-date or anything.

She texted Magic Guy: *Let's do something fun before working. Kayak?*

What she'd actually typed was: *lets do sumth fun b4 werkon. kayak?*

Magic Guy might have made excuses to avoid Suzyn, had he been aware of the error-filled version, but since he didn't see the original words, he did respond. Autocorrect is a marvelous thing for texters who are *almost* grammatical.

As it was, he replied: *Kayak rental ends at 6. Also, it's raining and about to get dark.*

He followed that up with: *(and barely 30 degrees)*

Suzyn snuggled her bare feet beneath the Ikea blanket on the couch, letting its warmth comfort her icy appendages. A coffee shop, then. Again. As usual.

Suzyn hated to think she'd reached a point where her entire life could be lived in coffee shops. Where were the parties, the drugs, the sex?

She managed to forget a party invitation she'd declined in favor of meeting with Magic Guy, the blow in her bag, and the creepy dude Morena had saved her from when clubbing at Nectar. Of course she forgot these things. It was morning. Or at least it was a time when she'd only been awake two hours. She texted back: *Your no fun.* >=(((She had to make her own emoticons. Hunting for the right ones on her keyboard took too much energy.

I'm very fun. =^.^=

From any other man, Suzyn might have taken that as flirtatious, but she knew better with Magic Guy. Which was lucky for her, because flirting back would have led to his making excuses, and their story game project would never have gained the necessary momentum to make it a viable small business, and she'd have died at age 36, depressed, in a car crash after stealing the car in a heroin-induced manic phase. But none of those things happened because Suzyn didn't flirt back. She knew he wasn't interested, and besides he was far too serious for her tastes.

Instead she rolled her eyes and returned to the evening's plans. *Where do you want to meet?* She sent it, then made her own coffeehouse suggestion because there was no way she wanted to go very far in the cold. *There's an Uptown near my apartment.*

But just before this second text left her phone, she received another from Magic Guy. *Liberty Bar?*

Liberty Bar had opened on 15th Street (Avenue? It was impossible to keep track) in Capitol Hill in 2006. Evenings, it was a sushi-lover's hotspot, open till 2 a.m. and frequented by the hip-yet-responsible crowd who wanted a luxurious bar scene without having to consort with the Broadway street rabble. During the day, however, it lived a double life. Before the hordes descended for the night, it provided amazing coffee to the local business people who knew to bypass the more-famous Victrola and Caffe Ladro and who needed something more exciting than the "secret" Starbucks shops (which did not fool savvy drinkers at all; these Starbuckses had been modeled after local joints, and only the foolish and unwary might believe they were actually small businesses).

By virtue of its being a bar, a morning patron who asked a Liberty barista *nicely* could get his or her coffee Irished, so long as they promised to drink it on the premises.

Suzyn rarely went to Liberty, as she was far more likely to party on Broadway or get her sushi fix in the Belltown neighborhood, but that was mostly because she wanted to save her own money instead of luxuriating in craft cocktails. She'd have felt guilty spending Morena's money in this bar where her roommate was less than likely to meet a hot, single, interested guy. She texted back, *You want to split California rolls?*

Magic Guy knew that meant he'd end up paying for them, but he agreed. Spending the extra money didn't faze him at all. However, if he'd known what a good time he'd have and how much he'd enjoy Suzyn's company, he would have avoided ever getting involved with either roommate.

It took Suzyn forty-five minutes to wash her face, slide into skinny jeans and an open-weave sweater, and find her ORCA card.

On her way out the door, she grabbed a puffy violet coat that her mom had bought for her in high school. It could have been down-filled; it could have been synthetic—either way, it was warm. Suzyn's mother had made sure all her kids stayed warm in the New York City winters. When Suzyn moved west, her mom had a moment of worry. Who would look after her baby? But she took comfort in knowing that her little girl was appropriately outfitted for any weather, even the sort of weather that Seattle didn't get. Everyone knew it didn't really snow in Seattle.

This fact everyone knew was, of course, false. The problem was that it didn't snow *very often* in Seattle. A true snow, the kind where inches upon inches stick to the ground, happens maybe every ten years. Just long enough for the city to sell off its snow plows as too expensive to maintain. About a year or two after such a sale, the snows will come, and everyone who lives on a hill—which is most of the city, really—gets stuck.

But it wasn't snowing that Friday night. No hills had closed down. No bendy buses had jackknifed on icy residential streets. Everything was as it should be, and that made it easy for Suzyn to get over to Liberty just as six o'clock came around. She stamped her booted feet hard on the entry mat, a habit that came with wearing her winter boots, and unwound her Sounders FC scarf.

For a while, everyone had Sounders Football Club scarves. They'd appeared overnight and proliferated through the city. Microsoft had ridden the popularity wave in 2011, making Microsoft Office scarves of the same size and weight available to Office employees only (who made up practically 30 percent of the city's population).

"Suzyn!" Magic Guy called out before she had a chance to feel lost and alone and like it might be worth flirting with a bartender in order to get something that'd calm her down.

Her not-date was sitting on a low black couch with splitting leather. The rest of the bar had high tables, and the adjoining room had normal tables, but the very front of the front room had these comfy sectionals. Perhaps they were meant to create an intimate atmosphere, or perhaps the low level of the table was meant to feel Japanese to go with the sushi.

Either way, Suzyn folded her long, denim-clad legs and still ended up falling the last few inches onto the cushions. She didn't let it stress her out, just picked at a pink-and-green concoction on Magic Guy's white, square plate. "Ooooh! What's this?"

He slapped her hand away from his treat and passed her a martini glass instead. It was full of clear liquid. A spiraling lemon peel, three inches long, balanced on the rim. "Drink your own drinks and stay away from my dinner."

Suzyn was pretty sure she could still get him to share a plate of California rolls, so she accepted her drink and her momentary defeat. "Whoa, that's strong."

She briefly remembered that you weren't supposed to accept drinks from anyone except a bartender because who knew what it might've been spiked with? But, really, if Magic

Guy spiked her drink, there wasn't much he could do that she wouldn't approve of. Just getting high for free? Score! Knocking her out and knocking boots? She'd just been bemoaning the lack of sex in her life. Deadly poison? He'd probably get arrested for murder after a tox screen.

Suzyn did not live a very safe, healthy, or self-respecting life. Not at that point in time. The author does not endorse this sort of behavior and cautions against ingesting poisons and/or date rape drugs.

She quaffed a healthy swallow and followed it up with a dramatic "ah" of exhale. "So, our game. We know it needs cards, right? Like, something that helps you set up character-istics and something else for major plot points, but then I was thinking maybe something more Fiasco-esque for character creation. What about you?"

Magic Guy couldn't help but find her sledgehammer approach to social niceties charming. After a few thousand years, he'd heard enough small talk. It had been one of his favorite things about living with Chidiock, actually: skipping over the tiresome chatter. There was nothing they'd needed to say to each other after centuries of best-friendship. Oh, they certainly were capable of chitchat when the mood struck, but it was unnecessary.

"I could see it going either way," he said. "I'm more con-cerned with game play. People playing a spy game are all go-ing to want to kill each other, and that's going to lead to some players getting kicked out way too soon for them to have a good time."

"Unless we give them different powers when they're dead." She moved her lips to the right side of her face, making a surrealistic Dalí out of the Thinking Man expression. "You know, like in that one superhero game—I forget which one—where you flip your character card over when you die and can do other stuff after, like walk through walls and read minds."

He tilted his head down so that he could peek up through his lashes to give her a better incredulous look. "You want to make The Undead James Bond?"

She tittered and took another swig of her vodka-and-whatever. "Zombies are very in."

"Tch. Zombies are so over."

Fashion is forever up for debate, and geek fashions take this even further. Geeks will be the first to say that trends don't force them to love something, though it's great when a whole community springs up around a topic you love. They'll also be the first to fight against the idea that they might stop liking something just because it's not cool anymore. However, there's a difference between *retro* and *so last year*, and zombies were starting to straddle the line. The question at that point was whether or not they'd jumped the shark as much as the expression "jump the shark" had done.

In the anti-zombie column, there hadn't been a great movie since *Shaun of the Dead* (itself a parody) or a worthwhile TV show (aside from the quickly declining *Walking Dead*), but there had been more than one Jane Austen knock-off. On the pro-zombie side, people still gathered in Fremont for the Zombie Flash Mob.

But probably the largest sign that zombie popularity was waning had been the zombie run episode of *Castle*. As a barometer of how popular something was, *Castle* let watchers know when something had gone from subcultural to mainstream. And once something went mainstream, it gained a lot of adherents—the kind who *did* care about whether something was fashionable for not. So, while zombies would definitely still be going strong for a core audience, they were done for the rest of the world.

Magic Guy made it his business to know what was fashionable and what wasn't, but he was also posing as a hipper-than-thou Capitol Hill cutie, so anything he said out loud was suspect.

Suzyn shrugged and gave in to the inevitable. "And if they aren't now, they will be in a year or two. Fine, no zombies."

Magic Guy waved down a skinny waiter and ordered Suzyn's California rolls. "Maybe we should ask Morena what she thinks."

Suzyn coughed and almost spilled her drink. "Oh, no. Bad idea. Bad bad bad. Didn't you see her face? If she hadn't really had a date, she'd have made one up!"

If he'd had a drink of his own, Magic Guy would have dropped it. He considered himself a more-than-decent interpreter of human expressions and body language, and it wasn't like Morena was bewilderingly young. "But she's the one who came up with the honeypot mechanic. She was interested, I know it."

"We can see how badly her date is going by trying to get her opinion right now. If she answers, it's awful." Suzyn smirked and took another hit of her drink. Usually, she didn't like to pick on Morena because she knew her roomie-bestie needed love and support. The martini must have been super strong to affect her so soon.

Magic Guy squinched up his eyes to make a negation face. He'd seen a teenager do it the day before while he was using a Broadway café's WiFi. "If you really think she doesn't want to, we shouldn't make her feel obligated. Hey, if you don't want to either..." He trailed off, giving her a way out.

A way she was definitely not taking. (Not because she knew it would help her stave off death at 36.) "I am so in on this!" Suzyn didn't believe in acting too cool. If people wanted to know whether she was excited about something, they had no doubts how emphatically her feelings ran. "I was focusing on the cards because I'm dying to make them. But we can talk about game play. We can talk about anything you want. This is going to be the Best Game Ever." She was already designing the Kickstarter page in her head. "We just need a prototype."

Kickstarter was *meant* for game launches. The first giant projects on the site were all for games, both big-ish companies and little indie goodies. Gamers loved Kickstarter. Kickstarter loved gamers. And Suzyn loved the idea of self-directed creativity with other peoples' money.

"Okay, then," said Magic Guy, a bit taken aback by Suzyn's vehemence. Also a bit taken in by her energy. He was helplessly swept up by her enthusiasm. "I was thinking we could do a version of the game where you played in teams. Like, that it would be possible to do individual, but that you could also be, like, a spy and a handler." He'd been picking up extra *likes* in his dialect for the past ten years, when it stopped sounding weird on young men. Now it just proved the "young" part.

"Good for groups of five to ten!"

And then they were flying, bouncing ideas higher and higher. Magic Guy suggested settings. Suzyn suggested giving handlers and spies completely different endgames and winning conditions. Magic Guy came up with TV watch lists for further ideas. Suzyn actually did spill her drink.

The drink would have fallen to the nearby floor. The glass

would have smashed, cutting her leg and calling the attention of the conscientious waitstaff. She and Magic Guy would have been sidetracked by the excitement and not finished plotting out the things a player character could do with only a convertible, a gun, and a library card.

But the drink did not shatter on the floor. Because Magic Guy caught it with his mind. Some brief cognizance and a hand gesture that looked as though he were conducting a tiny orchestra, and *poof!* The martini glass stayed in place on the table.

Suzyn, of course, noticed nothing. She was too busy sketching a variety of convertibles that might be favored by Mata Hari versus Sydney Bristow.

By the time three hours had passed, Suzyn was listing badly into Magic Guy's shoulder, and they'd completed two pages of very disjointed notes.

Suzyn giggled. "I'm a-gonna call Morrie," she slurred. "Gotta look after my girl." She patted her easily reachable pockets, then pawed ineffectually at Magic Guy's chest. "Soon's I find a phone."

Magic Guy held onto her arms before she attempted to fish around her bag. That could only end with her falling into it. He felt briefly guilty about plying her with so many drinks, but how was he to know that seven martinis in three hours would be too many? "Maybe not, my dear," he muttered into her hair.

Pushing into him affectionately, she giggled again. "Awwww. You're such a *good* friend."

She'd meant that he was a good person, and that she had come to consider him a friend in the course of their playing and during this particular evening, though possibly that feeling of friendship was heightened by the drinking.

However, there was a second interpretation: that she considered him a *good friend,* as in *a friend who is very close to my heart.* Of course, they weren't close friends. He barely cared about her (yet), and she knew nothing about who he really was (yet). But something about the way Suzyn said *good friend* made Magic Guy's fingers tremble. Yes, he wanted to take care of her because he had some modicum of fellow-feeling, but was that as deep as friendship?

Once, he'd had a close friend. A good friend.

In the wake of that fateful card game in 1820, very little had changed in the lives of Magic Guy and Chidiock. They still lived together and played together, but there was an underlying tension that Magic Guy couldn't let go. Whether or not Chidiock was aware, Magic Guy was too upset by their potential philosophical schism to ever relax.

The issue came to a head in 1835 when the English Education Act went live. The crux of their argument went something like this:

Chidiock would say, "Let people do what they want." By which he meant that human concerns were not *his* concerns and also that he didn't want to get involved in political affairs.

Magic Guy would reply, "This will have horrible repercussions." By which he meant that he'd seen this sort of artificial segregation before and that he didn't want the British Empire to be lessened by a disregard for education in India.

They went round and round until a great screaming match

culminated with Chidiock yelling, "I don't want to argue about something so pointless" and shooting his pistol straight into Magic Guy's heart. Thankfully, it wasn't loaded because they'd recently taken to using soft lead bullets, and those things flattened more than was comfortable for extraction.

Magic Guy threw on an overcoat and stomped outside. "That's the bloody point! It's an *important* issue!"

Two days later he'd stomped back inside and up the stairs of their townhouse to flop angrily on his bed and turn his back to the door whenever Chidiock knocked on it. Chidiock's weak apologies didn't penetrate Magic Guy's fog of annoyed despair, and it looked as though they might never speak to each other again.

So Chidiock had crafted a plan. If sincere apologies weren't enough—and if he refused to change his way of thinking purely in order to make his best friend happy—then he had to do something utterly non-serious to break them out of their vicious, cyclic funk. And so began the Great Prank War of 1835.

There is much debate, even in our modern day, over what makes a good prank. Does it require someone to be made a fool? How much hurt is too much harm? Must it involve tin foil? Taking these philosophical questions into account, along with Magic Guy's relative immortality, Chidiock began by instigating what ought to have been a harmless duel.

Having detached Magic Guy's sword hilt from its blade, Chidiock arranged for a clandestine meeting between Magic Guy and a lovely young lady of good family and breeding. He passed notes to both parties, signing all with the counterpart's name, until the pair was utterly committed to a rendezvous during an evening soiree. He then informed the young lady's older brother of the upcoming assignation.

In the cool evening air, Magic Guy and his potential lady love sat side by side in a private garden. The hedges rose high for privacy. The conversation was a bit stilted since neither had begun the affair or had any idea how to broach a topic deeper than *lovely weather we're having, what?* Worse, their bottoms were numbingly cold on the stone bench.

Magic Guy threw prudence into the compost bin and grasped the lady's left hand between his. Her fingers were like frozen carrots on his palms. "Darling," he began. The term of endearment shocked them both, their hearts beating faster, but neither allowed any outward reaction. "Your letters have given me such hope."

Indeed, her letters had been so forthright that he felt he knew her level of interest. He'd also enjoyed their later correspondence, the notes they'd actually written themselves, and knew she was a clever little thing. His perfect match, even if he couldn't recall ever seeing her before and had nearly no interest in her physical form. (Even in 1835, he'd found it difficult to be physically attracted to humans, maybe to anyone, but it wasn't yet acceptable to say such things.)

"Will you—"

He'd intended to ask if she'd come live with him and be his love, as the poet once said, but his scandalous proposal was interrupted by the arrival of the lady's brother, who was shocked by the entwined nature of their hands. His sister was not a normal girl of the times, but part of a genteel family that still believed in all the upper-crust signals and proprieties of the past one hundred years. To see her unchaperoned with a man who clearly planned to take liberties?

Well, he drew his pistol. "I shall have satisfaction, sir!"

The woman, Georgiana, crossed to her brother. "Nothing has happened. Magic Guy [who was going by some dull British moniker like George or Albert or Charles at the time, but which name was utterly unimportant to this narrative and shall remain "Magic Guy" for ease of discussion] was simply protecting me from the elements."

The would-be duelist frowned and pushed the lady behind him. "He seeks to stain your honor," he declared. "Protection from the elements? Nay! You need protection from those who seek to protect you."

He did not, sadly, see the humor in this statement. But these things happen when a person is led by emotion.

For his part, Magic Guy stood and tugged on his sword hilt, ready to answer the challenge. He hadn't thought to bring a pistol with him and was grateful now that he'd brought anything at all.

The hilt came off in his hand, bladeless.

The brother's frown deepened, a dark furrow forming above his nose. "You shall draw, sir."

Magic Guy looked at the hilt in his hand, then at the demanding man in front of him, then back at his failed sword. "I don't see how."

Georgiana's brother lowered his pistol and holstered it. "Let me help you." He reached out a hand for something. The hilt, the sheath, another piece altogether?

Magic Guy handed over the hilt and spread his empty palms. "Please."

Stepping close enough to smell dessert's orange residue on his opponent's breath, the brother attempted to reseat the hilt in the sheath and then pull it out again. In much the way that modern computer users advocate *turn it off and on again* to solve problems, this man hoped that he could start the process of sword-drawing over and that this time it would proceed in the expected manner.

Unlike a computer, however, a sword does not reset itself when sheathed, and the brother ended up next to his quarry holding a cord-wrapped grip that could certainly not be used for dueling.

"Perhaps," Chidiock suggested, having come freshly onto the scene, "you could also acquire a sword hilt and the two of you could pound each other with them."

As Georgiana's brother preferred pistols to pugilism, he was less than inclined.

Georgiana giggled, as she knew this about her brother. It wasn't the proper reaction for a well-bred young lady at the center of a reputational and moral crisis, but wouldn't you react the same way? All these idiot boys standing around and holding handles uselessly, too dismayed to use their hands instead of their tools... it struck her as funny.

Chidiock began laughing as well. Through his guffaws, he forced out, "You... clutching for no reason."

His mirth set off Magic Guy, and Georgiana's brother halfheartedly joined in. After all, if everyone present thought the duel irrelevant, cooler heads could prevail.

While Magic Guy and the brother marveled over the broken weapon, Chidiock and Georgiana indulged their humor over the sublime ridiculousness a bit more. They kept each other going, and then bonded over their preference for English country dances. Georgiana swore to save him a spot for the "Sir Roger de Coverley" set dance.

Though everything worked out for amusement and friendship, Magic Guy had his suspicions about who had sabotaged his dueling accessory and about how his romance may have begun. He swore prank-y vengeance. Of course he did. After all, this was a prank *war*.

Chapter Nine
Lost Girl

There are few things in the world more relaxing than curling up with a mug of tea and watching horrible TV on Netflix while you fiddle with a smartphone or laptop and chat with a friend. Some people believe that's too much to do all at once, but those people are all too old to have done collaborative homework over the phone (or, at least, don't have as many attention issues as does the author of this book).

On the Thursday morning following Morena's dating emergency and Suzyn and Magic Guy's time spent bonding over martinis and makership, none of our erstwhile protagonists were enjoying the relaxing activity described above. Each of them would have been thrilled to cuddle with tea and guilty TV—*Kitchen Nightmares* for Morena, something about gypsy weddings for Suzyn, and *Teen Wolf* for Magic Guy.

Instead, however, Morena was dealing with the aftermath of an unexpected server crash at work, Suzyn was awake and apologizing for being late to a potential client (it sounded like he wanted some food photography?) whom she'd forgotten even existed, and Magic Guy—well, Magic Guy was doing his usual thing, but he would have been happier to be relaxing with no expectations. Doing *anything* was the wrong thing as far as he was concerned.

Morena was in the midst of calling yet another operations person to find out what sort of workarounds were available for this computing disaster when she heard the buzz-beep of an incoming call. Since she wasn't getting anywhere with the ops guy, she let him off the hook. With a sigh, she hung up and flopped into her chair.

She hit the green phone button. "Hey, Vadim. Please tell me something good; this morning's been awful."

They hadn't been out since their Friday stay-in-shut-in, though not for lack of trying. Their schedules just hadn't meshed. If Morena had known then how hard it would be to get together, she might've cancelled her Monday night hair appointment. But she hadn't known, so she'd told him she was busy that evening and had gone to the Gene Juarez downtown.

Suzyn, by the by, would not have been caught dead in a Gene Juarez. She hadn't lived in Seattle long enough to know that the big hairstyling chain was far superior to many of the tiny boutiques. It was a complete reversal of just about every other city in the world. Where normally a person would get a cut and color with more panache and style from an artsy one-off store, the Gene Juarez chain had made itself indispensable as the place that poached all the best stylists. They had the most talented designers, offered the most continuing education, and usually had mall-adjacent locations with parking lots.

So it was that Morena's hair had bounce and body, and it had sparkled for a few days. But, while her hair had been impeccable, she had yet to see Vadim, and she did *so* want to see him. Their relationship was progressing at a sensible pace. Two dates in two weeks, lots of texts. She liked him. She wanted to know more about him.

She hoped he was calling to schedule a date.

"Lovely Morena, I have missed you." Vadim cleared his throat. "Perhaps, we get together today? Let us meet at the café where I first saw you. Say, at three?"

Perhaps she should have stayed in her office and tried to reconstruct her work of the last few months, but it could wait. She couldn't get much done anyway while the servers were down, and a spontaneous date with a man who just *had* to see her in the middle of the day sounded brilliant. "Three it is."

What Morena didn't know was that it wasn't actually a date. Vadim didn't *simply* want to let her presence brighten his day. He didn't miss her so much that he couldn't wait for the weekend. The truth was that he'd be gone by the weekend. He'd already been in the States for two months and had burned through his American prospects. His visa was up. His discretionary money was gone.

But he had what he hoped was good news: a prestigious job lined up in Lichtenstein and a sign-on/move-in bonus that could easily accommodate a significant other. So when 3 p.m. rolled around, he was waiting with her favorite drink (purchased with the assistance of the knowledgeable barista), a pounding heart, and a pair of plane tickets he hoped wouldn't be rebuffed this time.

"Darling!" He opened his arms for a hybrid hug and cheek kiss, then handed over the sugar-free mocha.

Starbucks mochas that have been made with the sugar-free syrup taste like birthday cake. There is no reason to get the sugared version. None.

Morena took a sip to give herself a moment to process. While she was thrilled to see Vadim, this demonstrativeness was a bit over the top for a third date. Still, it was charming that he'd thought ahead and purchased her favorite drink. "I'm glad you found the time to meet me this afternoon."

He ducked his head and blushed. It turned his ears an alarming crimson. "It is no trouble for you."

Morena felt her own ears heating up, either in sympathy or in pleasure. She wasn't sure which was worse. "I was thinking about this weekend. We could make a whole day of it on Saturday. Start with the Underground Tour, then get lunch, and maybe meet my roommate?" She figured they were getting serious enough that he should meet Suzyn. Not Mãe yet, but Suzyn.

"Ah. Um. Hmm. This weekend."

"Oh no." She reached out and patted his hand in mock sympathy. "Not again! We have so much trouble finding times to get together." She pulled her new Surface from her bag and opened up her calendar. "All right. When have you got? We'll find a time yet!"

But he didn't take out his own calendar. Instead, he waxed nostalgic. "Do you remember when we first met in this very place, and we talked about getting married?"

This was taking too strange a turn for Morena, who didn't really remember anything like that, but would be willing to believe she'd made a marriage joke. "So, I have Monday night, and I was thinking about leaving work early if the servers aren't one hundred percent yet."

Vadim pulled the tablet from her hands and rested it in his own lap since the table was too small to accommodate both coffees and electronics. He looked deep into her eyes, trying to convey how serious he was about her, about life, about the question he was about to pop. "Will you marry me now?"

She ran a nervous hand through the top layer of her hair and tittered. "I, ah. What?"

"I must leave tomorrow," he said. "You can come with me, and we can live *happily ever after* together."

"In the Ukraine?" Morena didn't even speak the language. And wasn't that close to Chernobyl? She'd swear she'd seen links to articles about the continuing fallout on her Twitter feed.

"In Lichtenstein!" Vadim smiled broadly, knowing that if location were her only objection, then she couldn't fault this one. A prosperous country with beautiful views and a populace that largely spoke English. She would come to love it there, as she must love him. As he loved her.

All Morena could think was, "You haven't even met my mother?" It came out as a question, when she'd meant it as a statement. In hindsight she realized it *was* a question with an implied *How can I marry you if.*

"Is that important?" He knew the words were foolish the moment he asked. Clearly it was. "We can do so tonight and leave in the morning." He flourished the plane tickets, much as he'd hoped to do on their non-starter trip to Las Vegas. "Business class."

As if business class could cancel out everything else. Morena huffed another laugh. "Lichtenstein?"

Vadim began to wonder whether she even remembered the most important question. "Darling Morena, please. You must say yes. Will you marry me?"

A couple at the next table, both in North Face jackets and with sustainable (REI-brand) thermos mugs, turned to watch. Morena noted their stares and felt her face heat. Sweat pricked her scalp and was probably frizzing her immaculate hairstyle.

"You barely know me," she said, her head shaking back and forth. Though Vadim opened his mouth to answer and persuade, she already knew her answer, her only possible answer. "No. No, I can't. I don't. I can't." Tears cooled her cheeks, and she spared a thought for her mascara, then got mad at herself for worrying about makeup during such a moment. "I'm sorry." She stood, leaving her mostly full sugar-free mocha on the table and her Surface forgotten on his lap. "Good luck in Lichtenstein."

She left for her office and didn't remember anything that happened for the rest of the day. Vadim went to his lodgings to pack and tried to return his second ticket for a refund. He contemplated staying, but her rejection had hurt him too deeply. At least he had an almost-new tablet to remember her by. It was a worthy parting gift from an American.

So he got on the plane and went off to his new job. But since this story follows the iPhone in Morena's handbag, Vadim no longer has a part to play.

Still in a haze, Morena picked up a rotisserie chicken from the PCC grocery store on her way home, its savory scent filling the back of the commuter bus. Normally, she'd be embarrassed about forcing other people to smell her dinner-to-be, but this wasn't a normal day. This was a day in which her work had blown up, her boyfriend moved out of the country, and she'd declined a marriage proposal.

Grocery-prepared food offers the best cost-to-effort value version of "homemade" in the known universe. It combines the idea of paying someone else to do the hard work with eating at home... and with not needing to tip one's server. It also gives the purchaser a chance to feel more involved in the food choice and preparation.

For instance, Morena could have gone to QFC to buy her rotisserie chicken, which would probably have been cheaper, but it wouldn't have given her the satisfaction of knowing she'd 75 percent surely bought an ethically sourced chicken— or at least an organic one. Plus, she'd managed to buy local. Supporting PCC was like supporting a small business, just a small business that had grown into a giant chain that could afford ever-increasing building rental fees.

It was like Starbucks in that respect. And Morena felt all kinds of warm fuzzy loyalty to her employer.

The roasted chicken's aroma kept Morena company in the cold between the bus stop and her apartment. She'd forgotten to put on gloves, and the paper bag handles dug fiery lines into the fingers of first one frozen hand, then the other. She didn't stumble in the dark over any of the holes or hills in the sidewalk, moving on automatic. Her brain had fuzzed out around 3:10 p.m. and hadn't come back online.

Finally, she reached her apartment building. Her pinkened fingers fumbled for her key ring, and eventually she made it inside. She kicked off her Oxford-style booties and let her full-skirted designer wool coat fall carelessly to the polyester carpet.

Suzyn was setting out the rest of the evening's ingredients in the windowless kitchen. She called out, "How was work?" Not giving her roommate a chance to answer, she ordered, "Bring me the chicken. You did get the chicken, right?"

And suddenly Morena was *there*, no longer stuck in a fugue, but fully aware and conscious and in her one-bedroom apartment with her barely-an-adult roommate. She could feel the lines of pain on her fingers, could taste the salty chicken fumes, could judder from her heart's pounding after the effort of walking so fast on hills... after the memory of Vadim's unhappy face.

(All right, so Vadim is *mentioned* once more in the narrative, but he doesn't show up again. Perhaps the author was not entirely accurate in her description of his continued presence a page or two ago.)

Morena slung the chicken bag onto the laminate counter, and Suzyn jumped back toward the refrigerator as it swung through her field of vision. But the Flying Chicken wasn't followed by violence or even by any further action. Morena just stood in the kitchen entryway, her hair limp and her eyes stinging, though they hadn't chopped a single onion yet. "What if he was the best thing to ever happen to me?"

Suzyn was pretty sure that no guy could be the best thing to ever happen to anyone, but she wasn't unsympathetic. She passed Morena a red onion and a knife. Gave her something useful to do. "Half rings." Unsympathetic, no. Hungry, yes.

Morena peeled the onion with more care than it deserved, then slammed the knife through the purple and white flesh. The knife also cut into the counter, but she wasn't really worried about the measly $250 cleaning deposit anyway.

That was less than a tenth the cost of the wool coat currently discarded in the doorway.

She yanked the knife out and proceeded to slice with perfect calm precision, as though nothing had happened, as though she were the Queen of England. An etiquette showpiece. "Vadim's gone."

Preferring to give her roommate some privacy during this revelation, while still providing a sympathetic ear, Suzyn turned away to open a can of hominy. "*Gone* gone? Or just gone on vacation?"

Morena didn't answer, but that didn't matter. Suzyn had only asked for clarification so that Morena would feel encouraged to continue speaking about what was bothering her. "He asked me to marry him. I said no."

"You've only known him, what, a week and a half?"

"I know, right?" For once, using the incredulous phrase of the younger generation didn't fill Morena with glee. "I think he really just wanted to keep dating, but didn't think I'd want that long distance. Oh, God." Her breathing sped up, which only made her inhale onion oils at a more dangerous rate. Her eyes watered. "What if I'd said I wanted to date instead of turning him down completely? Would he have been interested in that?"

It is a truth of the human condition: we go over all the options of things we *could* have said long after it's too late. Great zingers we didn't use against our enemies. Brilliant insights we didn't give when called on in class. Impressive language that might have influenced our boss or client. And, always always always, the perfect thing to say to a love interest to keep them hanging on.

Suzyn grabbed the chopped onions and tossed them in the

Dutch oven before they went from quarter-rings to finely diced. "If he'd wanted to date, he'd have offered it. But, wait, really. Marriage? I hadn't even met him yet."

Morena swiped the back of her hand across her eyelids, pressing in hopes of stopping the tears. At least they could be onion-inspired tears. "He liked me enough to marry me. He kept giving me these amazing gifts, like dance sessions and tickets to Las Vegas." Not that she'd been willing to go to Vegas, but the thought counted as more romantic and less creepy after the fact. "Cross-cultural relationships are hard, but my parents did it. What if I should have gone with him? What if I should have said yes?"

"Shred the chicken," said Suzyn.

Morena opened the plastic case and was assaulted by even more savory saltiness. She peeled off the skin like she'd peeled the onion and shredded white meat into a bowl. "I totally should have said yes, shouldn't I?" She shredded a few pieces even more viciously. Then her shoulders slumped in her pure-cotton, button-front shirt. "No, I shouldn't. The timing was terrible. What if we would have hated each other? What if I would have hated Lichtenstein?"

Suzyn paused in stirring. "Lichtenstein?"

"It's in Europe somewhere," said Morena, which wasn't what Suzyn was really asking, but it wasn't like Suzyn truly cared.

Well, Suzyn cared about her roommate. She wanted Morena to be happy and fulfilled and all that. And to keep paying for the apartment. But she also couldn't have cared less about the particulars of some guy who'd upset her friend and whom Suzyn had never even met. Also also? She really wished Morena wouldn't cry while making dinner. At least it was soup—well, posole, technically—so it shouldn't matter too much.

Morena sniffed one more time, loudly. Decisively. She set to shredding with a vengeance. "Well, maybe he was the best thing ever. But he's gone now, and that's what's going to have to be the best for me."

Suzyn nodded, not that Morena could see, and poured a can of tomatoes into the pot. "I'll still be here, and we can totally find you another guy. There's a better one out there. One with good timing and an interest in story gaming."

"And a really hot accent?" Morena didn't even sound all that upset anymore. "Vadim had a really hot accent."

Suzyn wended an arm around her roommate's shoulders and pulled her in tight. "You can't have everything," she teased. "Now change into sweats while I get this up to boiling, we're going to watch some trashy TV and enjoy life."

When Morena came back to the kitchen, her hair was pulled back in a scrunchie that was older than Suzyn and she wore colorblock cashmere sweatpants with a Starbucks corporate t-shirt. Suzyn had already turned out the kitchen light and had two DVD box sets in her hands. "*Buffy*?" She shook one hand, blurring the main character's blond hair and predatory expression. "Or *Lost Girl*?" She shook the other hand, blurring the main character's dark hair and predatory expression.

"Both?" suggested Morena. Two shows with snappy dialogue, focusing on supernatural problems that were unlikely to touch her actual life? She couldn't choose.

"*Lost Girl* it is," said Suzyn. She liked the idea of starting with a show about friendship. Because there was nothing better than the first season of *Lost Girl* for friendship in the face of adversity.

It is a strange fact that fantasy TV shows are the most realistic ones on television. Think about your favorite show that isn't fantasy or science fiction. You have to admit that even if the situations the characters find themselves in are plausible—is this week's issue whether or not someone gets a new kidney? A date?—the way the characters interact with each other is not. On the other hand, Buffy and Willow and Xander have a complex set of relationships, and they band together the way that real people do in order to face utterly unrealistic problems, like vampires taking over the city of Sunnydale. The mayor's turning into a giant snake might not happen in your town, but you can bet that there's a girl out there Faith's age who needed love and affection and sold her loyalty to the wrong sort of man in order to acquire those things.

While the soup simmered on the electric burner, Morena and Suzyn snuggled together on the couch and watched Bo and Kenzi snuggle on *their* couch. While Morena and Suzyn sipped their posole, they watched Xander give Buffy CPR so that they could overcome the bad-guy-of-the-month together.

While she served their second bowls, Morena realized that this was two-thirds of what she wanted from a romantic relationship. She wanted someone to come home to who would listen to her problems, cuddle on the couch, and watch cult-classic television with her. She wanted to live her comfortable life. But could this be enough? Could she just live with Suzyn in their cozy '80s apartment forever, making posole and watching supernatural shows? Could she really avoid meeting, and being ultimately disappointed by, new people?

The fact that Morena had to ask the question made her realize her current living situation came darned close. But it wasn't enough. And if she didn't want to put herself out there anymore, if she'd rather revel in the relationships she had than hunt down romantic possibilities, then could she ever find what she truly needed? What if she'd become too tired to try anymore? What if she was going to be alone forever? Doomed to cycle through ever-younger roommates, never finding the stability that she so envied in her parents' marriage?

Unlike Suzyn, who was in the "make my own way" phase of her life, and unlike Magic Guy, who was running away from his peers' society for a few hundred years, Morena had always wanted the comfort of family. She wanted someone to care for her when she was sick, and to care for in return. She wanted someone to do things with her, and who she'd love enough to do the things they wanted to do. She wanted to grow old *with* someone, instead of being forced to trade them out for a younger model.

Suzyn and Morena paused *Buffy* to put away their leftovers, and Morena called her mom. Since it was eleven o'clock, her mother didn't answer the phone, but Morena left a message anyway. "Hi, Mãe. Just wanted to call and say I love you. And that I met a guy, but he's gone, so I'm back to square one. (Laughter.) But that's okay. I still have you and Suzyn. Anyway, love you. Bye."

When her mother received this message in the morning, she was justifiably worried about her daughter. It was a pretty distraught phone message, to a mother's ears.

Chapter Ten
Not Always an
Operations Research Problem

Morena had missed the previous week's brunch with her mother, having cleared everything from her schedule "just in case" she chose to spend the weekend with Vadim. But Vadim wasn't a problem anymore, was he?

So Morena stumbled out of bed on *this* Sunday morning (stubbing her toe on the bare metal bedframe) and mumbled Suzyn into wakefulness. Normally, a mere mumble would not have woken Suzyn, but the younger woman had spent the previous night keeping Morena mopey company, and so she was mostly bright-eyed even at 10:30 a.m.

Morena tugged a harsh paddle brush through her hair and twisted the strands into a tight bun like a ballet dancer's, with no pretty tendrils slipping out anywhere. The style pulled the corners of her eyes tight, a physical pain which she hoped might distract from emotional ones.

The unusually unfashionable woman wrapped herself in a warm college sweatshirt formerly crumpled on the back of her closet floor and buttoned her loosest jeans. This change in routine meant she was ready to leave long before Suzyn, so Morena pulled out her phone to chew some time while she waited.

Once again, the phone that slid into her hand turned out to be the iPhone, not the Samsung. But that was perfectly fine for generic time wasting. She thumbed the iPhone's unlock, and immediately a bright green heart filled the screen. On reflex, she hit the *Randomize* button.

Ding ding DING!

What was she even doing? Either the app was a joke, or it had gotten her into this trouble in the first place. Besides, she didn't need romance. Not now. Not after Vadim.

She thumbed the *Randomize* button again.

Ding ding DING!

The sound cut a clear and comfortable path through her sudden headache, muting the timpanis behind her eyebrows. *No!* Morena threw the iPhone onto the bed. She'd gotten too used to having it on hand lately. She resolved to take her beloved Samsung to brunch today. It would serve just as well if some emergency cropped up at work... or if she felt a desperate urge to kill time with *Candy Crush*.

Suzyn skidded into the bedroom where Morena was flopped on her back, staring at the ceiling. She took in her roommate's outfit, incredulous. "Is *that* what you're—" But wow, did Morena look awful. Circles under her eyes, pasty cast to her usually golden skin, and an utterly vacant expression.

Suzyn amended her question to, "You ready to go?"

The iPhone stayed behind, all forlorn, while the women adjourned to the Smart, to the nearest Starbucks drive-thru, and then to a cute little café in Issaquah that billed itself as a Caffe * Bar * Tavern but only appeared to have breakfast foods on its menu. The off-white floor tiles were cracked, but in a way that looked artisanal rather than shabby. The door opened onto a large single room redolent with humid omelet-scented air. Happy blue stools sat at the bar, and a spiky metal-framed mirror imitated a small sun framed by liquor bottles.

Luiza was already seated in a '50s-diner-style booth that had been done up in black instead of red vinyl. She had a cup of tangy coffee resting on the chrome-and-laminate tabletop and was chatting with her server about the waitress's upcoming wedding (and waiting for a chance to mention flowers, but if she never got that chance Luiza would still be happy to have met the young woman and to have gotten her coffee freshened).

On spotting the roommates, Morena's mother gave her ex-fashion plate daughter wide eyes and an amused mouth twist, much as Suzyn had done. "I see you're doing well, *minha filha*." Which was such an obvious lie that it invited Morena to disclose any terrible secrets.

But that didn't happen. Morena just kissed listlessly at her mother's cheek before sliding into the booth next to her. "How's your business going, Mãe?"

The waitress went to get more coffee cups, and Suzyn dropped into a sprawl on the opposite side of the booth.

Luiza let her daughter steer the conversation toward business. Partially because she knew her Morena would speak when she was ready. And partially because the first stages of owning a small business were fun! "It's great. I've been going into all the little shops in downtown Issaquah and chatting with the people who own them. I've even made friends with the kids who put up all those Seattle Geekly fliers."

Morena didn't say anything in the face of her mother's enthusiasm.

Suzyn took up the slack. "Really? I met a flier person recently. They do wonders with wheatpaste." Suzyn, it had to be admitted, knew absolutely nothing about guerilla marketing, different pastes for hanging flyers on walls and garbage bins, or a single person who actually worked for any company that did this. But she had seen an ad once in a discarded roller derby program, and that was good enough to keep a conversation moving along, she thought.

And she was right. It was the perfect amount of engagement to keep Luiza chattering about her business's growth so far.

In an alternate universe where Suzyn hadn't said anything, Luiza would have dropped the topic altogether and been forced to find another, which would have led to asking Morena about her atypical appearance which would have led to Morena's getting defensive which would have led to Luiza's worrying aloud that her little girl would be lonely and unmarried forever. And all of that would have been very uncomfortable for alternate-universe!Suzyn, so it was a good thing that this Suzyn had spoken about flyer techniques.

"And whenever I go into a Starbucks," Luiza continued, "I make sure the people there know my daughter also works for the company. That gets me invited to more things. Why, just the other day someone invited me to a board game night. You two do board games, right?"

"Sort of," said Suzyn who'd never had much luck explaining the differences among board games, card games, story games, and videogames to her own parents.

At this point, the waitress returned with coffee for two, water for three, and an exhaustive knowledge of available meat cuts. Apparently, the Caffe * Bar * Tavern was attached to a charcuterie, though none of the women had seen it, and it had a hipster city-dweller's array of sausages.

"So, why flowers, anyway? I didn't know you had a garden or anything, Mrs. Blake." Because that was a much more comfortable topic.

Luiza patted Suzyn's hand. The younger woman was such a good complement to Morena, even when Morena was sulking. "I decided I'd like to have a local storefront where community members come in and spend time in the beautiful atmosphere. Plus, flowers are so romantic."

Unbeknownst to Luiza, Morena perked up at the word *romantic*. And Suzyn wished in hindsight that she hadn't asked about flowers. (Alternate-universe!Suzyn would still choose the flowers conversation, rather than the one in her own reality, and wants to make it clear that her opinions differ from our Suzyn's on the matter.)

"*So* romantic," Luiza repeated. "People buy flowers for their significant others. For their mothers, their weddings. It's so sweet. All those positive feelings mixed with all the best scents. Someday, Morena, you'll have a wedding with beautiful flowers everywhere."

At that, surprising no one except Luiza, Morena sniffled, curled up into a ball that put her boot-clad heels on the booth vinyl, and hid her head in her sweatshirt's voluminous sleeves. Because she *could* have had a wedding with beautiful flowers, and her mother would have loved it all. But she didn't. And now maybe she never would. And that would... be bad. Yes, bad.

Morena couldn't say all that, though, because her nose, mouth, and eyes were all buried in dusty cotton like an external sinus infection.

Suzyn sighed. "Morena's had a breakup."

Luiza nodded sagely. Morena had more breakups than Luiza ever had, that was for sure. In Brazil, Luiza had dated three boys before she'd met the visiting Scott Blake and never looked back. If only her daughter could have the same sort of clarity, but that couldn't happen for everyone, she supposed. "That Vadim boy?"

Suzyn nodded. Morena sniffled again into her sweatshirt, which was getting uncomfortably hot and muggy.

The waitress came by again, hoping to take their orders, but observed that it wasn't a good time. To Luiza she mouthed, *Is she okay?* Luiza nodded, hoping it was true.

Tugging her little girl against her side, Luiza let warmth and motherly embracing give all the affection and comfort it could. "Clearly, that Vadim was like all these young men you meet. No offense to your age group, Suzyn."

Suzyn held up her hands in the universal symbol of surrender, a gesture doing double-duty as *I certainly don't mind*.

"These young men," Luiza pontificated. "They're a date and a goodbye. You need someone serious. Someone ready to dedicate his life to you and to always be there. Someone to love you and care for you, like your father and I did for each other for thirty-eight long years."

Morena's shoulders shook with sobs, and Luiza *shush*ed her. "Não, não, baby. Don't cry. These men are out there.

We'll find you one."

Suzyn raised her arm like a schoolchild waiting to be called on by the nuns. "Ah, Mrs. Blake. Vadim proposed."

And since the pair was obviously broken up, Morena had clearly turned him down. Suzyn returned her arm to rest on the laminate-and-chrome table.

Luiza cast about for something utterly unrelated to romance. "I need that logistical mind of yours," she said.

She extracted an arm to pull a napkin out of the table dispenser and accepted a pen from Suzyn. "See, I've got two storefronts that want to carry my tropical flower line, and three suppliers in Brazil and Argentina who want to supply me. Oh, and a wedding boutique in Oregon"—she hoped Morena could handle the mention of weddings in the abstract since that was where most of her business came from so far— "with a family that wants me to make up kits for them."

As with all small business owners, her focus (when not on her daughter) was entirely on her work these days. Luiza hated to involve Morena with the details of her business, but family was more important than independence.

Morena's sweat-red face peeked over the edge of her sweatshirt's forearm. "And you don't know how many things to make? Or what to buy?"

"Exactly!" Though half of those items Luiza had listed were ones she'd made up on the spot. So far, she only had one supplier, one family in Oregon, and had given her cards to two local stores that hadn't gotten back to her. God would forgive a white lie to cheer her daughter.

Morena unfolded herself and took the pen from her mother's hand. "This is the poster child of OR problems," she said.

Luiza pursed her lips to keep the smile from spreading across her face. *Perfect!* She'd successfully distracted her daughter from sadness. "You *always* say that."

And it was true. But Luiza had learned enough in the past decades to know when Morena's analysis was right, versus when she simply saw Operations Research everywhere because it was what she knew how to do.

"Yes, and this time it really is. It's classic!"

And thus did Luiza and Suzyn spend brunch getting a linear programming lesson. Both of them were pleased to raise Morena's spirits, even if they didn't care about fiddly mathematics relating to fictional business problems.

Because that's what friends and family do. They love you in spite of your problems, and listen to you talk nonstop about your favorite topics.

For a few hours that Sunday, Morena didn't feel alone, Luiza bonded with her daughter, and Suzyn was drug-free (since 10:03... the night before).

Chapter Eleven
Eliminate the Impossible

By the following Tuesday's story game meetup, back at the marvelously geeky Wayward Coffeehouse, Morena settled down to being only a *little* mopey. Still, she'd become so lethargic that she'd contemplated—only for a moment—asking her naturopath about an elimination diet to determine her sensitivities to all kinds of food. Just in case that was what had been making her body so sluggish and unhappy.

Sure, unprompted elimination diets (where people decided they wanted to be sensitive to foods that didn't actually bother them) had become all the rage, but Morena wasn't the type to go in for them needlessly. In large part because if one worked, she'd probably have to give up coffee or milk, and that just was not on for a half-Brazilian girl employed by Starbucks. As a child, she'd laughed at anyone who gave something up for Lent. She wasn't about to start now for fashion or science-y reasons.

So Morena was drinking a Mudder's Mocha that Tuesday, full of both milk *and* coffee, and sitting with Suzyn and Magic Guy while they waited to be served their Wash Bagels. The trio had shown up half an hour early to chat about their story game designing, but that wasn't what had happened.

See, while Magic Guy had been at the counter, waiting in Tuesday night's interminably long line, Suzyn had commandeered *the phone*. Which was to say that she'd brought it with them in her messenger bag and had pulled it out to fiddle with it until Magic Guy returned from The Wars, AKA the ordering counter.

Morena looked up from her Samsung, on which she was obsessively checking the Starbucks HQ server health stats. She'd do that for a few more weeks until complacency set in again. Well, not complacency so much as *trust in professionalism*. Honestly, what large, multi-national company has unstable computing power? Good thing it didn't affect day-to-day operations and that no coffee drinkers had defected to Peet's or Ladro or any of the myriad local one-off shops.

Right. So Morena looked up from her Samsung and noticed Suzyn playing with an iPhone. She didn't immediately conclude that it was *the* iPhone, but she knew that Suzyn didn't own one and had, in fact, coveted the gift from Morena's ex. "Oh my god, woman." Morena slapped an ineffectual hand against Suzyn's shoulder. "What are you doing?"

Suzyn, as usual, was slouched in a broken chair. The steam from her chai wafted past her wrists where they pointed toward the roof, her head thrown back so that the ceiling lamps backlit the phone's screen. "Finding you a new guy," she said. She would have shrugged, but it was hard enough to worm her body into a slouchy sprawl that included the broken back of a wicker chair without adding extraneous movement into the mix.

"Oh my god," said Morena again, this time in a hissing whisper. "You can't just use that thing. What if it's forcing people?"

For *that* piece of apparent stupidity, Suzyn sat up and looked her best friend straight in the eye. "Morena. It's an iPhone app, not a satanic love spell."

Morena's vertebrae slumped, and she waved a permissive hand back at the phone. "Yeah, I know. I just got worried for a minute there. Like, what did Vadim see in me to get him started, you know?"

Suzyn arched her spine and wedged it against the spikey pale wicker once again. "Dude, that guy was so into you." She forced out a laugh.

Trying to make any talk of Vadim into a joke was harder than romcoms made it seem, Suzyn found. Not that she watched romcoms much. Except at Christmastime when Disney, the WB, and even the Hallmark channel made some horrible but funny ones.

A choked-off sob came from the other woman, but Suzyn refused to look away from the phone. (She was too unsympathetic to be a good friend when the messier emotions got involved, so she prudently avoided them.) She set the age range for 21-26, then thought the better of it and went for 27-35. That was still a little younger than Morena, but not so young that it'd be weird.

"I'm going to be single forever," moaned Morena. "Why don't guys want me?"

Magic Guy finally came back with his hot apple cider and one of their Wash Bagels. "Because other men are morons who don't appreciate you. And I just saw Rebecca get in line, so we should start rolling our characters soon."

Rebecca was another local Seattle story gamer. As far as this narrative is concerned, however, she only exists to fill table and plot space in chapter eleven and has no other functions. The reader has not missed anything crucial by only noticing her appearance at this juncture.

Suzyn kicked her feet up onto Morena's lap to provide her friend with more tactile reassurance and to increase the area of her own sprawl. "Don't worry, Ems." Sometimes, especially after guiltily watching *Gossip Girl*, Suzyn was taken by the desire to give people diminutives based on the initial letter of their first name. She didn't do it often. "I'm gonna find you a hottie in a point-three-mile radius."

At this point, Suzyn and Morena devolved into some good-natured bickering about whether or not to increase the radius to 1 mile or reduce it to 0.1 miles, with a tangent wondering why people who made geo-relevant apps didn't think 0.5 or 0.75 seemed like a good increment. Those were still walkable in the snow. One mile was pushing it. And three miles as the next level up? That was where cars started. There was no difference between three and ten miles, really.

But Magic Guy didn't notice this conversation, even if he might have been interested by its insight into the casual city-dweller's psyche. No, he was too busy reeling from the vibrations in the air. Not the auditory vibrations from JACK-FM playing over the speakers, or the imperceptible (to humans) spray from the milk steamer. Not the shivering air currents from the people setting up Pathfinder miniatures at the table next to them, nor the emotions focused in his direction by the woman with an impeccably styled gray bob from the writers' table in the back.

No, these were *bad* vibrations he was picking up. They were the opposite of the Beach Boys song. His lungs lurched, and his heart contracted as the vibrating sensation strengthened, then washed over and through him. He grabbed the table to stay upright and was half-offended that his companions hadn't noticed. (The other half of him was relieved he wouldn't have to explain anything.)

Someone was performing dangerous magics nearby.

The dark power made his thighbones quake with the urge to run somewhere safe. But this was his place, and his story game circle didn't deserve to have him abandon them with no warning.

He ignored the fear that they might not care. It wasn't a fear, after all. He'd worked very hard to not make "friends," but acquaintances still deserved some consideration. Unfortunately, Suzyn already classified him as a "friend," and he was soon to realize he felt the same way. Poor Magic Guy. His plan to remain lonely and untouched by human emotions had failed.

He closed his eyes, the better to block out the *Firefly* art and other distractions. He sent out his magic senses through the room, trying to follow the unfriendly wave that had so jarred him. He turned, following a ripple in the ambient magic. *There!* He slammed his eyes open when he pinpointed the vile practitioner, the better to catch them in the act.

His quarry was Suzyn. Suzyn, whose feet still warmed Morena's lap and whose fingers still tripped over the touchscreen of a sexy new iPhone. She was saying, "No, I haven't liked any of the guys it's sent you. I'm changing your underlying search settings."

Morena grabbed for the phone, but she couldn't reach the full length of Suzyn's body and seemed disinclined to shift her best friend from a supposedly comfortable position for such a little thing. "You figured out how to get an options dash?" She made frustrated wavy motions with her fingers. "Show me!"

And Suzyn obligingly sat upright, tilting her chair in such an alarming manner that Magic Guy was sure she'd fall over. The two women crowded around the phone, and Suzyn poked at an icon while Morena jittered with anticip—

Magic Guy swooped in and scooped the iPhone out of their hot little hands. Well, little compared to his own hands, anyway. Well, Morena's were. Suzyn had extremely long fingers for a female of the human species.

"Hey!" Suzyn objected.

"What gives?" Morena's slang was more out of date.

In his hand, the phone felt oily and wrong, and not because it had one of those strange military-grade cases (it didn't) but more as though it had been molded out of some unethical putty which had never once attended sensitivity training and didn't think it was important to discuss consent or permissible acts with a new sex partner. This phone was the worst kind of PUA (pick-up artist), and he didn't know why such beautiful people (soul-speaking) as Morena and Suzyn would own it.

The only possible reason he could see was that they couldn't sense its brainwash-y vibes. They didn't feel skeeved out by its presence. And of course they didn't. They weren't magical beings. The closest they got to that sort of thing was playing Monsterhearts, which Suzyn didn't even like.

Morena made grabby hands for her phone. Again.

Because OMG everyone wanted to take her stuff these days. Especially the stupid phone. She shouldn't have kept it, really, but it was so pretty. So sexy. Such an Apple product. Though, she was pretty sure Apple was going to take a downhill swing any day now.

"No," said Magic Guy. His voice wasn't teasing, even as he engaged in a bizarre game of keep-away in which two women came at him—one taller than he—and both leapt for the item in his hand. Somehow, they were repelled. "You don't want it."

"It's mine."

Suzyn was more scathing. "It's an iPhone. If she didn't want it, she could sell it on eBay for serious cash."

Magic Guy pocketed the phone, tucking it into a hiding place outside this dimension.

Holding out her hand, Morena agreed with Suzyn. "That's worth at least a pair of shoes. Hand it over."

"No," said Magic Guy again. He slid sensitive tendrils of magic into the lining of his jean jacket, feeling out the phone's presence where he'd left it. Secure. Far away from this woman, this woman he knew and had spent hours with and realized now, suddenly and completely, that he actually felt some modicum of affection for. Worse, he worried that he might have actually become *friends* with her. Because, if they weren't friends, he should have just left. He should have taken the phone and buried it.

He should have realized sooner that he was coming to enjoy the company of these gamers who admired his historical knowledge. He should have abandoned them for a different story game meetup, maybe one that met way out in Renton.

Because he now had incontrovertible proof that he considered them friends: he wanted to warn them about the dangers of the phone. He didn't want to steal their things, only to protect them. And his first idea for doing that was to tell them the truth. The truth! The truth was that he was a 6,000-plus-year-old elf with trust issues and magical powers and that his experience let him know the phone was loaded with dangerous magics. He couldn't tell them that!

...or could he? Magic Guy thought through the likely consequences.

In the best-case scenario, they would take his information in stride and ask him to dispose of the iPhone.

In the worst-case, they'd send him to Crazytown (he couldn't remember if that was just a hip reference or if modern America had insane asylums anymore; not like the Middle Ages, he didn't believe, but he'd heard horror stories about drugs and isolation and pain treatments) or have him dissected by government agents to find out what made his abilities tick. (He mixed-and-matched a lot of SyFy horror movie plots to make this worst-case scenario in his distraught state.)

Reader, don't be too worried on Magic Guy's behalf. He won't end up as a laboratory test subject or a drooling mental patient. First and foremost, this novel is a piece of crack. That means, in less slang-y terms, that it's something of a comedy, and the author does not find incarceration of any kind to be funny. In the end, Morena and Suzyn will choose a scenario somewhere between the two that Magic Guy has posited.

The internal debate raged. Until Magic Guy couldn't tamp down his instincts any more. His heart told him that he didn't want his gaming partners—he refused to call them his *friends*—duped or changed against their will.

"Your iPhone is a dark magical object," he said. "I know, because I'm not what you think I am."

At the table of Pathfinder players, one eavesdropper who someday hoped to be the GM for this group was also listening in. He didn't think dark magical iPhones were cool enough. He figured the gamers behind him were just hipsters playing at being gamers, not serious ones like at his table. Now if only David would take his turn already. The eavesdropper rolled his d10, just for something to do, and tuned back out of the conversation our heroes were having.

Suzyn ceased trying to worm her fingers into Magic Guy's pockets for the moment. "What are you then?" she asked curiously.

Magic Guy answered Suzyn's question with complete honesty. "I'm a six-thousand-year-old elf. I've felt magic like this before. It's evil, insidious. It's doing something to people's minds, maybe to yours." Even as he spoke the words, he surprised himself. Did he really trust these women so much?

Magic Guy was too blinded by his inner turmoil to think of a better approach to the situation. For example, he could've told them that this model of phone had been recalled and then bought Morena a new one with ready money from thousands of years of investments. So he divulged it all.

Morena gave him an eyebrow-twisting look that said *Seriously? That's what you're going with?*

Suzyn snorted. "Yeah, you played that character a few weeks ago."

"Argh!" Magic Guy sank into a chair and covered his hair with his hands.

It was a posture of frustrated defeat, and Suzyn felt bad for disbelieving him. After all, they'd become friends over the last few weeks, and he always had entertaining stories, whether or not they were true. Maybe this was another story, and it had gotten away from him a little bit. She patted him on the shoulder, tentatively at first, then more strongly when he didn't pull away. He could be her pet storyteller. They could play two truths and a lie. Storytelling chicken. They'd laugh about this situation. Someday. "It's just an iPhone, sweetie," she said, all conciliatory and calming. She wanted him to come back to reality and be a normal guy again.

Encouraged by Suzyn's success with soothing, Morena smoothed the denim on Magic Guy's other shoulder. "Do you want to check the rest of our phones?"

Suzyn kicked Morena under the table. They didn't need him getting any more confiscatory ideas.

Magic Guy sank further into the chair and buried his head so deeply that his words were barely audible as a mumble. "It's a magic iPhone. Why don't you believe me?"

Morena, more sensitive at times than her best friend, tried to project serenity. "Look, Magic Guy," she started, "we respect that you're part of the Pacific Northwest Wiccan-Druid Alliance, but that doesn't mean that we... ah..." She trailed off, unsure how to tactfully say what she wanted to say.

Luckily, for a given definition of luck, Suzyn was more blunt. "Magic doesn't exist, okay? We try to be nice about your whole pagan thing, but taking our techy stuff is just ridiculous."

This wasn't an outcome Magic Guy had expected. Fear, anger, these were acceptable. But outright disbelief? He had to prove it. Not that *he* was magic, but that the phone was.

He turned his head to look at Suzyn, who had been doing *something* that had pinged on his radar. (He was so proud of using that expression. It was new enough, yet had complete English-language penetration.) "What were you even doing with it a minute ago?" He tried to infuse his voice with confrontational cuteness. It was a thing.

Suzyn was sufficiently distracted by the mention of her entire goal for the evening. "I was trying to find Morena a date now that you-know-who is gone."

Two tables away, a huge Harry Potter fan looked up when she heard someone discussing Voldemort, but she couldn't figure out who it might have been and went back to her laptop.

Suzyn continued, "The phone came with this romance app, so... yeah."

Magic Guy leaned back so that he could watch both of their reactions. "And how does this romance app work?"

Morena shrugged. "It's like Urbanspoon, I guess. You give it some parameters—age, financials, location—and it sends someone your way. I've met a couple of people with it, we think. But maybe not. Guys are so weird sometimes."

Magic Guy chose to ignore the editorializing for the moment. "Yeah, but how does that work? I mean, you give it some details, and then what?"

Suzyn barked a laugh. "And then it *finds a guy*. Or gal. I didn't really play with that setting."

Morena added, "I think there's an 'other' as well."

"Not the point." Magic Guy sighed. He could see Rebecca finally heading their way with a drink in her hand and hoped to finish off this conversation before she made it. He didn't want her to know about magic, about him. "So you give it some info about you, and how does it find someone?"

Morena shrugged. "It probably scours the social media profiles of people in your immediate vicinity."

Some smartphone owners might take that as a warning to make sure all their privacy settings were turned on all the way. Others could be excited by the idea of meeting those with similar interests so easily. It is telling that social media professionals tend to keep most of their information set to public while computer programmers usually set it to private-as-private-can-be. On the one hand, the social media people are intimately familiar with what can be done with that data in particular and the benefit of leaving it out there for the world. On the other hand, the programmers understand Internet security.

Magic Guy patiently walked them through the next steps. "That explains how the app can tell you about people nearby, but how can it get you a date?"

Morena growled her annoyance. "I don't know! Does it matter?"

"Yes!" Magic Guy bit back a scream. Why wasn't she seeing the problem? "It's dark magic."

A Pathfinder player rolled his d4, bored. He really ought to buy some new dice, he thought. Some wooden ones instead of resin. That could be cool.

"It's not dark magic," said Suzyn. She made weird spirit fingers for *dark magic.* "It's an iPhone app."

If the writers' table had been listening, being comprised largely of science fiction and fantasy practitioners, one or more of them would have offered something about "sufficiently advanced iPhone apps." But they weren't listening because that would be rude, and also they were *working.* A lot of busy type-y, type-y motions going on over there.

"Oh, really?" Magic Guy sneered. He'd had it with these ignorant humans who wouldn't listen to their elders. "It *really* makes more sense for an app to trawl nearby profiles, which may or may not be privacy-locked, to find just the right match for you?" He jerked a thumb at Morena. "And then to send a push notification to those phones, owned by people who probably don't have the app. And those notifications work on some subliminal level to send someone stumbling into your path who *happens* to actually be interested in starting a romance with you?" His voice had risen in pitch and volume so that when he ended it with "And *that* sounds more reasonable than *it's dark magic* to you?" everyone in the café could hear him.

Passionate conversations that boiled down to *unlikely science* versus *unrealistic magic* were quite normal for Wayward Coffeehouse. Magic Guy was lucky they'd had this conversation in that location instead of at Wednesday's Cupcake Royale. There, someone might have noticed. No, probably not. The three friends were just another group of gamers/writers/sf-fen.

"Give me back my phone," said Morena slowly, "or I will call the police." She wouldn't have, but that wasn't the point.

"Fine." Magic Guy slapped the slick plastic into her palm, anger overriding his good judgment. He couldn't believe that they didn't believe him.

"Hi, everyone," said Rebecca as she arrived at the table.

As the group settled in to choose the evening's game, Magic Guy spared a moment to miss living with people who *did* believe in magic. At least he'd never had to hide his true nature from Chidiock. He snorted into his cooling apple cider. They'd had some good times before Magic Guy had moved out and moved on. Even during that horrible year of 1835.

Magic Guy had retaliated for the whole sword/hilt/duel thing by letting Georgiana know that her original correspondent had been his best friend, rather than himself. He suggested that perhaps thoughts of romance came so easily to Chidiock because the man was already desperate for her love.

While this was not, in fact, true, it *was* true that *someone* was desperate. Namely, Georgiana's parents. As Georgiana had turned an almost spinsterly age, the old-fashioned family had fallen on hard times, and her parents had been pushing her to settle down with a nice respectable man... preferably one with money, reputation, and a not-too-picky nature. When her brother had confessed to the near-duel for Georgiana's honor in the gardens, their parents were horrified, but not because their sweet daughter had come so close to ruination. No, the family was horrified that Georgiana's brother had scared off a potential suitor. If he should have agitated for anything, it was a swordspoint wedding, not a fight to the death.

So when Magic Guy planted the seed of romance in Georgiana's mind, the practical girl sent Chidiock a letter of her own. It was rather forward, but the gist of it was that she had enjoyed their previous correspondence and would like to continue; also, had he been to the newly opened St. James's Theatre yet?

Egged on by Magic Guy, who had his own correspondence with Georgiana now on the topics of Indian education and colonial growth, Chidiock replied that he too had enjoyed their conversations and would be happy to meet her at St. James's Theatre whenever she told him of her attendance; he'd seen a magnificent opera there the other week and had heard that Queen Victoria herself frequented the establishment.

Also prodded by Magic Guy, Georgiana contrived to leave Chidiock's letter about the house. The letter, with its proclamation of past private conversations and the attempt to set a time and location for unsupervised outings, scandalized her parents most deliciously, and the whole family trooped out to Chidiock and Magic Guy's home as a four-person unit.

After forcing their way into the townhouse and being ushered into a sitting room, Georgiana's father paced and paced and paced until the master of the house appeared. "You have ruined my daughter!" he announced to the first person to enter the room. Sadly for him, this was Magic Guy. "You must take responsibility."

Magic Guy blushed and ducked his head.

Georgiana rubbed her temples with a white-gloved finger. "No, father." She sighed. "It's the other one."

Her mother gasped in overplayed shock. "What *have* you been up to, my dear?"

Leaving the seated ladies behind, her brother stood and crossed the room to stand sheepishly at Magic Guy's side by the fireplace. "Please do forgive me for our first meeting."

"No harm done." Magic Guy smiled wide, wider, widest. This was definitely the best prank ever. Chidiock was going to *love* this family of emotionalists. "This time, though, you'll have to get the right man."

The young gentleman nodded so hard his brains could've rattled about (if he'd had any, a fact on which many people of the moment had their doubts). "Don't you worry." His hand fell to his sword hilt.

Georgiana snorted, much to her mother's embarrassed horror.

Chidiock entered, took in the tableau, and turned to Magic Guy. "I shall leave you to your guests."

He didn't manage to complete his retreat. For, as you readers know, he'd been wrong in his assessment that these were Magic Guy's visitors. Nay, they were Chidiock's unlikely callers, and Magic Guy was only around to watch the pantomime unfold.

Georgiana's father roared his defiance. He then paused

and touched a delicate hand to his now scratchy throat, amazed that such a noise had come from it. Recovering quickly, however, he laid his hand on Chidiock's arm, determined to arrest the man's departure. "You have ruined my daughter!" he declared again. "You must take responsibility." He glanced over at Georgiana to make sure he'd got the right man this time, and assumed it was so, for his daughter was nodding and leaning forward on the low couch.

Chidiock giggled briefly, but no one else was laughing. The whole room was silent except for his ill-timed mirth, which turned now to nervousness. It felt to him like one of those sensory-deprivation chambers where a person couldn't hear anything but his own laughter, his own heartbeat, his own badly chosen words. "Errrr," he stammered out.

Georgiana flicked imperious fingers in Magic Guy's direction, and he picked up his best friend's slack. After all, it had been his plan that had brought them here. "Chidiock," he said, enunciating the name for their visitors' benefit, "you remember Georgiana."

And she picked up her cue beautifully. She gushed, "I do so look forward to each and every one of your letters."

At the mention of letters, her mother found her voice. She was much less outwardly pleased than her daughter. "We were all struck by the one about escorting my young, unmarried child to the theatre without a chaperone."

"You *all* read her letters?"

Magic Guy didn't even hide his smirk. He knew Chidiock had sealed his fate with that remark. Instead of denying the allegations or mitigating the issue by claiming he'd planned to call on the family as a whole under proper conditions, he'd made it clear that he was guiltier than Jack the Ripper. (Jack the Ripper, of course, wouldn't be around for another fifty years or so, but this was Magic Guy's internal narration from his vantage point in 2013. He worked hard to mix his historical allusions in order to give off an air of *I can always look up the right timing on Wikipedia.*)

Within two days, the papers carried word of the "young" couple's engagement, since Chidiock would never be so heartless as to back out and ruin the girl whom he'd involved in this Prank War with his own first volley. Besides, the elf men both rather liked her and her conversation.

Within two months, the pair was married. Georgiana was resplendent in a cream gown with the world's puffiest sleeves (as far as she'd ever seen, leastwise). Chidiock cursed and thanked his friend for forcing their involvement. The happy pair moved to a country estate for a little while. And for a little while, they were happy there, laughing over the story of how Magic Guy had brought them together and wishing their friend would come to visit.

Chapter Twelve
Finding The Path

Magic Guy emerged from his flashback (an hour after it began) to find himself playing a Civil War general in the night's story game. It had been more of a rumination than a flashback, so he'd managed to keep up with no one the wiser.

Well, that wasn't entirely true, because Morena and Suzyn *had* been wiser. They'd kicked him enough times—Morena with her round-toed, pony-hair pumps, and Suzyn with her self-gel-penned Converse high-tops—to get his attention. Thankfully for all concerned, the elf man could spin a yarn with three-quarters of his brain elsewhen.

After the final time Morena kicked him, she put her foot back down, expecting to touch shoe to area rug. Instead, one glittery sole slipped on a pebble. No, it was too tall to be a pebble, with sharp sides she could feel through her sparkly shoe leather.

A man leaned over from the next table. "I'm sorry. Excuse me. That's my dee-twenty you're stepping on." He had close-cropped, ash-brown hair that was trending toward gray at the roots, a boyish smile that didn't crinkle his eyes, and the telltale line of contact lenses over his café-au-lait irises.

"Oh right," said Morena, and she shifted to fold herself in half so she could reach under the table and pick up his die.

"No, no. I'll get it." He made negatory hand motions, but he didn't bother to get out of his chair. If he'd been asked, he'd have explained that the waving was more to show off his lack of wedding ring than anything else. In his age bracket, all potential romantic interactions began with checking for evidence of outside involvement.

Morena grunted her acknowledgement of his statement, but she was committed at this point. Sure, her skinny jeans dug into her hip bones and cut into her flesh as only stiff, denim waistbands could, but she'd been raised to be helpful. And the die under her shoe was annoying. Triumphant and a bit flushed, she resumed her seated position, the pressure on her midsection alleviated.

She handed over the die. It was a swirly blue and white. "Here." She smiled to signal the interaction's end and returned her attention to her table, where Suzyn was trying to convince Rebecca's character that they should run away and steal office supplies together while the General was walking the camp boundaries.

Rebecca's character wasn't going for it, but that was because she was playing an enemy mole. She had better things to do than steal office supplies. Unfortunately, she couldn't come out and say that—thus getting Suzyn to leave her alone—because then her cover would be blown.

"My name's David." The man with the formerly missing d20 slid his chair closer to Morena's. "Pleased to meet you."

David's tablemates were not pleased by this development. They were in a multi-round combat scene, and if he wasn't prepared to roll for his chosen action the moment his turn came around, they'd be stuck playing this one battle for even more hours than necessary. Some people like protracted tabletop battles. Others hate the turn-based system. Either way, all seasoned players respect their comrades and come ready to play.

Except that apparently David was more interested in chatting up a woman at a neighboring table than in demonstrating regard for the people he knew and socialized with on a regular basis. If he kept this up, they were going to be very angry with him for the next few months of this campaign, at which point he'd be disinvited from joining their party again.

Morena held out her hand to shake. "Morena." She bit her lip and looked away from him to her own group. They were managing without her, but paying attention was important in a game like this. She looked back. "Nice to meet you?" She hated to give anyone the brush off. "Perhaps some other time?"

"Of course." David tugged his chair closer to its old spot. The other Pathfinder players glared at him. "What'd I miss?"

"It's your turn," gritted out their cleric.

"Still," added the tank.

The GM shook his head. "Guys, please." It wasn't quite an admonition, just a reminder that they had to get along in order for the campaign to continue.

David saw that his miniature wasn't where he'd left it on the map. "Uh, where am I?"

"Rrraaagh!" growled Tariq (the cleric). Tariq had run out

of patience about the time that David had dropped the die, long before the sort-of flirting started and only a little bit before everyone's characters had been displaced on the board by an enemy sorcerer-wolf thing.

Back at the story gaming table, Morena had caught up with the flow of the narrative, and her character was engaged in a duel in a graveyard at midnight for the right to marry the General's daughter. The General didn't think Morena's character had good enough prospects post-war, which was ridiculous since she planned to become President-Dictator of the Confederate Union, not that the General knew that... and not that it was particularly likely, especially if Suzyn's character kept stealing all the office supplies she needed.

It was a whole thing. Story gaming is awesome.

The story gamers wrapped for the night on a cliffhanger wherein everyone was in the graveyard and having duels at cross-purposes. Readying to go home, the players rooted around the floor by their chairs, pressing electronics safely into bags and wrapping themselves in scarves.

Suzyn grabbed at Magic Guy's arm before he could stand and take off. "We meeting on Friday to discuss the game?" The game didn't even have a title yet, which frustrated Suzyn to no end. She wanted to start designing the box it'd come in, but she couldn't do that without a title. Or some more direction, really.

Magic Guy shrugged his casual acceptance and tugged on his green-and-gray-striped gloves that worked with all touchscreens. "Friday's good." He slid a gray fingertip across his phone to unlock it and made an entry in his calendar. "We can discuss the specifics at our other game tomorrow?"

Magic Guy might have gamed with Suzyn and Morena

two days a week, but he played much more often than that. He was so determined to keep up with this new development in social entertainment that he was a member of five different groups. He knew that if he couldn't adapt, then people would sniff him out. And they'd be more interested in pitchforking or government-agenting than Morena and Suzyn had been. Actually *making* a game would be the pinnacle of his addiction to this latest craze. If only he could do this himself! But he couldn't, and, besides, Suzyn had all these uber-modern mannerisms.

At the next table, David broke away briefly from his party. He'd heard the story gamers packing up and, worse, making plans with each other. He couldn't let the hot woman with the glitter-soled shoes leave without setting something up, not if she was going to go off with other people instead.

This feeling is well known to many. It's one thing to think that your quarry has no interest in ever doing anything, with you or with others. But the moment that person seems like they might be willing to go/do/interact with someone else, there's this mix of jealousy—*why not with me?*—and opportunism—*clearly, they do things!*—that fills a potential pursuer to bursting.

"Morena!" David reached over to where the woman in question was folding her character sheet and grasped her fragile wrist in his hand. She tried to twist out of his grip, but he held on tight. She couldn't leave, not yet. "What are you doing on Friday night?"

"Friday?" she echoed.

Suzyn winked and nudged Morena with a foot from across Magic Guy. For his part, Magic Guy frowned at the pocket where he'd last seen the woman's iPhone. Neither of the younger-seeming pair suggested that Morena needed to join their game-making strategy session.

David shot to his feet, upsetting his table so that the miniatures fell over and a few rolled away from the squares where they'd been. The guy playing the cleric pounded his head on the table while the GM tried to reset everything. David remained oblivious to all that while he stammered, "Maybe we could do something?" He tried to be cute: "I owe you for nearly tripping you with that die, right?" But the cute didn't work so well since it's hard to trip someone who's sitting down. "I just... I thought... maybe, y'know?"

Inarticulate as he was, Morena *did* know. And, what was more, she was really starting to enjoy going on dates and talking to strangers who didn't immediately offer to shower with her. The iPhone was opening her up to new experiences. "Sure." She scribbled her number onto his character sheet. "Text me."

"Yeah," he breathed.

She edged around their tables and headed for the door, Magic Guy and Suzyn in her wake.

David's comrades reclaimed him and alternately glared in his direction and congratulated him for getting a date for the weekend.

All in all, it had been a strange night for our protagonists, each of whom had learned something.

1. Suzyn had learned that she really didn't enjoy story gaming all that much, at least not when she wasn't high. This had been her first game without an escape for a line or a smoke, and the whole make-believe lark hadn't been nearly as thrilling without the pharmaceutical assistance. Apparently, she depended on her drug-increased talkativeness to make role-play interaction fun.

But she couldn't get complacent and go back to her old addictions. Not now. Because she did her best planning while sober. Some artists, they tell you they're brilliant on uppers or downers or what-have-you. Most of them are lying. A few are telling the truth. And Suzyn was self-aware enough to know that she shouldn't even try the lie.

She laid out her projects sober. The end. (The art itself... sometimes she needed the focus. She was aware of the false dichotomy here, but had never before cared to overcome it.)

2. Morena had surprised herself by chatting with another stranger. She didn't entirely look forward to their date, but she figured it'd be a good experience. She'd also learned that Magic Guy was serious about his whole magic thing. Come to think of it, it might have been during that conversation when she first started referring to him as "Magic Guy" in her mind, though not out loud. Not yet.

3. Last, Magic Guy had given himself away, not that it mattered. Moreover, he'd learned that he had accidentally acquired friends. He couldn't help remembering Chidiock. It was a moment of weakness to remember the good times, and he missed Chidiock with such fierceness that it knocked his heart into his ribs and pulled at his brain through his nostrils as if he were being embalmed alive. He wondered if they could still be friends, whether they'd ever stopped being friends.

With the ladies gone to their Smart, Magic Guy walked over to the supernatural post office that had set up shop in an abandoned light rail-to-be building. It was the perfect location for a supernatural way station: hidden from humanity yet utterly obvious, intended for movement yet closed and therefore static, and conveniently located in a part of the city that got plenty of bus traffic. There was another one downtown, but this one was right by Wayward.

Maybe he shouldn't have, but the bolt of homesickness prompted him to write a quick note. Just an *I miss you, but I don't know if I'm ready to talk yet.* He left it in a special post box that he knew would deliver the message to wherever Chidiock happened to be.

The box dutifully "ate" the message and magically flagged Chidiock's location to let the other elf know he had mail for pick-up next time he was near a postal location. Then it swallowed the image of Magic Guy's paper-based words down beneath the city, below the Underground Tour (spotlighting Seattle's original city plan) and into the magical miasma that flowed everywhere and nowhere all at once. The message took itself to the closest post box to its recipient and reformed from component atoms till the very swirls of the curly p's had been reassembled. Chidiock could read it whenever he was ready.

Back in Seattle, Magic Guy wondered what would come of his sudden whim. *What if we aren't "besties" anymore?* For all that he'd been the one to leave, Magic Guy had always expected to have a friend to return to when the dark feuding feelings had lightened and melted to nothingness.

But what if I don't?

At least Magic Guy still had Suzyn and Morena, his new friends, the ones who had jumpstarted his emotionality. What if they were all he had?

What if they weren't?

Already, he missed being the poster child for the Seattle Freeze.

The following evening, Suzyn and Morena lazed in their apartment, physically close together but largely ignoring one another. Morena knelt in front of the oak coffee table (craigslist find!), half-watching a DVRed episode of *White Collar* on the 32-inch screen while painting her nails a sparkly shade of coral. (She'd thought of giving up on the latest *WC* season altogether, but some niggling piece of her soul demanded completion.)

Suzyn wasn't watching the show at all, even though she'd started out as a huge fan. *White Collar* was practically a love letter to New York City, and it made her sweetly nostalgic for her family, for her school friends, and for her neighborhood haunts. But then it made her homesick. Hot men and competent women couldn't make up for the sudden attack of *emotions* whenever Neal looked over the city from his rooftop balcony.

Instead, Suzyn lay on the sectional couch with her laptop and created an OkCupid profile for Morena. For "three words that describe you" she'd gone with: statistical, fashionable, worthwhile. She could work on it more later. She wasn't sure that last one conveyed what she wanted it to.

Suzyn pulled out her phone and angled it down so the camera framed the back of Morena's head. "Look at me," she half demanded, half questioned.

Morena twisted away from her nails, careful not to smudge. "What's up?"

Click.

"Perfect." Suzyn emailed the photo to herself and posted it as Morena's default profile picture.

"Don't you have enough photos of me? Better photos?" Morena squinted at her roommate as though she could divine the younger woman's intentions. She briefly wondered if Magic Guy thought that he could divine anything with his weird magic obsession. "What are you even doing?"

Suzyn could've replied *an experiment*. Morena would have accepted that answer and thought nothing more of it, content with her polish and her TV show. But Suzyn said, "Updating your OkCupid profile."

Morena frowned at her nails. She'd have to do a third layer unless she wanted to pull out the remover, because that last pinky had gotten a bit wavy. "I don't have an OkCupid profile."

"Hey, someone's checking you out." A number on the left column of Suzyn's screen counted how many people were viewing the profile at any given moment.

"Ohmigod," Morena rushed through the word. She took a moment to screw the top onto the polish bottle before scrambling to her feet, careful not to use her fingertips for balance in any way. "What did you *do*?" She leaned into Suzyn's space as well as she could without tapping her extremities against anything.

"You wanted to find love." Suzyn switched over to another tab, where she had saved a bunch of profiles that ought to fit Morena's criteria. "Tell me this one isn't a super hottie."

This one was a fit thirty-something wearing a suit in his profile picture. His three-word description was "kitten-loving Microsoftie."

Morena couldn't help but appreciate the kitten lover's uber-sharp cheekbones. She breathed a little faster, ready to give in. "What are his hobbies?"

Suzyn scrolled down. "Ugh. Camping and meeting planning."

Morena pulled back from the screen and made a grossed-out face that involved an open mouth with a tongue sticking out the side in an unbecoming manner. "Hells to the no."

Suzyn giggled. "Don't say that. You sound ridiculous." She was firmly of the opinion that Morena was too old for cute sayings. Gen Xers weren't supposed to act like young people.

Morena would've swatted Suzyn across the head, but her nails were still tacky and it wasn't worth potentially scoring lines in the paint. "Besides, I have a guy already."

Suzyn rolled her eyes as strongly as she possibly could. It kind of hurt. "You haven't even gone out with this guy once yet. You're not *taken*." She checked her email. "Aha! I already have five matches who have checked you out and rated you highly with the selfie-style profile picture. In an hour, I'm going to change it to a glamor one from our Gas Works shoot."

And that was the truth of the matter: Suzyn was only partially interested in using the site to help out her roommate. The rest of her clamored for market research. She wanted to see which of her photos resonated best with the untrained observer. She thought it would improve her art.

Sadly, Suzyn hadn't thought this plan through. Because these weren't untrained *art* observers, but rather trained *romance* hunters. A selfie said one thing, and a glamor shot said another. What a person wore, how they smiled, the angle... these all communicated the Oker's interest in sex versus love, in sports versus couch-surfing, and so on. Any data Suzyn acquired would only tell her how many guys wanted certain kinds of relationships.

Another email popped up. "Aaaaand someone wants to meet you."

The message was basic. It read:

heyy cutie....what ya doin 2nite. party at my place...yea.

And that was just... no. Suzyn deleted it with an embarrassed cough.

"Take it down." Morena knew you couldn't really delete something from the Internet, but she didn't want to deal with stuff like that email. Not ever.

"Oh, come on," Suzyn wheedled. "It's for art research. Besides, you could use it to do quizzes! Ever wonder what happened to pointless Internet quizzes? They all went to OkCupid."

Morena had often bemoaned the lack of quizzes in the last decade or so, and Suzyn had no compunctions about taking advantage of this fact, but the elder roommate's face was still stony, so the younger tried again. "You don't need to look for a *romantic* partner. What about a karaoke partner? Or volley-ball! You've been wanting to meet other volleyball people. I'll do a search..."

"Take it down, please?" Morena wasn't good at telling Suzyn no, but she didn't see the point in having a profile on this website. "I mean, when you're done with the research." Because she always supported Suzyn's art. Always. That was the prerogative of a good best friend.

Suzyn tried again. "And it's not just my research. OkCupid has the best statistics! Look at their blog!"

They really did compile neat statistics, and mathematical modeling was the path to Morena's heart, but no one needed their own profile in order to read the conclusions.

The friends had reached a stalemate: Suzyn wasn't going to give up; Morena didn't want to deal with annoying emails.

In the end, Suzyn was going to win. They both knew it. Morena didn't care enough to fight about it, not when it made Suzyn happy and all the emails got shunted to the younger woman's email address. Compromise was the heart of any successful relationship, after all.

Morena's nails were almost dry, so she reached for her new iPhone to play with the other romance-finder in her life. "When do you think I need to charge this thing?"

She charged her Samsung every night, but in the weeks since she'd gotten the iPhone from her ex, she hadn't come near it with a plug. It hadn't even come with a cord, now that she thought about it.

Suzyn fiddled with Morena's profile a bit more. She set *rather not say* for the income category, then proceeded to rate ten guys. "Maybe it's magic," she offered. She right-clicked another hot guy to open his profile in a new tab—this one's favorite color was green, and he enjoyed fostering cats and reading late 19th-century literature—then paused, played back what she'd said, and laughed. "Like Magic Guy claimed it was."

"Like: long cat is long, and Magic Guy is really magical?" she offered. "Seattle pagans can be pretty weird." Morena didn't mean this as a bad thing. They tended to be weird in the best ways: the most fun, the best at crafting, the greenest thumbs. "Not that magic is real or anything."

But the phone sat in her hand at full battery without ever being charged.

On Suzyn's computer screen, a note popped up saying that a green-loving man was checking out her (well, Morena's) profile. Yes, this is the same Green Man who has appeared earlier in the narrative. No, he will not yet meet our heroines.

"Right," said Suzyn. "Believing in magic would be crazy."

Morena's thumb hovered over the romance app, not sure if she should open it. While she deliberated, the screen changed of its own accord. The familiar wheels beckoned, practically begging to spin and find her a match.

"Crazy," Morena agreed.

The ladies did protest too much, to quote (with grammatical fixes) The Bard.

Chapter Thirteen
Why Dating Is Awful

It wasn't the snowiest winter Seattle had ever seen. Not even the snowiest in recent memory. That had been in 2008: Snowpocalypse. Some people called it Snowmaggeddon, but those people were wrong. In those days, LiveJournal had still been A Thing, and the LJ-erati from Seattle had all agreed on Snowpocalypse.

During the 2008 winter, buses had jackknifed in the streets and been abandoned like unintentional robots or like the modern art in the Olympic Sculpture Park (always free to visit). Capitol Hill had been cut off, its grocery stores going unstocked for too long. The cab companies had made apologetic calls to stranded locals who wanted to go to the airport that Christmas. People only got out of the city if they had snow chains and/or four-wheel-drive vehicles to put them on. And, well, if you had those things, you probably didn't live in the city itself.

But while this 2013 winter wasn't as snowy as that 2008 one, there was a light dusting on the ground before the sun rose. Suzyn built a calf-high snowman in the shade of their apartment complex, and it took half an hour to melt.

This was March, after all, and snow couldn't last for long. It was still cold, though, and Morena agonized over what to wear on her date with David, the discourteous Pathfinder player.

"Do you know where he's taking you?" asked Suzyn in an attempt to be helpful.

"Grrraaagh!"

"That's a no then."

Eventually the roommates decided on a wintry palette to sparkle in tandem with the last of the season's snow: gold sweater, pine-green cords, tree-bark-brown boots with silver soles like a hint of frost. The outfit was classy, tasteful, and this side of casual, which should work for most dates.

Clothes chosen, Morena spent an hour and a half on her hair. Suzyn played makeup artist with a flair helped along by YouTube videos from an aesthetic institute in London and a precocious high school freshman in the Midwest.

All Pathfinder David (for Morena had started calling him this in her head; she hoped she wouldn't say it out loud when she met him) had told Morena was that he planned to pick her up at 6 p.m. sharp and that he was going to wear navy blue. The first part of this meant she had to watch the clock carefully, it being a Friday, in order to leave work and get home and dressed in time. She'd put in enough hours and had things working smoothly, so no one outright objected to her schedule, but she hoped they weren't going to be eating fatty foods—ugh, she hoped Pathfinder David wasn't a paleo—because her stomach was already over-tight from letting a date with a near-stranger come before her career (in the form of continuous overtime).

The second part, about the navy blue... that was just confusing. What did it matter what color(s) he wore? Was he sending a signal that she should do the same? Or that she should stay away from navy so that they didn't get too matchy or too almost-but-not-exactly-the-right-shade clashy? Morena's final color scheme would complement his choice either way.

What the friends hadn't expected was for him to be dressed in a suit and tie. Both navy blue.

"What are you *wearing*?" Pathfinder David said the second Morena opened the door, tone utterly aghast.

He didn't comment on her meticulous hair. He didn't notice her Marilyn Monroe eyeliner, complete with white stripe as suggested by the Midwestern YouTube artist. He didn't say how lovely it was to see her again or compliment her sparkly sweater, which fit her shoulders exactly so that it fell in soft perfection to a slightly nipped waist.

No, he criticized. "That's all wrong for an awards dinner. You'll have to change."

Suzyn recovered first. A bit. "An awards dinner?" she echoed.

"My firm has a table. I reserved a second seat for my plus one."

Morena huffed. He didn't get to treat her like an idiot when he sprang this on her. "How formal is it?"

He lifted incredulous eyebrows, like clumps of earthworms dead in a rain puddle, and gestured to his suit as if to say, *Like so.*

It is important at this juncture to understand that Pathfinder David truly did not see where he'd gone wrong. He thought that telling her his color scheme in advance would lead her to extrapolate *formal*. Moreover, he didn't understand that though a suit and tie for modern men could cover anything from business not-quite-casual to we'd-really-prefer-if-you-wore-black-tie-but-we'll-still-let-you-in, women's clothing had finer gradations. So possibly we can forgive Pathfinder David for being a total moron about this part of the scene. Possibly. Morena certainly did so, knowing that some men in her socially-disinclined city missed these delicate points.

We needn't, however, forgive him for being a total jerk to her by skipping out on the common courtesies. If Seattle could claim anything as an overarching personality, it was being polite. (Well, polite and caffeinated.) People smiled, people offered help with groceries, people noticed your hair or your new bicycle. They didn't have to like you or invite you to their house, even after they'd been to yours, but they certainly had to bring wine as a host gift if they came over.

Oh, but what can we expect from a player who flirts instead of tracking the combat-in-progress at his weekly Pathfinder campaign? (Excepting that awful breed of "ladies' man" who would do the same in the gaming situation, but at least would be smooth and charismatic on the dating side.)

With no further cues from Pathfinder David, Suzyn and Morena adjourned to a bedroom closet, where they chose a black crepe cocktail dress. Above the knees and simple, it could pass for party-informal. Dry-clean and classy, it could work up through almost-black-tie. It wasn't perfect, and Morena was frustrated to have mussed her hair and mascara in making it work (between the sweat and the disrobing), but it would do.

When they rejoined Pathfinder David in their living room, he was stubbing a wing-tipped toe into their matted doorway carpet and punching angrily at his phone screen. "Are you ready yet?"

His tone and impatience settled a granite ball between Morena's collarbones that made swallowing more difficult than usual. She didn't want to upset the new mountain in her throat by speaking, so she simply picked up her beaded peacock clutch and transferred her keys, cards, and sexy iPhone into it. She pointed behind him to the cashmere-wool coat hanging beside the door.

Pathfinder David rolled his eyes in frustration. "So put it on!" And went back to his phone. It didn't occur to him that he should pass it to her, maybe help her slip into it.

Suzyn gave Morena a sympathetic eyebrow arch and got a rueful shrug in return.

And so Pathfinder David pulled Morena out the door, still not acknowledging her existence in any useful sort of way, and escorted her to his car. It was a black Audi TT (with the top up) that sported salt-stained tires and a crooked front bumper.

Who even drove Audis anymore? They broke down all the time. Morena bit her smiling lower lip, holding in a laugh. And if a person did drive one, it tended to be something flashy to showcase their status, not a semi-broken thing.

It was hard to feel intimidated by someone who drove a messy Audi TT.

Morena swallowed and cleared her throat. "I thought you'd have a Subaru." Many people at Wayward who owned cars did, indeed, drive practical Subarus, but this was just a gambit. Morena hadn't given any thought to what kind of car Pathfinder David might own until that very second. She could have just as easily offered a Toyota, a BMW, or a Fiat Panda.

He didn't strike her as a Panda guy, though, not from his looks and hobbies.

What he said was, "No."

Her clutch buzzed against her leg, and Morena surreptitiously pulled out her iPhone to check the message—even though she knew it was bad manners to use one's phone while on an outing with friends. She didn't even have to thumb it open to read it. Her mother's words showed up in a text block on the front:

Need a delivery girl. Come help me?

Finally! After a month of needling, Luiza was willing to ask for help with her business. Morena had been dying to do something that would make her mother's life easier. So, of course that happened when Morena was on a date. Then again, it wasn't like driving things around was such a big help, not like business planning or website updating. Which was good, as far as Morena was concerned, because she was going to have to decline her mother's invitation to chauffeur.

Slowly, and slyly eyeing her driving companion to stay unnoticed, Morena unlocked the phone. A big, green heart filled the screen, and Morena used her second hand to cover it. Even ruder than taking a message while on a date: using a romance app while on a date!

Still... she had it open now.

Morena gave the phone a little shake and covered the speaker with her forefinger. She felt more than heard the *ding ding DING!* that meant she had a new match. Why had she done that? Why was she being so unfair to Pathfinder David?

And then, *Why did I unlock my phone in the first place?*

Sorting through all these questions gave Morena a small headache, so she put her phone back in her clutch and stared out the window until they reached a downtown parking lot somewhere between the two malls and underneath one of the city's many towers (all of which had glass sides so that a person might look out onto the Sound, even when all a viewer could really see were more buildings with this exact same architectural quirk).

A fount of friendliness, Morena gave discourse another go. (She'd tried twice more in the Audi and been shut down as handily as with the car discussion.) "Brrrr." She shivered a bit, knowing her legs were goose-pimpling both where they were bared to the air and where they were covered by her dress.

Pathfinder David contemplated not replying to this gambit. He knew that commenting on a lady's wardrobe could go horribly wrong. He also knew that he'd been a terrible date in the car, not even buying her flowers, or whatever it was that people did nowadays according to TV shows. He settled on a neutral: "You should have worn something more practical."

This statement was decidedly not neutral from Morena's perspective. After everything she'd gone through to please this guy! But then he offered her his arm—the one not holding a hardbound book—like a Victorian gentleman, and she thawed. Her legs felt warmer, at least, or maybe she simply didn't notice the cold as much. She could tell that he'd realized he needed to step it up, and she decided he must be apologizing for his demeanor with his actions.

Neither of these things Morena thought she knew was, in fact, the case. But it made her feel better, which meant Pathfinder David was observably improving as a date. A fact that single men of the world should lament because, damn it, they worked hard to make themselves desirable and interesting and appropriate and polite, yet jerks who managed to successfully ask girls out were the ones who got the chance to treat them badly!

Or something.

They strolled to the parking garage's elevator, shoe heels loud over the sound of squeaking tires (still wet from the rain and snow) filtering in from other levels of the structure. Once inside the elevator, Pathfinder David pressed a chilly button for the third floor of the skyscraper above. He cleared his throat, and Morena looked away from her reflection in the striated steel walls, ecstatic that he was finally loosening up enough to talk to her.

"The last date I brought to something like this left with someone else. I hope it goes without saying that that's rude."

Morena found herself nodding already by the time his words sank in, and by then she was committed to agreeing that (a) yes, it was rude and (b) she would never think of doing something like that and (c) his condescension was totally okay with her. She could see why someone might have abandoned him, but this was a first date and she was determined to make it work. He might just be socially awkward, she rationalized, and needed her to give him more chances until he could show her his true nature. Not everyone did well on first dates.

All the same, to demonstrate her disapproval, she gave him the silent treatment till they'd entered the banquet room. The room smelled of Old Spice and Indian curry. The tables had been set far enough apart to make the room look luxuriously large, and each one was crammed with officemates.

A low hum concentrated over each table, but no conversations hopped from one seating area to the next. No interaction between companies, not even to subtly interrogate or gloat.

Surprisingly, for a building like this, the organizers had

chosen a windowless room, so she couldn't look out over the water and pretend to be somewhere else, wearing a romantically wistful look on her face until Pathfinder David was so overcome by her effortless artlessness that he needed to know her thoughts. This fantasy would have to remain fantasy, and not just because of the window issue.

Pathfinder David grabbed her wrist and tugged her along a winding path between white-clothed tabletops. He stopped briefly to drop a heavy book in front of one attendee. Silverware rattled, and chatter at the table stopped.

Pathfinder David flashed the seated group a false smile. "Just returning a library book to Frances here." He clapped Frances on the shoulder and pulled again on Morena's wrist, startling her into a brief stumble.

"Are those your coworkers?"

He winked. "Nope. Frances is going to have a hard time of it for a while."

As far as Pathfinder David saw it, you had two choices in business: to be helpful to everyone so that you all got ahead, or to sabotage your competitors and step over them on your way to the top. The reader has witnessed his inability to be helpful and, thus, will understand that he chose the latter course.

They paused at the buffet table, from whence emanated the scent of curry and cheesy paneer pakoras. When Pathfinder David finally dropped her wrist, she made a show of rubbing it with her other hand, though it was perfectly fine. He didn't notice.

"Aren't we joining your workmates?"

Pathfinder David shrugged. He wanted to be sure his boss saw him attending, but knew he'd get more useful information from the catering table. "I'm supposed to organize the holiday party this year, so I'm scouting caterers early."

He didn't know anything about organizing a party, but he'd volunteered after the last one, three months prior, in order to prove he could take on more event-related PR. He tended to get stuck doing a lot of data analysis and (whenever he couldn't get out of it) cold calling. He was more of a let-me-design-your-social-campaign kind of guy, but that wasn't paying right now, not when the interns did that stuff for free. So: event planning. It had to be easier than calling strangers and asking what their current PR firm really did for them.

"I can help you with that!" Morena smiled broadly, not that Pathfinder David was looking. She was ready to wow him with her beautiful teeth and knowledge of how people coordinated stuff like this.

Dismissive, far more interested in discovering what had prompted the event planners to pick Indian (which could be very polarizing), he said, "That's all right, honey."

Morena's spine curved away from him like he'd sent a Sounders soccer ball into her ribs. She had certainly never given him permission to call her "honey." And not like *that*. Still... she forced herself to straighten up and step closer to his warm body. Maybe she could convince herself it was sweet that he'd given her a pet name on their first date? "I work in the food industry. I know this stuff."

"You're a waitress?"

She gave him a scathing look, which, of course, he missed, too busy pulling covers off the food, sniffing, and putting them back. "I'm a logistics and distribution engineer. In the food industry."

"Of course you are." Pathfinder David noticed a person wearing all white at the end of the table. "Excuse me."

He proceeded to have a half-hour discussion with the catering manager, which they had to continue out in the hallway while the keynote speeches began. Pathfinder David learned all about how much things cost and how the company had been initially contacted. The upshot was that this restaurant didn't usually do large events but that the restaurant owner knew the event organizer. Useless. Pathfinder David's night wasn't going well.

Without date or direction, Morena leaned against a wall next to the yeasty naan and listened to the speeches, politely clapping whenever someone won an award. By the time Pathfinder David returned and asked why she hadn't taken a seat with his firm, she was more than ready to leave.

Instead, she waited another two hours, making polite chitchat with the people at the table Pathfinder David finally escorted her to, her side smashed against a bearded man who'd drenched himself in Old Spice. All the women at the table wore business suits, except Morena in her crepe cocktail number.

She didn't let that get to her. She was long used to being the best dressed in a room, even when no one else knew it. She could just pretend they'd all made mistakes in wearing business attire to a more formal function.

Three hours later, when Pathfinder David dropped her off at her door, she was ready to tell him she'd enjoyed meeting him but didn't think they'd make a good couple. Morena couldn't see a future with a guy who didn't even like her. Before she got her chance, he said, "I had a really good time tonight. All because of you. Could we do it again sometime?"

He looked so sweet and vulnerable, gazing up at her through long lashes on a downturned face. And he'd said he liked her. If she didn't want to be alone and loveless forever, if she wanted someone to grow old with and to care for, she needed to make the effort. How many other men would she find in her age bracket who were single and city-dwelling and interested?

"I'd love to."

Morena shuddered. What had she gotten herself into?

Now she had to go out with him again.

Chapter Fourteen
Not The Real Thing

While Morena was out with Pathfinder David, Suzyn and Magic Guy were rocking specialized footwear, last fashionable in the early '90s. They'd chosen not to patronize a bar or a café for their latest business meeting, but had gone instead to TechCity Bowl. Home of hot dog grease, unfortunate karaoke singers, and a cosmic floor glowing blue and red.

Magic Guy had shown up at Suzyn's apartment around 6:30 with a car2go Smart and teased her that "you'll feel right at home," since it was the same model as Morena's. They'd driven across Lake Washington and along twisty roads into the middle of what felt like nowhere but was still Kirkland, a relatively metropolitan city.

As transplants, they believed that Kirkland was near enough to Seattle that it was worth driving to for the promise of multiple bowling lanes, no matter that all their new friends would recoil in horror from heading into suburbia on a Friday night. And so they dealt with the traffic (which they mostly ignored while listening to 107.7 FM, The End, and lamenting how cool it had been at New Year's when the station had played their entire library in alphabetical order and why didn't the DJs do that all the time?, but then it'd be programmable like JACK-FM, which they agreed was much less cool), because it didn't bother them at all.

Suzyn's bowling ball, a ten-pounder, rolled down the slick wood, almost pink in the red floor lights. "C'mon, c'mon, c'mon," she cheered it on in a near-whisper. The globe veered to the right and hit two pins.

"Yes!" she crowed. "Take that!" In the fifth frame, her score was 34. Magic Guy's was 89.

He snorted and plucked his own ball, fourteen pounds, from the carousel. "When I win, you owe me a soda."

Already, the little plastic table where they'd punched in their names—and argued over score corrections—overflowed with empty soda cans that they may or may not have been allowed to have down in the bowling pits. They'd given up on ordering from the alley's bar with its karaoke aficionados (*voted second-best karaoke in Western Washington!*) in favor of visiting the vending machine when necessary. They'd been trading off rounds.

"I'll get you a soda anyway."

Suzyn abandoned the lane to buy two Diet Cokes. Behind her, pins knocked against each other in a crash that overpowered the karaoke on one side and the thumping cosmic bowl beats on the other.

She returned to find Magic Guy's score now at 108. She didn't bother scowling. She wasn't like the serious group in the last three lanes who were all scoring 200-and-something.

Bowling was for fun, not for talent. (For Magic Guy's part, he was a little annoyed about getting a strike-nine, but he too was playing for fun, not for status.)

Magic Guy accepted his can, condensation dewing onto his fingertips. He cracked the top and took a short, too-bubbly sip followed by a long draught. "Gosh, that's good."

He'd been sad when Coca-Cola took the cocaine out of their products, marking the first big change in the formula, but he adored the comparatively new Diet Coke. It wasn't The Real Thing, as far as his memory was concerned. Rather, it was a definite improvement.

"We totally need to get a vending machine when we live together," said Suzyn. Her eyes closed, and she leaned back precariously in one of the plastic chairs, her feet up between the empties.

Magic Guy's stomach clenched hard around carbon dioxide remnants that felt too big and sour now.

She was a study of relaxation. "I always wanted a vending machine, but my parents said they were impractical. What is that even about? One day they say *find your dreams*. The next day they say my dreams are impractical."

Magic Guy didn't know what to approach in that revelation first. Suzyn had opened up to him, told him something true and emotional about her life. He understood her now more than he did before, and he wished he didn't. It made her more elven in his eyes.

So he tried to ignore it, knowing he could only do so on the surface, and not inside his brain. "Whoa whoa whoa. When we live together? *When?* This isn't a date."

Maybe, he feared, she'd thought it was, what with him picking her up and taking her out on a Friday night and paying for her bowling shoes because she was mostly broke.

"I know." She sat up and twisted to look at him, her eyebrows screwed together in confusion and slight derision. As if to say *duh!* Though he was pretty sure kids didn't say that anymore. "You said you were ace." Which was true, he *had* told both Suzyn and Morena that he identified as asexual way back in Chapter Two – Let You Tell Me a Story.

She said it as if that explained everything. And, in fact, it should have. It *did* explain why he, at least, wasn't on a date. He appreciated her casual acceptance, knowing that people even thirty years in the past would have had a harder time of it. But Magic Guy still didn't understand why she felt that they'd live together at some point.

When, not if.

The last time he'd lived with someone (and the last time he'd gotten a cool new housewares gadget, like a vending machine), it had ended in disaster.

A few months after their wedding, Chidiock and Georgiana had returned to the London townhouse and joined Magic Guy in every activity. For instance, the threesome shopped together, breaking apart for bare minutes to frequent specialty merchants, only to reform again. All three would go to the sweet shop, then Georgiana and Magic Guy would visit the antique bookseller, after which they'd rejoin Chidiock at the curiosity shop to marvel at the shrunken heads, and so on. They quickly became an inseparable trio about town.

Some of the old biddies found it scandalous, a lady of Georgiana's breeding and stature living with *two* men, but she had married one of them and came from an impeccable family, so said biddies sent dinner invitations for three instead of for two whenever such occasions arose.

The trio preferred to dine at home, however, than to attend salons. A person can only be a guest at so many parties before wishing to sit in one's own relatively quiet home to *agree* about politics (something Georgiana rarely had the chance to enjoy at society functions), discuss fiction, or play a decent game of cribbage without losing an outrageous amount of money in the process.

Betting without risk was a novel concept of which Georgiana in particular was quite fond in light of her husband's talent for coming in second.

Magic Guy knew their peaceful coexistence couldn't last. The paused prank war was made of Damocles steel now that he'd escalated it with the forced marriage. He could barely wait to discover what retaliatory trick Chidiock might invent. He looked forward to the idyll's end with an impish smile on his face and a trill in his heartbeat.

But Magic Guy waited patiently, enjoying the games and the discussions and the widows' speculative looks. Chidiock was his best friend, and Magic Guy had come to love Georgiana as well as he'd ever loved any human. He was in no hurry to move things along.

For his part, Chidiock bade his time until he was sure Magic Guy wouldn't expect a new maneuver. Then, he employed an inventor from Threadneedle Street to help him make a kitchen automaton that could chop vegetables. He brought gold tubes and copper sheets to his eccentric employee and ordered cogs of metal and wood.

To speed the assembly process, Chidiock taught the inventor small magics suitable for frail mortal bodies to wield. Soon, the innovator could shape impossibly smooth wheels (nearly frictionless!) and precision lenses.

So it was that it took but a few months before Chidiock had a human-height doll, shaped in elongated ovals of copper plate. The automaton could chop vegetables, throw them in a bowl so long as the bowl was properly placed by the user, and stop chopping when it ran out of produce.

Chidiock thanked the inventor, paid him a last installment, and absconded with his new possession to the basement of the London townhouse the threesome called home. There he drew on the elven-only magics he knew.

He breathed aether into the metallic mouth. He wove the copper skin with ley energies. He poured enchantment over the unthinking head for fourteen midnights. Until at last it was truly complete.

He taught his automaton to move itself about a room in response to the vibrations of a human voice. It would follow those to their source and chop in the direction of said voice— not at the join of the neck where the voice box might be, but slightly to the right.

He didn't want to kill his friend, after all.

But he knew quite well that Magic Guy tended to go down to the kitchen in the evening and make off with vegetables intended for breakfast the following morning. The next time Chidiock's best friend tried to nab a piece of pepper, he'd get a kitchen blade in the shoulder. It would heal, but it would also be a shock—and possibly keep Magic Guy out of the crisper for good.

Chidiock jittered with anticipation. He desperately wanted to see how it would work out *immediately*. And so he installed his creation in the townhouse's kitchen the moment he'd finished it.

Unfortunately, the first person to visit the kitchen unannounced wasn't Magic Guy.

At six o'clock of the evening on the day the automaton joined the household, Magic Guy and Chidiock were warming themselves by the sitting room fire. Its crackling smokiness made for a cozy reading area, letting the friends sit together without needing to entertain one another (a feat which had proven difficult, and not necessarily desired, in the recent few decades of their comfortable companionship).

The evening's relaxed harmony burst on discordant screeching. The screaming continued and continued. So it wasn't a staff member surprised by a spider, then.

Alarmed, they sprinted toward the sound. Toward the kitchen.

Magic Guy knocked his shoulder into a corner as he ran faster. The bruise faded in seconds.

The screaming stopped.

By the time they reached the kitchens, a rhythmic *thunk*ing had taken over. A *pound, shhwhirr, pound, shhwirr*.

The door was closed.

Chidiock's bowels quivered with fear. He swallowed down bile, pushed ahead of Magic Guy, and flung open the door with a clanging crash. He was sure he knew what had happened, though not to whom. Perhaps his mechanism-and-magic mixture hadn't been ready to experience the world.

Behind the entry, the automaton's back was pushed into the brick wall. Its knife was embedded in the wooden door.

Had it feelings, the automaton would not have been pleased by this change in its status. It had done exactly what had been asked of it (protected the kitchen with blows to the voice box of intruders), and all it got in return was a bloody mess and a door that was much too hard to easily chop into pieces. Its gears cranked harder, whining with the strain, until the utensil came free.

It slammed the knife into its oaken nemesis once again, as it had been created to do.

"Oh dear Lord," breathed Magic Guy. For he had seen the automaton's earlier work, the source of the screams.

A lady's body decorated the floor. Its mutilated, rusty-smelling flesh was strewn about the feet of the kitchen island, as if a chef's knife had come down over and over and over to finely dice the throat and shoulder.

The vibrations from Magic Guy's voice called to the automaton, and it wrested its knife from the door before heading mindlessly toward the sound. It needed to chop, to mince, to protect against the intruder.

Magic Guy fell to his knees in the blood pond by the lady's unmolested head. Her eyes would never again twinkle and tease. Her mouth would form no more words in defense of some unfashionable cause. "Oh, Georgie."

For, as you have undoubtedly guessed, the corpse in question was Georgiana, the eternal victim of this foolish prank war. First, Chidiock had played with her emotions in order to set Magic Guy up for a duel. Then, Magic Guy had forced her to marry or else have her reputation destroyed, as if marrying her were a prank-level annoyance. And now—now her life had ended, never more to tolerate her boys' games.

Chidiock tackled the automaton before it could chop up his dearest friend's throat. He needed to keep his mistake from doing any further damage. Could their kind come back from decapitation? He'd heard campfire stories that went both ways and had no desire to find out the truth of the matter.

He'd mourn for his dead wife later.

The automaton, as one might expect, was significantly stronger than Chidiock, seeing as it was made of metal. It was not, however, in charge of its own destiny. Chidiock inhaled, drawing his aether back from the metallic mouth. He unraveled the ley energies from his creation's copper skin. He pulled at its enchanted workings with his own anima, reclaiming his magical potential and leaving the monster lifeless.

The automaton *clunk*ed to a halt. A musty, singed aroma came from its overworked vents, clashing with the copper-and-meat smell of Georgiana's lamented body. Its innards ticked as they cooled down.

Chidiock panted from the effort of stopping his abomination.

Saltwater tears filled Magic Guy's mouth. "Why?"

Magic Guy knew he was in shock. His eyes saw as though he were underwater, where everything was blurred and far away. His limbs shook with chill. This knowledge did not help him to focus on his surroundings.

He imagined Georgiana twenty, thirty, fifty years in the future. She would have friends and children, would host salons, would spearhead a major cause and force the House of Lords to pay attention. Not anymore.

"I didn't mean for this. It was an accident. You were supposed to come to the kitchen first."

"You meant to kill me?" Magic Guy didn't move, just cradled his friend's unseeing head. He and Chidiock had been so close for so long, killing each other ought to have been like killing themselves. If Magic Guy hadn't already been floaty and miserably unsurprised, he would have been now.

"No!" The shout was overloud in the small space, echoing

off cast-iron pots before getting swallowed by the crimson floor. "It wasn't supposed to kill you. It was just part of our prank war."

The love letters had been a prank. A rock under a seat cushion would be a prank. Drawing blood is never a prank.

Magic Guy laughed without joy. "The Great Prank War of 1835." He shook his head, tears flying to the floor with a rapid *plink plink*ing. "What an auspicious future we've built."

"I'll fix it."

But Chidiock couldn't fix it. Georgiana was dead.

Magic Guy said, "I'm leaving. Give me half an hour to pack a valise. That will be enough."

"No!" Chidiock yelled again, but this time the denial was quieter, eaten immediately by the objects in the room. The sound had no impact. "You shouldn't be alone. We can grieve together."

Magic Guy stood, his knees stained sticky with congealing fluid. "We've been together long enough, don't you think? Do you know who you are alone anymore, who I am?" He pushed fashionably innocuous, curly hair out of his eyes, idly noting that he needed to cut it. "If you can be shortsighted enough for this, what does that mean for me?"

Because he understood that this wasn't intentional and could believe that no one was at fault for Georgiana's needless death, but he wanted some time away to internalize this.

He understood now why his parents constantly traveled when he was young, though travel was dangerous even for elves in 4000 B.C.E. They'd needed the distance, the comforting constancy of always being an outsider. Magic Guy had rebelled and settled down, and what good had that done for him?

For Georgiana?

He also understood that magic and machinery were not meant to mix, at least not for frivolities.

In 2013, Magic Guy hoped to avoid any future roommate disasters. And though Suzyn had trusted him with her vending machine story, he couldn't share this particular memory with her.

He had to admit that he'd fallen off the proverbial wagon when it came to wafting, untouched, through life. Still, he wanted to acknowledge his growing friendship with his mortal, human woman. So Magic Guy said, "Yeah, we'll get a vending machine someday. Who cares if it's practical? Plus, we can stock it with all our favorite things. Like Diet Coke."

He tipped his can to her, and to Georgiana's memory.

Suzyn laughed a breezy few notes. "Ooooh! And Jones Soda! I loved that Thanksgiving turkey flavor."

They traded a few more light quips about potential sodas and why a vending machine was cooler than a soda fountain, and in the back of Magic Guy's mind a certainty formed:

Morena *must* stop using her iPhone.

If it truly were a machine/magic hybrid, and he'd become fairly sure it was, then her very life could be in danger.

Chapter Fifteen
You Make Me Sick

We are all—yes, even you, dear reader—hurtling through time and space at (relatively) the same pace as one another. This fact was no less true for people who lived in Seattle, Washington (planet Earth, etc.), in the first half of 2013.

However, time does not move in exactly the same way for characters in a fictional narrative as it does for us in reality. For them, events speed up or slow down at the whim of the storyteller. An author may skip the hours of sleep, then allot pages of detail to ridiculous observations like the one you're reading at this very moment.

And so it is, that two months have passed for Morena, et al, since the end of Chapter Fourteen – Not The Real Thing.

In these two months, Easter had come and gone, an occasion on which Morena and her mother attended Mass and Skyped their family in São Paulo. Suzyn had not joined them at church, being stridently non-Catholic, but had turned up to eat an early dinner beforehand. Brunches had become less frequent because Morena had been busy, so Suzyn had been invited to dinner even though she wouldn't celebrate Easter.

Also in these two months, Pathfinder David had taken Morena on a variety of awful, terrible, horrid dates. And after each one, Morena told both Suzyn and Magic Guy all about it. Yes, *and Magic Guy*. Because Magic Guy had become a fixture in the best friends' household.

If their cheap, tiny apartment in Lower Queen Anne could be considered a household.

Magic Guy came by after work most nights, eschewing his other story gaming circles. He told himself this was only because he was learning so much about contemporary American culture via more in-depth association with two prime examples of it, but this excuse fooled no one. With every evening in the roommates' company, he fell deeper and deeper into friendship. (He wondered sometimes about whether his *previous* friend could still be counted as a *current* one, as Chidiock had yet to reply to Magic Guy's letter, but after almost a century since their last communication, he tried to convince himself that he wasn't too worried. Moreover, he had no idea how long it took Chidiock to pick up his mail these days.)

Some nights the trio worked on their story game concept, which was still sort of an amorphous blob of *spygame!* ideas. Other nights, they merged their Pandora stations and held impromptu dance parties in the living room. Still other nights, they made dinner and watched the SyFy lineup. They barely went out anymore. Suzyn found herself enjoying a long period of complete sobriety, having never invited her dealer to visit the shared apartment.

Making dinner in the small apartment was a communal effort... and very cramped. An *intimate* affair, if you will. The kitchen was large enough to comfortably fit one person on either side of the sink, but all three smushed themselves in with jabbing elbows and sock-blunted feet.

Suzyn and Morena found it difficult to object to their nearly permanent houseguest, who always left by 11 p.m. because he insisted on cutting all the vegetables for whatever they planned to make. This wasn't such an onerous duty on nights with rice and rotisserie, but whenever someone felt the urge to make a Chinese soup, things were a bit more effortful. Plus, Magic Guy never cried when he cut onions, a fact that sometimes made Suzyn wonder whether he really did have magic powers after all.

Lest you think that Magic Guy was some sort of free-loader, he *did* invite his accidentally acquired friends over to his own apartment, but that was an even tinier place. He rented a studio efficiency on the other side of Lake Union. With the greater total distance (distance per person multi-plied by number of people traveling) and the fact that his craftsman-hotel kitchen could possibly fit twice inside the 1980s laminated one whose floors he slid across in socked feet most nights, the ladies politely declined every time.

But we weren't talking about Magic Guy's XS apartment or even the myriad nights he spent in our heroines' company. We were discussing the two months that had passed and how during those two months Pathfinder David had managed to discover all the worst places to take Morena.

In a cold snap at the end of March, he'd booked a campsite; Morena was more of a "three stars is roughing it" kind of lady. In the beginning of April, he'd bucked local convention and only chosen restaurants where the food was defiantly gluten-heavy. (Not that Morena was gluten-free, but what kind of place didn't even advertise that their chicken skewers were celiac-friendly? It really said something about the quality of the establishment in a city known in the relevant circles for its sensitive population, whose dollar signs jumped above $$.) In mid-April, he'd divulged an interest in polyamory during a double date on which he introduced Morena to a couple who would be interested in joining forces with him alone, but not with Morena under any circumstances.

During these unexpectedly awful dates, Suzyn and Magic Guy spent time together. And on one memorable instance, they rented a car and drove over to Issaquah because Luiza had texted Suzyn for the first time ever with an urgent request to help her pack up some UPS boxes for pick-up "since Morena is too busy for her dear old Mãe."

Luiza had become intensely lonely with just her flowers and her card-playing circle for company.

As Magic Guy sneezed over the tropical lilies in Luiza's townhouse, the Brazilian transplant sighed about her little girl. "Other than her teenage years, Morena has always been the sweetest. And she seemed so enthusiastic about helping out before." An excited note made her next question rise to an even higher tone than one might have expected. "Is something wrong with her?"

Luiza was ashamed to hope that her daughter had a difficult life problem. Any mother would be. But in the competition of *upset-daughter* and *mom-is-too-clingy*, Luiza hoped the recent sullen silence stemmed from trouble at Starbucks or a controlling boyfriend. To hide her immodest interest, she ducked into the kitchen to grab a bouquet from her stainless-steel refrigerator.

"Well, you've heard about David?" Suzyn slotted a wedding-arrangement kit into the packing box in front of her on the plush carpet. "I'm not sure about him."

Magic Guy mumbled, "Pathfinder David may be awful, but he's not Morena's main problem."

No one listened to him. He didn't expect them to. If he had, he'd probably have spoken a little louder.

Luiza gasped and rushed back to the dining room table. With chilled, dewy hands, she pulled at Suzyn's shoulders until the two were eye to eye. Luiza had to crouch to manage it, and the motion wasn't good on her knees. But that didn't matter. Her little girl was what mattered. She hadn't really meant to wish a controlling boyfriend on her daughter. "Is this new guy good to her?"

"Well..." Suzyn trailed off, unsure what to say. Pathfinder David was kind of irredeemably awful, but Morena had to see *something* in him. (Then again, Suzyn didn't know that all Morena appreciated in Pathfinder David was his potential stability. As soon as she married him, she'd never be alone again. Though, if she'd once said that out loud, Suzyn or Magic Guy would've undoubtedly pointed out that she might not physically be alone, but she'd surely still *feel* lonely because Morena and her boyfriend had nothing in common. They didn't even play the same games!)

Luiza let go her pinching grip on Suzyn's shoulders and paced her thick carpet. "I want her to be settled! But only because it will make her happier. It's no good to settle if you're miserable."

Nothing decided, the three finished packing the rest of the

boxes, and the two Seattleites were sent home with *cajuzinhos*—a nutty treat which they shared with Morena when she arrived at the apartment after her latest terrible date. That had been the night of the oh-so-fun polyamory surprise, and the sweet, cashew-shaped confections made Morena's evening that much better.

When she unlocked her iPhone to write a "thank you" text to her mother, the pond-scum green romance app opened itself as per usual, and she forgot all about what she'd been doing before shaking to find her perfect match.

But that's enough of the two month interlude. *This* is Chapter Fifteen. It's the new now.

And on this particular Wednesday evening at the beginning of May, Pathfinder David showed his darkest colors by being conspicuously absent.

Magic Guy had made chicken noodle soup from scratch (except for the noodles, because who does noodles from scratch anymore?), and Suzyn was pouring Morena's second glass of orange juice after emptying out a basket of tissues, which Morena had filled fairly quickly because Morena was quite sick.

Sick people usually enjoyed the tender care of their significant others when said SOs were available... and Pathfinder David had already gotten home from work and sent Morena a "feel better; my day was as awful as you look" text. Sick people, when awake, preferred to be visited by friends... and all Morena's closest friends, except her universally reviled boyfriend, were in attendance.

Yes, Pathfinder David was very much on everyone's minds on this day.

Morena couldn't smell the soup Magic Guy brought her,

no matter how many gurgling nose-clears she tried. (She buried her face in the steam anyway.) But it tasted like cumin-and-ginger-flavored affection. "Thanks," she said. The simple phrase was too small to encompass the enormity of someone's going to the effort to make soup *just for her*, but it would have to do.

"No worries." The phrase might have been Aussie in origin, but everyone was saying it these days. "I also brought DVDs of old stuff that's not on Netflix yet. How about *Flight of the Conchords*?"

She gurgle-sniffed again. "I don't want to disturb you guys." Because Morena expected that Magic Guy had come by to see Suzyn and to work more on their game, possibly with her input for once since she was a captive in the apartment. When Morena was sick, she became very accommodating.

Magic Guy hadn't, in fact, come over to work on the game. "I love the first episode." He shook the DVD box till it rattled with temptation. "That *Robots* video is something special." He remembered the days before English speakers called them *robots*, back when they were simply machines or automatons or contraptions.

Suzyn bounced onto the couch, making its wooden feet creak ominously. "Ooooh, we could add a robotic spy to the game. Or a spy whose handler is a giant Turing machine." She was sure that was the name for a machine so human-like that it could fool psychologists. Unless it wasn't. No one corrected her, so she felt confident. She took a bubbly sip from a fresh glass of Diet Coke, then offered it to Morena. "Drink?"

Morena held up her orange juice in negation. Her friends had plied her with more than enough liquids at this point. She was starting to think they'd done some unfortunate Internet research and come to the conclusion that she'd die if she weren't constantly imbibing something. Maybe they'd heard about it on *All Things Considered*.

Struggling with the plastic case, Magic Guy hobbled to the DVD player beneath the TV. He popped in a disc and grabbed the remote from its regular location in the drawer underneath the channel guide. In that moment, he realized how far his life had deviated from his expectations.

His ears tingled, and his fingers followed suit (so he gripped the DVD remote harder, trying to subtly work blood flow back into his extremities). He knew where the DVD remote belonged in this little apartment. He'd cooked a soup without asking where to find the cooking equipment.

When had he practically moved in? What would he do when they moved out?

On the couch, Morena coughed chartreuse phlegm into a super-soft Puffs Plus tissue.

Magic Guy's face turned a matching shade of greenish yellow. He should leave now, he thought, before he couldn't anymore. Before his life was so intertwined with theirs that he trapped himself in the bonds of obligation, shared interest, and codependency. Before they died in a scant century (or less) and all of this became irrelevant in the face of his lonely misery.

He was about to say something like, "I should really head out. Lots of work tomorrow. Clients and stuff. See you at Wayward for the next meeting or what-have-you." But Morena had put her mostly full soup bowl down on an end table and shuffled deeper into the couch with a whisper of pajamas on a fleece blanket, and that Would Not Do. So what he ended up saying was, "You'd better finish that soup I made you."

Morena thought he sounded like a parent. Her mother had called in the afternoon and promised to come by the next day with groceries to help out. Suzyn had spoken to her and reassured her that everything was under control but that her presence would be welcome whenever she wanted to drop by... and that they'd appreciate the food shopping.

On the TV screen, Bret and Jemaine attempted to woo a beautiful woman. They were doing a horrible job of it. Through her laughter Suzyn said, "And still they're better at this than Pathfinder David." The friends always referred to David as *Pathfinder David*, so long as he wasn't around.

Magic Guy swatted her thigh from his place in front of her on the floor, but it was too late.

Morena sniffed back some bubbles that wanted to drip from her nose and into her soup and asked, "Why isn't he here?" He'd have been able to soothe her headache, maybe.

That particular sniffle might have been more sadness than sickness.

"Aww, honey," Suzyn started.

She intended to follow that up with the usual platitudes when a boyfriend's actions were lacking: *you know he wishes he were here; he still loves/likes you; maybe he'll come by later to surprise you*. But she stopped herself. Because what she'd seen of Pathfinder David made him seem like a self-centered jerk who had no interest in helping Morena or caring for Morena or even noticing Morena when it didn't suit him. So she finished with, "Are you sure he's the right guy for you? You never seem to be on the same page."

Which was a polite way of saying that Morena tended to unclench with relief whenever she got home from a date with her odious boyfriend.

Magic Guy could have backed Suzyn's play. He could've vociferously recalled some of the horrible activities Morena had complained about—like when Pathfinder David volunteered her for Hempfest and took her to a planning meeting without telling her in advance, or when he signed them up to hike Mt. Rainier with a singles activity group (Events and Adventures). It was like Pathfinder David had been passive-aggressively daring her to break it off.

In the end, Magic Guy bit his tongue because sometimes people wanted to complain, not to hear bad things about their loved ones or to do anything about those complaints.

Holding his tongue had been the right idea, as evidenced when Morena actually sat up straight, in spite of her illness, in order to glare at her best friend. "He's my boyfriend. Of course he's right for me."

It had been so long since Morena had a steady boyfriend who wanted to spend time with her and who didn't move out of the country after only a few weeks of dating. She was creeping up on *over the hill*, whenever "the hill" was. Most guys her age were married (or divorced) or uninterested in ever marrying. As far as she knew, Pathfinder David could be her last chance to find a permanent companion.

She didn't want to grow old alone! And wasn't he better than some of the creeps who'd hit on her lately, like Flash Me Your Tits Guy and Please Enter My Pick-up Guy?

She wanted someone to care for her when she was sick and who she could accompany on excursions. (Morena willfully ignored that her boyfriend *wasn't* caring for her when she was sick, and that she really hated all of his planned excursions.) She was the last of her family, locally, aside from her mother. And what would she do when her mother was gone?

So, no. Morena had no plans to give up on Pathfinder David. He was a romantic prospect who liked her and did things with her and sought out her company. She'd hold onto him till her fingers turned white and bled from the effort.

Suzyn had had enough of that sort of argument. "Yeah. He's your boyfriend. Congratulations!" She made sarcastic jazz hands. "Yay! A boyfriend you don't like and who doesn't even visit when you're sick."

Morena slumped down into the couch's microsuede with a heavy *thud*. She was tired. And sure of her argument. "I don't need him to visit. I have you and Magic Guy." She gestured to Magic Guy as if expecting him to nod along and agree with her.

He very carefully made no movements or sounds, as still as the Seattle P-I globe when the power went out.

"Yes!" Suzyn jabbed a finger into Morena's toes, conveniently located in her lap. "You have us. You don't need that loser." She soothed the area she'd just stabbed and added more gently, chidingly, "And I notice you didn't protest how you don't even like him."

"I do *too* like him." But it didn't sound very convincing. More petulant. "I don't want to break up with him," she whispered. That was much more credible.

Suzyn smacked the back of the couch hard enough to make it bounce. "Why not?" Her voice rose. "You're better off without him."

Morena drew a deep breath and then hacked a series of coughs that spluttered and choked her with phlegm. Suzyn passed her a tissue to *hew* into. When the fit passed, Morena's voice came out clear and strident over the strains of "I'm Not Crying" from the television.

"You just want me to stay home and work with you and Magic Guy!" She flung a hand out at their permanent houseguest-cum-friend as she yelled. "Because that would make *your* life easier. Well, I won't do it! I've been fooled before. It'll be great right up until you leave, too."

In her sick and distraught state, Morena conflated Suzyn with every other friend who'd loved her and left her for a different lifestyle. Cycle after cycle for decades.

But Suzyn wasn't all those other women. She was her own person.

"I'm not leaving!" Suzyn screamed back. "And Pathfinder David isn't even here!"

"You'll leave someday! You're barely more than half my age!"

Magic Guy wished he could hide from all the exclamation points. On the television, Jemaine's "girlfriend" finished breaking up with him and walked out of his life forever.

"What does my age have to do with anything!"

"Everything!"

"Nothing!"

"You don't want me to have anything nice!"

Magic Guy couldn't help it. He had to point out, tentatively, hand up in the air like he'd seen young people do, "Ah, Pathfinder David's not really all that nice."

Morena's fevered gaze lasered onto him. "Are you ganging up on me?"

They hadn't planned it, but Suzyn glommed onto the idea. She grabbed Morena's feet and put them back in her lap, soothing and rubbing, trying to calm her best friend. "It's an intervention."

Morena yanked her limbs away, kicking the couch cushions to produce a gentle *thud* that turned into a double-*clank* when the couch vibrated enough to rattle the end table and knock her soup onto the floor. No one moved to sop up the mess on the carpet. It was a rental, and the argument was much more important.

"Maybe I don't want an intervention!"

Magic Guy knew it hadn't initially been an intervention in the sitcom sense, but he felt compelled to point out the flaw in her logic. "Uh, the intended subject *can't* want an intervention. That's kind of a prerequisite."

Suzyn talked over him, as if he hadn't spoken. She wanted to keep them on topic. "We can all agree he's no good for you! Why do you even want him?"

"I already told you!"

"We can find you someone else!"

If she'd had a tablet on hand, Suzyn would have pulled up the email she'd associated with Morena's OkCupid account. It was so inundated that Suzyn had started deleting the *[name] is checking you out right now!* messages and the ridiculous *[name] likes you!* emails. Because if those guys were really into Morena's profile, they'd have sent her a message to go with her other fifteen messages per day.

"There won't *be* anyone else!" Morena screamed back. "There's never anyone for me! I don't want to be single anymore! Stop pushing me!"

"Maybe you need me to push you!"

"Maybe I need to not be alone!"

"Well, fine! Maybe I'll leave! And then I won't push you anymore!"

A few lingering drops of the spilled chicken soup dripped onto the carpet with a *plink-plink, plink-plink.* On the DVD, Bret and Jemaine dressed up as makeshift robots. Morena hacked more phlegm into a tissue she had scrounged for herself because no one passed her one; they were each in their own space bubble, and touching suddenly seemed anathema. The two women prepared to never touch again.

Magic Guy should have been relieved by this idea, by the gang breaking up. He wasn't.

Suzyn's hair stuck in sweaty scraggles to her forehead. She didn't know when she'd started sweating.

Morena clutched the squishy tissue in her right hand. For once, making a fist didn't make her feel stronger or more powerful, just grossed out and tired. She whispered, "Would you really leave?"

Morena couldn't remember the point of this fight. Keeping Pathfinder David was the sensible thing to do, the safe thing, the thing that would keep her company for years to come... if he stuck around. She couldn't calculate the probability of his remaining by her side for even a full year; they'd only been dating two months. But Suzyn. Suzyn had been her best friend and roommate for that year already, and they'd expected to continue as they had been for a while longer. What was the point of this fight if she lost Suzyn? How could Morena claim to want companionship if she lost her current companion over it?

Suzyn answered her question with a too-casual shrug. "Probably not."

But the threat had been issued, and the consequences had been weighed. Morena had to admit that she loved Suzyn more than she did some random guy who'd picked her up and taken her on some excruciating excursions. She giggled through a bubble of snot. "Remember when he took me to the Monty Python quote-along at Central Cinema even though he knew it was my first experience with Monty Python?"

Suzyn launched herself at Morena and carefully landed on top of her sick roommate, tackling her back to the couch cushions with a strong hug, uncaring of the oozing mucus that could infect her at any moment. "God, yes. You didn't even know the title of the thing they were quoting."

Magic Guy knelt on the floor, watching them reconcile, and wondered if there was any space for him in their little world. He knew there was space for them in his. He bit his lower lip on the inside, invisible to others, and decided to be practical if he couldn't be beloved.

He found Morena's phone, the Samsung model, and brought it over to the couch. "You should probably call Pathfinder David."

Morena tugged the offering from his grip and pulled him into the huddle on the couch. He overbalanced and toppled onto Suzyn's pointy elbow. Morena's hot, scratchy breath teased at his neck.

Yeah, they had room for him in their lives.

"I'm gonna miss you guys," said Magic Guy, thinking about their inevitable deaths.

Morena worked her arms upward until she could see her phone and tapped out a message to Pathfinder David. It said: *I don't think this is working out. Let's break up.*

It was a bit callous, yes, but she was sick, damn it, and that should excuse a lot. She could feel bad about it later. She needed to spend more energy on the real goings-on in her life, in her own apartment.

She tossed the phone down, narrowly avoiding the squelchy chicken soup, so that she could worm an arm around each of her friends. "You don't have to miss us.

We're right here." Morena breathed out a nervous huff, hoping her next statement was true. "And Suzyn tells me she isn't going anywhere."

Suzyn encircled Magic Guy's waist with her right arm, grabbing a scratchy denim belt loop and pulling him even closer. "I'll prove it. When this lease is up, we'll get a place together. New lease, new promise of at least a year."

Magic Guy levered himself out of the assertive cuddle with help from the arm rest in front of his squished nose. "We could get your vending machine," he teased.

Suzyn stayed where she fell when Magic Guy moved, tucked into Morena's side and rubbing her cheek against the jagged blanket. "Nah. A vending machine is too big for an apartment." Well, it was too big for the kind of apartments they had right now, anyway.

"Not too big for a house, though," Magic Guy countered. He kind of missed living in houses. Much as he loved the centrality of his studio, he wanted space to stretch out. He could use storage, an extra room for his home servers, someplace to put guests if he ever had guests again.

Morena petted Suzyn's crunchy hair, crusty from hairsprays and gels. "You wanna buy a place?" she slurred, adrenaline crashing and fever spiking. "All three of us?"

"Oh. My. God. Best idea ever! We'll get a room for your mom." Suzyn had no idea how much houses cost, but it couldn't be impossible. She squeezed Morena's hand.

Magic Guy folded to the floor in front of the couch and rested his head against Morena's hip, looking upwards to take in both their faces. "It's got to be a house so expensive that none of us could ever afford to move out." They scrunched their eyebrows at him, so he explained: "Proof that we're going to be together forever."

Well, for as long as his friends survived, anyway. And as long as none of their income streams got cut off, though Magic Guy was sure he had enough saved under various names to take care of unexpected eventualities.

Nodding her head and almost nodding off, Morena agreed. "Mansion in Capitol Hill. My mom'll love it."

"Uh, guys?" Suzyn's face was hot from more than the blanket's friction against her cheek. "I can't afford much, like, at all."

Morena volunteered, "I can do most of your part. Ten thou' a month max for our contribution, though," she cautioned.

Magic Guy crawled away from them on the fuzzy floor to get his laptop out of his messenger bag. A quick check of mortgage rates, and he figured, "So we can manage a place that's around five-and-a-half million, assuming a twenty percent down payment."

Suzyn gaped at both of them. "Then why do we all live in such tiny old apartments?"

"Shoes," said Morena.

"Efficiency," said Magic Guy.

"You guys are nuts," said Suzyn. But she reached over Morena to tug Magic Guy into her pseudo-hug. "And I love you both."

Magic Guy shuddered and took a deep breath. Saying it would make it real. "We love you too."

Morena didn't say anything. She was already asleep, dreaming happy dreams of all living together and cuddling like this for years and years and years.

Magic Guy smiled softly and smoothed down the blanket on his way to get paper towels from the kitchen and clean up the spilled soup. To Suzyn he said, "And we'll get your vending machine."

Her eyes were bright circles. "The height of home technology," she declared.

Chapter Sixteen
Obsession: Not Just for Perfumes and Sociopaths

Buoyed by her friends and cared for constantly, Morena recovered from her cold-flu thing in five mucus-filled days. In that time, Magic Guy found a mortgage lender who specialized in working with the supernatural and pushed through his part of the financial paperwork. He'd rushed to get it finished before Morena could be healthy enough to notice which bank accounts his down payment would draw on and why his credit history traced back hundreds of years (though he'd only been with Diners Club for the last fifty).

Morena's pre-approval paperwork for a mortgage was much simpler. She had a steady job, only one social security number, and the kind of brilliant credit that comes from regularly buying high-end clothing online using a variety of cards. So, by the time she was well enough to face the world:

- Suzyn had submitted a photojournalistic essay to *The Stranger* and been rejected.
- The threesome was pre-approved for $6 million in mortgage loans (though they couldn't afford payments on anything over $4.6 million).
- Magic Guy had mapped the best available mansions on Redfin.

Unfortunately, they couldn't take *themselves* to look at houses. Whether they wanted one or not, they needed a real estate agent. Magic Guy emailed a random woman from Zillow's website, and Morena demanded that they meet in a café before looking at houses because she was *not* gallivanting about with a stranger to make potentially life-changing decisions on no caffeine.

Which is how they found themselves at the Peet's Coffee in Green Lake at 8 a.m. on a Saturday morning, waiting for their realtor. There was a Starbucks only three blocks away, but the realtor had chosen the spot, and Morena hadn't argued about it.

Green Lake wasn't convenient to any of their current residences, nor to the mansions they'd bookmarked, so the trio wasn't entirely certain how they'd ended up there.

"The lake is pretty, though," offered Suzyn, whose untied Converse sneakers drooped with exhaustion.

In the overcast morning light, the silver lake water rippled like a living Zen garden whose sand was made of smoky glass. A long field of muddy green separated the cozy café (with unexpectedly calming classical music) from the 2.8-mile path populated only by marathon trainees and dog owners at that time of morning. Which was to say that it was doing brisk business, because more than half the neighborhood owned dogs.

Morena grunted, her back to the floor-to-ceiling windows. Her entire focus was trained on the beige-and-brown marble (quartz?) countertop where her drink would appear. Any second now.

Magic Guy was aimed at the entrance. His stomach trembled with anticipation every time someone walked near the door, but most of the time it was a dog walker about to cross the street, or a person with a stroller heading to one of the shops further down, or someone with a buzz cut or a bald spot. He was ready to jump on anyone who looked like the thumbnail picture of the realtor as seen on his smartphone, a woman with long hair.

Speaking of smartphones, Morena had two in her pockets: her Samsung and the magic iPhone that she hadn't looked at in days due to illness... and due to Magic Guy's hiding it from her during that time. Before the threesome had left for their meeting, the Apple product had called to her from her sock drawer, and she hadn't resisted the urge to put it in her pocket.

Fifteen whole seconds passed without caffeine's appearing on the barista bar, and Morena distracted herself from the lack of wake-up juice by toying with the iPhone. Hey, if she'd brought it along, she may as well let it entertain her. With a listless finger she tapped the pond-scum-green icon and opened the romance app.

A slow shake of her wrist later, and it went *ding ding DING!* She didn't bother looking down to see the standard message ("Rest easy! Your perfect mate is on their way to you.") before shaking again.

Ding ding DING!

Shake.

She really needed some caffeine. She was getting a horrible headache that was doubtless brought on by this accidental detox.

Ding ding DING!

Shake.

Ding ding DING!

"Oh my god," said Suzyn at her side, annoyed. "Will you *stop* that?"

The barista said, "I have a triple large almond-milk mocha for Morena."

Magic Guy said, "You have got to stop using that thing." With every *ding*, he'd felt a pull on the air around them, something that seeped cold into the space next to Morena as if she were a humidifier that the iPhone had set to *creepy magical lethargy*. "It's not good for you."

There were very few reasons a human would exude an otherworldly chill, and none of them was healthy for the human in question. Besides, he'd learned his lesson during the Industrial Age: magic and machines didn't mix. He wondered whether the phone had been the cause of her recent sickness or if it had been a normal case of cold-flu thing. Mortals used to die of influenza. Did they still?

The realtor breezed in while Magic Guy was distracted, recognized him, and said, "Hello. Sorry I'm late." The realtor could best be described as friendly, flighty, and organized. This odd combination of natural and learned traits had made her one of the most sought-after in the business. She was as fun to spend time with as she was competent at selling houses. She was not, however, used to showing the kind of homes whose commissions would pay her bills for the next two years.

Morena's iPhone buzzed, and the screen read: Mãe. She rejected the call and returned to shaking her app. *Ding ding DING!*

The realtor pulled a sheaf of papers out of her briefcase with MLS data for the relevant addresses on them. "Let's take a quick look at the listings you sent me and one other I found that you might like, while you tell me what you're looking for."

Morena hummed, more interested in sipping her life-giving beverage and shaking her iPhone again. *Ding ding DING!*

Magic Guy led the realtor over to a table, pulled his laptop from his ever-present messenger bag, and showed off his spreadsheet.

Still at the counter, Suzyn slumped against Morena's side, feeling a bit left out since her financial contribution on a purchase like this was barely a rounding error. She'd never felt so much like a child. Her cheek ached where it pressed into Morena's bony shoulder, the perfect height to watch the "adults" discuss monthly payments and square footage. She wasn't sure the realtor had even looked at her, just taken in her age and her threadbare zebra-print sweater before deciding to spend all sales energy on Magic Guy.

Suzyn supposed she could just walk out now. She knew how to take care of herself without Morena's patronage. She wasn't dependent or anything. She'd managed to do exactly what her parents had done—and been so enamored of—namely, bootstrap her way out of nature's plan for her. Once their game got off the ground, she'd be making some serious money. All she had to do was stay sober for a few weeks till all the blips blurred into a smoothly plotted future.

Morena's arm slid around Suzyn's zebra-printed waist and

tugged her close, grounding the younger woman in warmth and *now*. "Ztu urly."

"No kidding," Suzyn agreed. It was far too early for her to drop out of their friendship yet. What would she do without Morena? What would she do without a soulmate who modeled and played and loved, and all because Suzyn requested it?

Over at the table, Magic Guy said something about numbers of bathrooms and room to grow. The realtor nodded emphatically like he was explaining the finer points of recycling a #5 plastic tray.

Morena drew away from Suzyn to pull the iPhone from between their bodies. "Wanna play?" Morena was half interested in killing some time with the hotly contested app and half interested in showing Magic Guy she didn't care if he thought it was bad for her. What did he think, that the app gave off cancerous radiation?

Magic Guy felt the pall descend again, like a metaphysical fire blanket draping lower and heavier every time his friends shook the iPhone. He wanted to stop them, but he was too busy answering questions about natural light. Plus, Morena had already shut him down on this topic. He just had to hope she'd get distracted soon. Besides, she was surrounded by strangers and would probably have to take a break.

So many times, he'd hidden her phone or put it into his own pocket, only to see it in Morena's grasp a few hours later (including once while she was too sick to take side trips to hunt for her phone instead of falling asleep over DIY network shows in anticipation of home ownership). The device's insidious presence could not be overcome by subterfuge. He needed to find a way to make her *want* to give it up. And with the way it dragged at him that morning, he knew he needed to (pardon the pun in a book about story gamers) step up his game.

When Morena looked up from her screen, she was surrounded by bodies that crammed against her like espresso grounds packed down by a tamper. She snagged Suzyn around the waist again and tried to push her way (politely: "excuse me, miss") through the crowd at the counter to the relatively empty tables to the right. Had she truly been so oblivious that she hadn't seen all the other patrons waiting for their drinks? Was she such an unobservant ditz? Her face went blood-hot.

Morena's mocha was empty by this point—perk of an app she could use one-handed—and she subtly shoved past people until she reached the recycle-and-compost bin. (The two functions were shared halves of a single can; the trash was back the way they'd come.) She stared at the instructional picture above it with half-cognizant eyes, cataloguing the items in her hand against whether they counted as compost or recycling.

She had once gone to a conference in Chicago where restaurants had a single bin for all waste. It had been confusing. She'd hunted for the compost and recycling every time she'd finished coffee or lunch.

"Hey there," said a deep voice behind her. It was the kind of voice that made your bones rumble and your toes curl. Morena didn't want to turn around. She knew she'd only be disappointed. "They make these things so difficult, right?"

A least Deep Voice's small talk was good. Maybe he could help her figure out whether the cup was compostable. She'd already decided about the sleeve, the napkin, the plastic travel lid, and the swizzle stick, but not the cup itself. Starbucks HQ had tested compostable cups, but she wasn't sure if any had trickled out to the franchise stores yet, and this wasn't even a Starbucks. How could she know for sure?

"A-hem." Suzyn knew Morena didn't like strangers and wished Morena wouldn't abandon her for them. What was the deal with that? Like, a second ago there had been an arm around her, grounding her, and now what? Morena would rather chat with some old guy than hang with Suzyn? Ugh.

A crash from the espresso machines pushed the crowd away from the counter and back toward Morena—and Morena's phone—at the compost-and-recycling station.

A teenage girl wearing candy bracelets and aqua-streaked hair patted Morena's hand gently to get her attention. "Let me help?" the girl asked breathlessly. She'd surprised herself by actually *talking* to the beautiful woman who probably had better prospects than some high school junior. But Morena *smiled* at her. The girl was going to have a *kick-ass* month after this, riding the high of facing her fears and not getting rejected. Not that she said anything else for Morena to reject, but Morena hadn't told her to get lost or anything.

No, the teen didn't say anything else to Morena because a jogger with three dogs came in off the street. The jogger was a thirty-year-old man who had clearly been out at the lake for a while, turning his white-pale winter skin into a kaleidoscope of red legs under yellow spandex running shorts. "You are so beautiful." His dogs jostled the aqua-headed girl out of the way. "I will pay you to go out with me."

He must have gotten all his lines from pop songs and cult '90s films.

A senior citizen in jeans and hiking sneakers with a scarf wrapped four times around his neck laughed at the jogger. "Like she'd be interested in a young thing like you."

Luckily for everyone involved, Magic Guy and the realtor packed up their things and collected their excursion-mates at this point. Morena tossed her cup in the recycle half of the bin.

Disappointed admirers mourned in her wake.

The house hunters carsolidated, leaving Morena's Smart behind so the realtor could drive them all. Magic Guy watched the dashboard GPS from the passenger seat, while Suzyn and Morena sat in the back and played with the iPhone some more.

"Set the first wheel to 4001+," Suzyn suggested. "I want to see what it does. Cuz I'm pretty sure it's not supposed to be an age category."

"No!" yelled Magic Guy. He was pretty sure it *was* supposed to be an age category, and he was the closest 4001+-year-old around.

"Geeze, okay," said Suzyn. She pulled the iPhone out of Morena's grip and reset the first wheel to 20-26, saying, "You want someone younger than Pathfinder David was."

Morena snorted hard enough to bounce her head off the BMW's leather headrests, releasing the decadent scent of dead cow. "Don't make me think about Pathfinder David."

After the realtor finally managed to get the lockbox at their destination's door to open with her specialized iPhone app, they toured their first house. The house was okay.

It had a grassy front yard that was larger than their apartment building's parking garage. Morena loved the ceilings' plaster moldings with swirling vine patterns etched in.

But the location was too far away from anything really cool (other than the lake), and it was only 5,000 square feet, which didn't provide room for them to grow into over the next 70 years. If all three of them met a significant other and then had 2.5 children, fifteen residents needed to fit.

The second place the realtor took them was more central, in the northern part of the Capitol Hill neighborhood. It sprawled over 12,000 square feet and had its own elevator that had been installed in the 1920s. Suzyn and Magic Guy loved the elevator and all the balconies. The house was swimming in balconies. But north Capitol Hill was a residential area and not really walking distance from either Broadway or 15th. They wanted to live *near* things. All of them agreed on that.

Morena didn't actually see the inside of the second house and, thus, had no opinion on the elevator or the balconies. At that house, the listing agent had insisted on being present to show them around, and Morena didn't feel energetic enough to deal with a stranger who wanted to sell her things. So she made some gentle excuses about fresh air, blah blah, and loitered at the end of the drive. She knew her phone could keep her company for thirty to sixty minutes.

Morena could have used the time to check work emails or returned her mother's earlier call. She could have tweeted about house shopping or watched cute kitten GIFs on tumblr. Now that she had an iPhone, she could have downloaded some games from the App Store and played Candy Crush or Angry Birds or Wordament.

As you may have guessed, Morena did none of these sensible things. With the calming scent of rain-washed grass in her nose, she fired up the nameless romance app on her iPhone and shook it. *Ding ding DING!*

Again and again and again.

Spin, spin, spin.

Drowning in victorious *ding!*s, the residential sidewalk was the loudest it probably ever got at this time of day.

An incoming text from her mother interrupted her game. It took over half the display for five whole, obnoxious-to-Morena seconds: *I don't know where to buy good soil. This is an OR problem, no? :)*

Morena's arms shook—whether with exhaustion, ennui, or exasperation—and she stabbed the *Home* button to get the stupid message off her screen. Maybe her mother was trying to be cute, but it couldn't be an OR problem unless there were multiple choices and multiple destinations. And if it had been, it wasn't like Morena could solve linear programming problems while out looking at houses!

She reopened the mysterious app, and its big green heart gave an animated beat before nestling back down into the central column. Morena didn't set any options. She just shook.

Ding ding DING!

A man with arms as thick as his legs and five yowling cats on leashes moseyed up to Morena. She gave him and the cats a brief once-over, then returned to her phone. It would've been rude to judge his troubles with herding felines, and she preferred to look busy.

The man said, "Whatcha doin'?"

And they somehow segued into a conversation about cat walking as a business, Clarke's Third Law, and the new Seattle Sun Tan ads ("Everyone Has Their Own Reason"). They were joined at that point by a woman with skin the color of damp sand and a yoga mat slung over her shoulder who wanted to tell them how wonderful the vitamin D from tanning beds felt ("not that I need a tan for its own sake, of course").

By the time Morena's companions rejoined her, they needed to extricate their friend from a smiling and laughing crowd of joggers, neighborhood stroll enthusiasts, animal walkers, and yoga aficionados who frequented a studio only a few blocks away. Most were residents and called after Morena, saying they hoped to see her around the area soon.

For a person who didn't care to make small talk with strangers, Morena held up remarkably well, probably because everyone adored her before she even opened her mouth. Whatever the reason, she was giving serious thought to becoming an extrovert.

The third house was one the realtor had found for them, not one Magic Guy had sent her. "You'll have to do some cosmetic maintenance on the third floor, but so long as you don't need it immediately, you can handle that, right?"

The third house was magical. (No, not literally. Ah, "literally." A word only starting to lose its meaning in our heroes' timeline.) It was a 1919 Tudor with a brick addition. Eight thousand square feet. Terraces. A rose garden. Cozy light slanted into the kitchen, which was itself laid out in Magic Guy's ideal triangular plan where the sink, the fridge, and the stove formed an isosceles triangle.

The third floor was, as promised, a bit icky, with exposed wiring, insulation puffing out of the attic access hatch, and an unfinished bathroom that had a half-knocked-out wall. But, as the realtor pointed out, the three of them didn't need the third floor yet, even if the windows overlooked the green rolling front acreage. Best of all, it was two blocks from the Broadway corridor and had a view of Lake Union. Less good, it was pushing their exorbitant budget at $6.2 million.

Morena said, "We need to think about it."

Now that this was becoming a reality, she wasn't sure she wanted to commit to $10K a month. What would that do to her shoe collection next season? What if she wanted to pick up some new jewelry but was too house-poor? She'd worked hard and lived accordingly so that she could have nice things. Did she really want to change her lifestyle to include extravagant shelter, but no fresh wardrobe?

In the car on the way back to the Green Lake Peet's, where the three friends could pile into Morena's Smart and head back to the Queen Anne apartment, Morena agonized over these issues. She tapped idly at the iPhone's romance app with one hand and massaged Suzyn's overstyled hair with the other. (Suzyn had collapsed sleepily against her side nearly immediately.)

Morena thought that if the choice were between shoes and a mansion, she'd choose shoes. But if the choice were between shoes or the certainty of Suzyn in her life forever, she'd choose Suzyn every time. (And Magic Guy, of course, but since she wasn't massaging his hair at the moment, Morena's situational-fondness levels were skewed.)

The realtor dropped them at Morena's car and disappeared from the rest of this narrative. A fate that pleased the three friends, who would have preferred to lead their own home tour, even if it meant never seeing the third, "magical," house.

Magic Guy claimed the backseat to spread out and talked nonstop on the ride back to Queen Anne. He updated his spreadsheet with desirable features from the three homes they'd seen that day. Suzyn couldn't imagine why he bothered; if they were going to do this, clearly the last house was the only real option. She leaned back enough to worm her Converses onto the dashboard. With every small turn that Morena made, Suzyn's shoelaces ticked against the car's plastic.

They parked in the apartment building's underground garage, a place that felt newly small and claustrophobic. It *was* pretty small, only enough space for fifteen cars and the trash/recycle/compost bins. Suzyn was tall enough to touch the ceiling's exposed ductwork—though Morena and Magic Guy couldn't—and that was a far cry from some of the living rooms (parlors? salons?) they'd just seen. But they'd never found it cramped before.

At their apartment door, Suzyn pushed on the smooth, laminate, '80s faux wood. She and Magic Guy went in, but Morena didn't follow them. Her upper arm was grabbed by someone in the hallway. A man's fingers pulled and pinched at her skin beneath her coat; his grip was that tight.

"Let go!" she yelled. But he didn't, and no one came to her aid.

The man yanked her around to face him. Pathfinder David! His graying ash-brown hair was matted in some places and stood at all angles in others, as though he'd run sweaty hands through it over and over. His usually boyish smile had been replaced by a feral snarl. "What were you doing today?"

Morena did *not* have to deal with this. "We broke up," she said. "Let go of me."

He didn't. "You shouldn't be looking at houses without me."

"Why would I need you?" She packed as much derision as she could fit into a laugh. It was more for her than for him. She had to remind herself that she didn't need him, not when she had Suzyn and Magic Guy and the sudden ability to handle small talk on the streets of Capitol Hill. "We're not getting back together, David."

He continued as if she hadn't asserted herself. "And you shouldn't be looking at places on that side of Lake Union. We can get a place in upper Queen Anne if you need someplace big. Or the residential section of Ballard has great views of the sound. Magnolia!"

Her eyes narrowed in suspicion, clichéd but true, and that's when it hit Morena: "Have you been following me?"

"I had to see you!" he burst out. "You can't leave me like this. I need you! I need to be near you!"

Aside from sounding like something a *Twilight* character might say, he'd already proven it a lie.

She scoffed. "You couldn't stand to be near me when I was sick."

Finally, he released Morena's arm. She didn't bother massaging it, just stepped closer to her threshold. As soon as she passed it, she could slam the door in his face and glare at Suzyn and Magic Guy for abandoning her to her ex. Her latest ex. There'd been a lot of them lately.

Pathfinder David didn't know why he'd tailed Morena all day. He certainly had better things to do than drive around Capitol Hill and watch his ex-girlfriend hang out with her friends. Yet every time he'd thought he should go home and do something more productive—like put oil in his car or practice duck-tailing his hair—he'd been drawn closer. Something deep in his psyche had cried out for *just one more minute*, and he'd given in every time. Why shouldn't he indulge himself when all it cost was a bit of gasoline?

Their stare-down was interrupted by a pink-faced teenage boy in a red uniform complete with pillbox hat.

"I'm here to deliver a singing teleg-ram." The teen's voice cracked on *ram*, which didn't bode well for the singing part.

Also, he was lying. He lived in the building, two floors up. When he'd felt this strong desire to be on the first floor, he knew he needed a good reason to head down there or else he'd look like an idiot. Luckily, he'd had this costume crumpled in the back of his closet from a sophomore year theatre production. Hence: singing telegram. He hoped no one made him actually sing.

Pathfinder David tried to give the boy laser eyes, but maybe his contact lenses got in the way, because it didn't seem to deter him. The teenager took a breath to start singing *something*, and Pathfinder David growled, "Can't you see we're in the middle of a discussion, kid?"

The boy gave an apologetic shrug that was totally negated by his incredulous bitchface. "I'm just trying to do my job."

He refrained from poking at Pathfinder David's age because Morena was right behind the annoying older man, and the teen didn't want her to think that he thought that *she* was old (because she was, but she was also totally gorgeous and amazing and the best thing that had ever happened to him, and he'd be so good for her if only she'd give him a chance, and he knew she wouldn't give him that chance if he insulted her).

Pathfinder David said, "Well, do your job somewhere else."

The teen said, "I gotta talk to the lady, man."

Pathfinder David said, "I'm going to break your face in."

The teen said, "I'd like to see you try, Gramps." Because he couldn't hold out on the ageist cracks anymore.

Morena ignored all of this. She'd grown bored and pulled out her iPhone. Shake. *Ding ding DING!* The sound pounded in her temples. *Great*, she thought, *just over forty years old and I'm getting my first migraine.*

There was a click at the end of the hall as the building's door opened. The smell of fontina cheese and pepperoni filled the hallway.

Pathfinder David reached for the teen's arm, as he'd done with Morena, but the boy dodged. "Hah!"

"Any of you order a pizza?" asked the delivery woman. She wore a thick leather jacket and had a motorcycle helmet under one arm while the other held an insulated pizza bag.

The teenage boy crouched so that he could lead with his shoulders and rushed Pathfinder David, slamming the two of them into a wall and clearing a path for the pizza woman.

Morena said, "I'm not sure. Can you wait a sec?" And then she called out to ask if either Suzyn or Magic Guy had ordered delivery from Zeeks.

Apparently, Magic Guy *had* placed an order, so Morena invited the pizza woman inside, then closed the door (gently, silently) on the physical squabble in the hallway. Magic Guy rooted through his wallet, and Morena relaxed. The delivery was his problem, and the idiots outside were the building manager's.

Out of habit, she looked down at the iPhone. She went to shake it, but her hand felt heavy, like the phone was made of lead or plutonium. The weighty feeling traveled up her arm, muscles going slack. The doorway looked bright, then dark, then bright again until the light pierced into her brain and she had to close her eyes.

"Hey," said Morena. But that was all she got out before she hit the beige carpet with enough force to jar every joint in her body.

"Let me help," insisted the pizza woman. "I have to be near her."

Crashing thuds banged against the door.

Pathfinder David screamed, "Nobody go near my Morena."

And the teenager tried, "Is everyone all right?"

Magic Guy reached for the energy in the room, preparing to redirect it and reassert a little calm. The area around Morena pulsed a shade of gray that reminded him of the Seattle sky for its 226 cloudy days of the year. He pulled hard on other sources of energy: in the air, the earth, and the waters. He sent out a tendril of directed power and easily freed the pizza woman and the teenage boy from the iPhone's influence.

So long as he concentrated hard enough, Magic Guy could see where these two most recent victims were affected on the astral plane. He didn't have to be a phrenologist to understand how changing a section of the brain could influence a personality.

The pizza delivery person took her tip, left the pizza, and departed. The teenage boy shrugged and slouched toward the stairway so he could go home and get out of his stupid outfit.

Pathfinder David, previously outside, switched places with the pizza woman—when she slipped out, he slipped in. Magic Guy had only *weakened* his desperate cord to the iPhone. The ex-boyfriend had been exposed too long for a painless uncoupling, and Magic Guy didn't know what would happen if he cut the man off entirely.

Pathfinder David dropped to kneel beside Morena's supine form. He had to be closer. "Oh my god," he said.

Suzyn, who had come to see the commotion, rolled her eyes at him. "Seriously?" But then she directed her attention to her best friend, who needed more from her than derision for her ex. "Okay, Ems," she said to the unconscious woman, "let's get you somewhere comfortable."

Pathfinder David pushed Suzyn backward before she could raise Morena up off the floor. "You can't move her! What if her spine's broken?"

Morena shifted minutely.

Magic Guy said, "Her spine isn't broken." He went to pick her up, planning to put her on the couch, but Suzyn choked a whine.

"What if he's right?" Suzyn asked. "We should take her to the hospital, maybe?" Suzyn didn't know where the closest hospital was, but she knew Morena went to a UW neighborhood clinic for her regular stuff, so maybe UW Medical Center over in the U-District had an emergency area.

Morena moaned from her place on the floor and turned herself over so she could bury her face in the nice beige carpet. It was scratchy and clearly polyester. The carpet, not her face. "Go away, David."

And he did, solemn and subdued.

"Someone help me up?"

Suzyn stooped to get her arms underneath her best friend, and together they hobbled to the living room.

Magic Guy watched them. Whoever had sent her that iPhone certainly wasn't a friend. It was killing her, he was sure. Even if it hadn't directly caused her recent sickness, the way it fed off her vitality had surely weakened her immune system.

Magic Guy wondered how he was going to get the iPhone away from Morena now that she'd gotten addicted to it. He had to do something, but what?

Chapter Seventeen
Friendship Is Magic

With so much time under the phone's influence, its hooks clawed deeply at Pathfinder David's astral soul. Which is why he came back the next morning.

This time, the unsuitable suitor went around the side and tried to break in. It was a testament to the strength of his desperate need to see Morena that Pathfinder David didn't think this through very well. First off, breaking in through a double-pane window is pretty difficult, since you have to get through both panes, which reinforce each other. To make any progress, he had to forsake the window itself and tear at the head-height window frame instead.

And, secondly, even if he had managed to breach the barrier before someone caught him, he'd have half-fallen into the apartment behind the living room couch. Suzyn and Morena may have been on the ground floor, but that didn't make their place easy to break into, other than in comparison to the rooms on the next floor up.

Luckily for the potential dent in his scrambled brain, Pathfinder David *did* get caught before he could do much more than scrape the building's exterior. (Was that plaster? Stucco? Did it matter?)

Magic Guy had slept on the couch Pathfinder David might have fallen into. He hadn't wanted to leave Morena and Suzyn alone after the hallway drama and Morena's fainting spell. That was what he told them, anyway, and they went with it because they were dead tired (even though, in the light of day, they would've argued about how neither of them were damsels in distress and they were perfectly capable of looking after themselves) and they appreciated that Magic Guy cared enough to sleep on their unsuitable furniture.

The unspoken part of his reasoning was that he was exhausted from trying to break the iPhone's will-draining cords. The magic was a powerful braid, like nothing he'd touched before. It wasn't his own magical style that manipulated local energies. It wasn't Chidiock's talent for ley weaves and aether manipulation. It had an earthier feel to it, stocky and harsh.

He definitely wasn't staying because he didn't want to be separated from his new friends after a traumatic event. Nope. That couldn't be it at all. He didn't do friendship, at least not that strongly. He didn't think so, anyway. Not yet. He couldn't. Could he?

So Magic Guy was on the couch, Pathfinder David was tap-tap-tapping at the apartment window, and Morena was deeply asleep in her bed with the iPhone at her side so that if she woke up and needed to check the time she could both do that and spin the romance app wheels.

Suzyn, this Sunday morning at 8 a.m., stumbled into the living room on her way to the kitchen, because if she was going to be awake and sober, then she was damn well also going to have tea and cereal. Which was why Suzyn was the one to look out the window above Magic Guy's slumbering body and scream at a shadowy figure peering inside and working at the edges of the sill.

Suzyn's early-morning hair was a lank, matted mess that smelled of lavender-scented pomade. Her oversized sleep shirt made her look alternately like a skeleton swathed in burial linens (in the light) or a giant mountain troll (in the dark, playing off her height). So when she screamed and pointed at Pathfinder David, Pathfinder David also screamed and pointed back at the massive humanoid with flapping wings who, he thought, was probably coming for him.

Magic Guy, woken by the stereo screaming, sighed, stood, and unlatched the window. "Come around the front," he told Pathfinder David through the screen. He closed the window again. To Suzyn he offered, "I can take care of this if you wanna go back to bed."

Pathfinder David may have noticed Suzyn's frightening appearance, but Magic Guy simply noticed her presence. His obliviousness to her lack of conventional beauty endeared him to her even more.

"Oh my god, seriously?" She threw a pillow at him, the same pillow he'd been sleeping on. He didn't catch it, and it fell to the floor with a quiet *thud*. "I'm gonna go wake up Morena. We'll *all* deal with this." She shivered for effect. "He is getting so creepy."

"I think it's the phone."

She gave him a stern glare. "We are not talking about magic stuff again. Not at this time of morning."

"You have to admit that the app seems to be drawing Pathfinder David to her."

Suzyn wound an arm around Magic Guy's waist, and he relaxed into her hug, still half in dreamland and not wary enough. She tightened her hold until his ribs suggested that they might be dangerously overpressured.

His soon-to-be mansion-mate ground his bones closer together and warned, "That sounds a lot like blaming the stalking victim."

Magic Guy couldn't push her away without hurting her. The energies in the room gathered around him in preparation, but she let him go before he needed to test his control.

He shook his head hard. "I'm blaming the *phone*. It's doing something. And she's addicted. You saw how she was yesterday."

Suzyn was more than a little familiar with addiction, and she didn't like it on Morena. "Yeah, I know." But she didn't know anything about iPhone addiction. Were you supposed to wean the junkie off or make them go cold turkey? Could you take them to rehab?

A heavy pounding shook the apartment door and the frame around it. *Sheesh*, thought Suzyn, *Pathfinder David is so rude*. She opened the door for him and admonished, "You know, other people live in this building. Keep it down."

Pathfinder David tried to avoid looking at the woman's Halloween-esque morning costume and scraggly hair. "I'm here for Morena," he said.

"Whatever."

Magic Guy turned on the hall light, thrusting them into

a wan starkness that was particularly displeasing on Suzyn when it made her naturally dark skin turn Seattle's average pasty-white. They really needed to get better light bulbs for this apartment complex, but it wasn't going to be our heroes' problem for much longer. Not with their mansion move-out plan.

"Why don't you come sit down?" Magic Guy gestured Pathfinder David toward the living room, where rumpled blankets made up the remains of Magic Guy's bed.

Suzyn said, "I'll get Morena."

Her statement soothed Pathfinder David, who had intended to protest if he didn't get what he wanted. It also made Magic Guy raise his eyebrows in an *if you must* expression, since he'd rather hoped that the two roommates would stay out of his way while he attempted to break the iPhone's hold on Morena's most recent ex-boyfriend.

While Magic Guy plucked experimentally at the cords tying Pathfinder David to the phone, Suzyn sat at the edge of Morena's bed and poked her bestie in the shoulder. Poke poke. Poke poke poke. Poke poke. Poooooooke.

Morena flopped over to get away from the incessant stabbing and flailed an arm in Suzyn's direction. "Lmmrgrmne," Morena grumbled.

Suzyn poked more. Poke poke. Poooooooke poke poke.

"Ugh!" Morena sat straight up, comforter pooling around her silk-clad hips. "Oh my god, what do you *want*?" She reached for the iPhone at her side to check the display. "What even *time* is it?"

The time was 8:07 a.m. on Sunday morning, and Morena groaned again. She fell back onto her pillows, phone held at arm's length above her head. "What do you want?" she repeated.

But she wasn't looking at Suzyn. No, she was opening the romance app and setting a few wheels before shaking it.

Ding ding DING!

Suzyn snatched the phone from Morena's sleep-slack grip. "You need to put this away."

"It's mine!" Morena practically screeched her annoyed agony. And *that* told Suzyn more than enough about phone's level of enslavement. Morena definitely could not stop at any time.

The younger woman remembered all the days and nights Morena had dealt with Suzyn's addictions: showering with her after a horrible trip, holding back her hair while she vomited, making sure no one took advantage when she was higher than a Kenmore Air seaplane.

"Honey, you've got to trust me on this." Suzyn smoothed a hand over Morena's formerly poke-abused shoulder. Calmed her like a feral thing. "Even if Magic Guy hadn't said it was evil. Even if we hadn't already worried about the ethics of using it. Even if!" Suzyn tossed the phone into a corner and gathered her best friend into a bony jumble of limbs and covers. "It's not good for you. Let's get you a new phone, okay?"

Morena struggled against Suzyn's hold. She wanted to get out. She could see the phone, mocking her with its closeness. "You want it for yourself," she accused. "You couldn't afford one if it wasn't my castoff!"

Which was a mean thing to say, if true, but addicts said a lot of mean things to people who tried to help them. Suzyn had said plenty to Morena when under a cold showerhead with her partying cut short. "We'll give it away. I won't get a thing. That good enough?" Suzyn usually *begged* for Morena's secondhand goods, but she didn't want this one.

She preferred to come by her fixations honestly.

Morena collapsed in the embrace, becoming deadweight, and Suzyn tentatively loosened her arms... only to have Morena lunge out of them and bang into the opposite wall.

Triumphantly, Morena cradled the phone in her hands. The warm *my screen's been on too long* radiation warmed her palms. "You don't understand. I *need* it!"

This jonesing was a lot further along than Suzyn had thought. "You don't need it. We'll get you a newer one. They're really pretty."

Morena hissed at her best friend and shook the phone. *Ding ding DING!* "I'll be unloved forever. Only the phone can help me. Only the phone understands me."

The phone did not, in fact, understand Morena at all. It wasn't a sentient sort of machine. It had fairly simple programming with three directives.

(1) Get used.

(2) Send somewhat inappropriate potential love interests to the owner (to enforce directive 1).

(3) Soak up energy on behalf of the originator.

If it could have understood Morena, however, it would have encouraged her misperceptions because they might inspire her to use it more. Directive 1 accomplished. But it didn't, so it couldn't, and it wasn't. At least, not on purpose.

Suzyn stretched out a hand in supplication. "I understand you. I do. And you'll always be loved. I'll always love you and stay with you." She inched forward, pleased when Morena didn't press back. "We'll be friends forever. And I'm way better than some random guy, right?"

Morena cocked her head to the side (which looked super animalistic and creepy but was actually her listening pose) because she could hear the rumble of male voices from the living room. She picked up Pathfinder David's stentorian tones saying something about his human rights and trespassing.

But it didn't matter what he was saying. Anything he said was guaranteed to be awful, in her estimation, and reminded her exactly where this stupid romance app had gotten her.

The phone skittered across the carpeted floor toward Suzyn, who grabbed it up before Morena could change her mind.

"I can get a new one?" Morena confirmed, voice tremulous.

"Hells yes."

"But it's so pretty." She reached to get her phone back. Surely she could keep the iPhone without succumbing to the app's allure.

Suzyn stuffed the phone into her underwear band (she was still in her oversized nightshirt, after all). "The newest model will be even prettier. They come in colors, you know. Oooh, we can get you a case on Etsy."

"Kay," Morena agreed in a small voice. She eyed Suzyn's waistband, but propriety (even with her best friend) kept her at bay. She knew she had to stop, and she trusted Suzyn to keep her from making any more mistakes with the phone.

Suzyn slapped cupped palms against her nightshirt-covered thighs, and the painful-sounding crack put a definitive end to the conversation. "Let's go out there and see what your ex wants."

Following Suzyn and the phone into the living room, Morena said, "I haven't seen him since before he sent me the... Oh, you meant *him*. Hi, David."

Pathfinder David and Magic Guy had heaped the blankets

onto a couch arm and now they sat stiltedly, with perfect Victorian posture, side by side in the place the blankets had previously been. Magic Guy was sweating from the effort of trying to separate Pathfinder David from the iPhone (not that anyone knew why his forehead was shiny at cold o'clock a.m.), and Pathfinder David stared straight ahead at the black TV screen.

When Pathfinder David heard his name on Morena's lips, he surged forward and grabbed her arm in the same place he'd nearly bruised it the night before. His nails dug painful slices into her bared biceps. "C'mon," he said. "Pack up your things."

"Ummm," said Morena.

Suzyn sidled over to Magic Guy, keeping her eyes on Pathfinder David the whole time in case he tried anything more detrimental than holding her roommate in place. She whispered, "I got the phone. What do we do now?"

Pathfinder David frowned harder than a person who thinks they've found a perfect parking spot and then realizes it's in an inexplicably zoned area. Zone 11? Zone 7? Zone 12? What do they mean? Could you park there for two hours or for two hours only with a zone permit?

"I know you have suitcases," he said. "You're moving. Today." His eyes strayed to Suzyn, whom he'd never cared for. For some reason, he found himself staring at her tiny waist; at least he thought it was tiny beneath her giant sleep shirt. Too tiny, perhaps. But there was something about Suzyn this morning that called to him...

Morena didn't know why Pathfinder David wanted her to pack, especially since the three friends had only seen three houses so far (well, she'd only seen two, really). They weren't moving yet. They hadn't even had the chance to discuss the options fully, since Pathfinder David had interrupted everything the night before.

On the other side of the room, Magic Guy felt the air vibrating, astrally wrong and discordant. He knew the iPhone was still working its magic and drawing Pathfinder David to Morena. There had to be something *more* to its ownership than transferring hands. If he concentrated on seeing the flow of energies, he could detect the phone in Suzyn's pocket (oh, how he hoped it was in a pocket).

The device sucked at Morena and had bound Pathfinder David so strongly to itself that he was watching Suzyn and Morena equally. Clearly, taking the phone wasn't enough.

Magic Guy whispered back to Suzyn, "How did Morena get it?"

"It was a present from her ex."

Which meant that it had been explicitly transferred. Maybe that was the key. Magic Guy would just have to convince the current owner to gift it to him. "Hey, Morena?"

Pathfinder David talked for her. "Shut up," he said to someone. Magic Guy? Morena? "You're moving in with me. Now! Move it!"

"Ummm, no?" said Morena. She wasn't at her best in the mornings. Couldn't Pathfinder David have brought a coffee or something before he started making demands?

No, no he couldn't have. Because he hadn't known what was going to happen before he tried breaking in. He'd only known he had to be near her.

Magic Guy approached slowly, not wanting to scare Pathfinder David into doing anything drastic. "Hey, Morena?" he tried again. In response, Pathfinder David's nails bit deeper into Morena's arm as he pulled her closer to him, tautening her skin in an unpleasant manner. "I think I've figured out how to deal with everything. Can you give me the iPhone?"

"Whatever," said Morena. "Can you get this guy off me?"

Magic Guy checked the energy flow. Nothing had changed. "No, really," he said.

"Yes, really." Morena tried to tug her arm back, only to cause a fresh trickle of blood to slide down. She was briefly glad the blood wasn't going to get on her dry-clean-only jammies before she remembered to be annoyed that her friend wasn't helping her escape this jerk.

Magic Guy slumped over in the full-body expression of ultimate exasperation.

"Fine!" she yelled, making Pathfinder David flinch back from the explosion of noise near his ear. They jerked together, connected, but he righted himself easily enough with a dark look Morena ignored. She could yell if she wanted to. It was her apartment. "You can have the iPhone. I give it to you."

"Thank you," Magic Guy graciously accepted the gift. Suzyn handed it over to him.

Immediately, the phone cleared its memory. It synced itself to Magic Guy's current phone. It changed its number to match his. It connected itself to his credit cards and iTunes account.

No one knew it had done any of this.

What Magic Guy did know, however, was that the energy flow from Morena stopped. He saw the cord (the one that had been stringing Pathfinder David along) wink out of existence. The phone ate no energy, affected no minds. It was inert, harmless, *waiting*. A bundle of potential.

Pathfinder David's nails squelched as he extricated them

from Morena's arm. "What the hell?" he accused Morena. "What are you doing?" He didn't let her answer. "Whatever. I'm leaving."

And he did. Forever. No one knows where he went next, and no one really cares.

Magic Guy felt the phone's tendrils curling around his hand, nothing draining or desperate like they'd been for Morena. Just tentative little tendrils suggesting he swipe to unlock. It'd be so easy.

But Magic Guy knew better. He'd seen what happened when Morena opened it: immediate app loading. He wouldn't be sucked in.

Its affinity for him was so weak that it took almost no effort to slice the threads that bound it to him.

The iPhone turned off.

Suzyn headed for the medicine cabinet in the bathroom. "I'll get you some Bactine," she told Morena. Suzyn still preferred Bactine to any sort of natural cleanser, so sue her. You can put the girl in the Pacific Northwest, but you can't make her choose organic locavore foofy products.

In Magic Guy's hand, the iPhone turned itself back on. It pulsed gently, such a miniscule throb he could barely feel it. The screen lit with a message: *I'm lost. Please return me to—* and a name and address that Magic Guy could only assume it had gotten out of an area phone listing.

He bit his lip and squinted his eyes, hunting for all the unsettled threads and snapping them. The iPhone turned off.

Now that she'd given the phone to Magic Guy, Morena couldn't imagine the desperation that had driven her only minutes before. Yes, she'd always chosen texting over calling, ever since she'd had the choice, but she'd never cared for the apps that smartphones made her pay to use. She didn't play games much, used Instagram for maybe two months in 2012, and ranted in frustration whenever a mobile site offered fewer features than the full one.

Something about owning that phone, though... it had done something to her. "Aren't you worried?" she asked Magic Guy.

He shrugged, and if it was more bravado than surety, no one had to know. "What's the worst it can do to me? Make me go on a date?"

They both laughed at the idea of an asexual aromantic being forced to go on a date. The phone wouldn't be getting what it needed from Magic Guy.

In his hand, the phone turned on again. This time, when it sent out its ephemeral tendrils, it also drew on the earth. *Hah!* Magic Guy had known it would run out of internal power eventually. The "battery" it pulled from reminded him of Chidiock, a deep well connected to ley lines and aether.

But only on the surface. It wasn't Chidiock; he could tell. Even if the other elf hadn't learned a lesson about merging magic and technology, it didn't *smell* right. Chili powdery on the astral plane. Thankfully, Magic Guy was not called upon to explain this conjecture because his friends didn't believe in magic.

The screen lit, blue with a photo of a Dalmatian. *Help! I'm a lost phone. My owner is waiting for me! Please call—* and another number that the phone had acquired from who knew where. Well, it wouldn't be fooling anyone into passing it on from here. Not this time!

Magic Guy reached for all the energy in the room, even borrowing from the power outlet's electrical spark. With all the force of his 6,000-year old-anima, he burned away the connections to the iPhone's power sink.

The nearby ley lines shriveled and shook and bent around their little corner of Queen Anne Hill. The aether in the air smoked and singed, though the human women couldn't taste it in the backs of their nonexistent astral throats.

And the phone, finally, turned to a lump of clay and clockwork in Magic Guy's palm.

At that very moment in a modest house on Threadneedle Street in London (near the Bank of England), a mysterious inventor cursed. "Damn!" he said. For this inventor was also the originator of the iPhone and had been siphoning its energy to make himself effectively immortal.

His walls were decorated with defunct models of the tools he'd used for this purpose in the past: a wind-up watch, a pocket calculator, pieces from a wooden treadmill (and *that* had been a horrible idea). "There went another one."

If he'd known about it, Magic Guy would have felt a mixture of satisfaction and worry over this reaction. But he'd used up all his energy destroying the connection between the phone and its benefactor. And he'd never have known to eavesdrop on such a particular location, even if he had the vigor.

He flopped onto the earlier-abandoned couch. "Besides," Magic Guy added when Suzyn reappeared with the disinfectant, "my magical abilities should cancel out whatever's been done to this thing."

He didn't miss the dubious look Morena and Suzyn traded, but it didn't bother him. Whether they believed him or not, his true nature—the one he only hinted at during story games—would help his friends, and that made his face hurt with how wide his smile got.

It didn't matter what they believed or what he believed.

What mattered wasn't boyfriends or wanting a boyfriend.

What mattered was friendship, pure and simple. Their love for each other would help them stand against the world, would help them love themselves.

Agape conquers all.

"So," said Magic Guy, "that third house ticked all the boxes." He slid the earthen lump (which had once simulated an iPhone) into a mostly empty coffee mug. He could dump its contents in the compost bin later, and no one would be the wiser.

Suzyn said, "Let's buy it." She put a *Hello Kitty* Band-Aid on Morena's upper arm.

Morena laughed, at the impetuosity or the Band-Aid or both. "Why not?" she agreed. "So long as it's near a coffee shop."

Epilogue
Spring Green

Two weeks after the threesome decided to buy their Capitol Hill mansion, they moved in. The previous owners added a greenhouse to the backyard at Morena's behest, with the incentive of our heroes' taking possession near-immediately. As apology gifts went, she thought her mother would appreciate having a dedicated plot whenever she came to visit.

The greenhouse, though, was the only room appropriately full. In the main house, the threesome's meager furniture barely took up a corner of the huge rooms. They'd unloaded everything from their U-Haul in one trip.

Two couches in the large sitting parlor made the adjoining entryway (almost as wide as the parlor) seem conspicuously empty. Walking on the century-old hardwoods created a clicking echo—if a person were barefoot, it was more of a thunking echo—that could be heard all the way to the kitchen. No décor or furniture ate the sound, so everything was amplified.

Morena chose a room on the second floor and claimed two bathrooms, one of which had a claw-foot tub likely as old as the hardwoods.

Suzyn took over two rooms on the main floor, one for sleeping, which was big enough for a king-sized bed (she owned a full-size) and five dressers (she had *one*, which she wasn't using thanks to the walk-in closet). Her second room had a bay window, a fireplace, and an inspiring view of the soon-to-be-overgrown backyard; it was the ideal workroom for a graphic artist.

Magic Guy put his bed in the one finished room on the dilapidated third floor, preferring a view of the lake. He chose to think he was like a lake, still and calm but also deep and old.

In a nook in the kitchen, next to the French doors that led onto their honey-colored entertainment deck, they'd installed Magic Guy's tiny dining room table. It was a circle that could fit three people at best and would have looked silly in the dining room under the Michelangelo-inspired ceiling.

All the boxes were in the correct rooms, waiting to be unpacked. (Morena mostly owned clothes, so she'd had an easy time packing wardrobe boxes and would have an equally easy time unpacking them.) Their musty-moldy corrugated cardboard scent was barely noticeable in the oversized home.

Evening was falling, dusk darkening the rooms till the three friends hunted for light switches and hoped the previous owners had left behind light bulbs. (They had.) Magic Guy lounged against the kitchen counter next to the eight-burner gas stovetop.

"So," he said, "dinner?"

Suzyn folded herself over the butcher-block island in the center of the room. "I don't want to go anywhere. Also, I'm pretty sure we're broke now."

Magic Guy grinned at her. "I guess that leaves Morena to hunt our repast."

Suzyn raised her hand, seconding the motion.

Morena shrugged. She wanted to go outside and see the neighborhood anyway. "There's a QFC on Broadway."

Suzyn gave her a dollar for some Santitas, the tortilla chips that always cost $2 no matter where you bought them. Magic Guy chipped in a fiver for another bag and some avocados, saying, "We could make guacamole."

They owned a mansion in Capitol Hill, and they were going to eat cheap tortilla chips and guacamole for dinner on their first night in it. Why not? Morena warned, "You'd better find the blender while I'm out, then."

On her four-block walk up the steep hill to Broadway, Morena called her mother. "So, brunch this week?" she said as soon as Luiza picked up.

Luiza could have said something snarky in reply like *Now you want your mother?* or *I'm sorry; who is this?* But she didn't say those things, largely because she could understand that her daughter had been all twisted up by this Pathfinder David guy—which was the story that Magic Guy and Suzyn had sold her on, anyway. Luiza had heard all about Suzyn making Morena realize that supportive friends were there to *help*.

"I shouldn't have pushed you into a romantic relationship. I'm sorry," said Luiza. "You have wonderful, supportive friends. You're not going to be all alone like I worried you would be. I saw too much of myself in you, *minha filha*, and it's been so hard for me to live on my own

246

since your dad..." Luiza trailed off but quickly got back on track. "You make different relationship choices than I do, and that works for you."

What's more, those supportive friends hadn't taken over Morena's life when they'd intervened. They'd simply *been* there, bolstered Morena so that she could confidently make her own choices in the aftermath of this weird relationship. They'd been an example to Luiza: she had to take her own relationship advice; she had to trust in her daughter and her friends. Letting them help with her new florist business didn't necessarily mean losing herself, only that she'd gain a new perspective.

"Oh, Mãe," Morena sighed down the phone scramble. (Though half that sigh was from walking too quickly while also trying to hold a conversation. Did she need to work out more? No. But everyone wonders that when they get out of breath.) "I'm sorry too. Sorry I stopped taking your calls for a while."

"You were busy."

It was easy to let the excuse lie. So Morena did, but she was still going to make it up to her mother. "Anyway, I need to save money and eat at home now. So why don't you come over to our new place for this week's brunch?" The cars zipping down Broadway got louder the closer Morena got to her destination. (There was also less zipping and more stop-and-go.)

"That sounds marvelous." Unbeknownst to Luiza, Morena also wanted to show her mother the greenhouse space. She had bought and spread exotic soil herself! "Did I tell you I joined a small-business collective? I'm going to be learning Korean from a nice gentleman with a karaoke bar on your side of the lake. He says it'll expand my prospects." It might also

have been a date, but Luiza wasn't looking for that. Though...
if it *happened*...

"No way?" Morena could see the QFC on the corner. "Oh,
I'm almost to the store."

How domestic it all was, Luiza thought. "I told you Suzyn
would be great to settle down with, even if you two aren't
having sex."

"Mãe!" shrieked Morena. Luiza's laugh let her know it was
the reaction her mother had been going for. "I'll find someone
someday, yes, but I don't *need* someone. I have my friends,
and we're going to be friends forever."

That last statement was a true fact. Unfortunately for
Magic Guy. Who would outlive them all.

By the time mother and daughter hung up, Morena was
more than ready to get three bags of Santitas, a few avocados,
and two lemons and then get back to her new house and kick
up her feet on the tiny dining table. She probably should have
thought about her footwear before starting the trek.

Next time, she was driving, damn it.

The QFC was more convenient than any convenience
store, being open 24 hours. It smelled of bleach and apples
when she walked in, and she assumed that meant it was
clean. Her double side-zip ankle boots squeaked on the lino-
leum as she walked past the no-bake cookies (*One for 75
cents!*) on tired hooves. The cookies didn't smell like anything,
a side effect of not baking. Maillard reactions were an
important part of the cooking process.

The store's avocados looked sickly even under the exces-
sively yellow lights. They were pitted and mottled with black
spots. Morena wasn't going to be choosy, however. She didn't
actually know much about avocados, only that the sign above

these spotty things said AVOCADO. She picked one up and squeezed it, but had no way to judge the firmness or scent, so she stuck it in a plastic bag with two of its mates. Avocados down, lemons and Santitas to go.

On the other side of the green-and-black avocado mountain, a man wearing all green offered Morena a crooked smile. He was almost as tall as Suzyn, just shy of five-ten. His cable-knit cap pushed warm brown hair into one of his eyes, and a little tuft escaped out the back like it wanted to play with the half-stubble-half-beard on his chin. His gray-green scarf wound around his neck and shoulders over an emerald wool pea coat. Even his eyes shone green, though maybe that was the store lighting.

He was simultaneously the scruffiest and the most put-together man Morena had ever seen. And he was definitely the most beautiful.

"A travesty, right?"

"What?" She hadn't expected the hot guy at the grocery store to chat with her. She checked her pockets to make sure she hadn't accidentally taken the iPhone back from Magic Guy, but no. She only had her Samsung.

The Green Man gestured at the mound of pock-marked fruits. "The avocados? They're a travesty?"

Morena couldn't have said yes or no, and her face reflected that truth.

He laughed, then. And extended a hand to shake. "I'm Nicholas." His fingers felt smooth, and Morena glimpsed perfectly manicured nail beds.

They spoke for a few more minutes and exchanged phone numbers. A few months back, Morena could never have had a polite conversation with a stranger (at least, not without some serious anxiety). And a few weeks back, she'd never have met a nice guy, not with the iPhone picking her paramours for her.

And now here she was: with live-in friends, a house that her mother would be proud of, and the phone number of a supremely good-looking man.

Morena was smiling as she went through the QFC's self-checkout, not caring anymore how sore her ankles would be by the time she'd climbed back to the mansion. Her life was looking pretty awesome right now.

And so ends the story of a girl and her iPhone. Or rather, of a middle-aged woman and her two best friends.

STOP HERE IF YOU'RE HAPPY WITH THIS ENDING.
NO, REALLY.
I MEAN IT.

Continued...

That's pretty much the end of the story for Suzyn and Morena, but what about Magic Guy?

Later in 2014

Chidiock backed the Spygame Kickstarter project. When his Kickstarter reward went out, Magic Guy sent a personal letter with it. Finally, Magic Guy was ready to see his old friend again, whenever Chidiock was up for it.

2034

Chidiock wrote back! He'd dealt with his abandonment issues and mourned their Georgiana. His letter suggested a reunion in the style of an evaluative coffee date, so Morena and Suzyn sent Magic Guy to a downtown Starbucks. They called him at 20-minute intervals so that he'd have an excuse to escape if it wasn't going well. Morena actually did suffer a small paper cut, which would have made an acceptable "emergency," but Magic Guy was having too much fun chatting about Chidiock's life in Johannesburg to come home.

2064

As Morena entered her nineties, Magic Guy decided that he really did want to have a long-lived friend around again. These newfangled ones didn't last. He and Chidiock became steady pen pals.

2072

Morena's age and the state of modern medicine came to an unfortunate intersection for Morena. This drove Magic Guy farther in Chidiock's metaphorical arms. The other elf flew to Seattle to keep him company until Suzyn died as well. Then the two of them left behind the Capitol Hill mansion to inhabit a cozy condo in Montreal. Chidiock liked to say he only wanted a roommate so he'd "always have someone to blame when the dishes weren't done," but it was clear that their centuries of affection only deepened with each passing decade.

Second Epilogue
2164: Friends Till The End

One hundred and fifty years is a long time for mortals. One hundred and fifty years can see the change from the Industrial Age to the Technological. It could change Seattle from a wild hinterland to a city with raised sidewalks to a place with a Ferris wheel that no locals would ride.

One hundred and fifty years was not, however, a particularly long time for Magic Guy. It was more of a rounding error. Or it had been. He'd lived alongside his mortal friends, encouraging their dreams and passions, watching the changes in their bodies and their situations. He'd become "Uncle Magic Guy" to two children, and then to the children's children and the children's children's children.

Suzyn and Morena's "happily ever after" had included lifelong friendship, a fashionable mansion, and families of their own when the time came. Magic Guy's happily ever after ended when they died. And then it began again, after reconciling with his old friend.

But on this day, this anniversary, one hundred and fifty years after he'd moved into the Capitol Hill home with his friends, he came back. He wanted to honor the ones who'd taught him to love again, to rejoin society.

He brought coffee with him.

"Wait here." And he left Chidiock outside with the transportation and rang the old-fashioned bell, which hadn't been changed since probably 1950.

A golden-skinned, acne-pocked teenager opened the door wide. "Can I help you?"

"Is your, ah, grandparent here?"

The kid shrugged and closed the door in Magic Guy's face, leaving him in the graying afternoon light.

The door reopened, and the man behind it gasped. His face split on a wide smile that showed off straight white teeth that would've been the envy of any octogenarian in previous generations but were now utterly unremarkable. "Uncle Geoffrey! Welcome home!"

He'd gone by Geoffrey for a while, he thought.

After a round of hugs, Magic Guy headed into the backyard. In one nearly overgrown corner of the acreage, hidden behind a koi pond and next to the greenhouse that Morena had built for Luiza, he found a stone bench. Its jagged edges pushed into the backs of his knees, and the cold seeped into his bones, but that didn't matter.

He poured a libation of coffee over each of five gravesites, Suzyn's and Morena's and their spouses' and Luiza's. "I miss you guys," he said, falling back into the early-2000s vernacular. "I'm still taking care of the kids and stuff, when I get a chance. Chidiock and I are cool again, thanks to you, so... yeah. Sorry I don't come around much, but you know how it is. Bigger and better places."

He took a sip of his own coffee. "I played the game last week with some friends who hadn't heard of it. They liked all the names we decided not to call it. I remember the three of us giggling over *spy vs. spy vs. spy vs. spy*, but no one gets the *Mad Magazine* joke anymore."

He stayed with his friends a while longer until the silence and the cold coffee became too depressing. Then he gave one last round of hugs to the kids and the kids' kids, etc.

"Come back sooner next time!" called the oldest.

The teenagers stayed in their rooms, avoiding all the cuddling with a family member they didn't even know because *ugh, no*.

And Magic Guy collected Chidiock, got in their vehicle, and let himself be driven to their shared home on the supernatural side of Portland.

"You gonna be all right, buddy?" Chidiock asked, also in the 2000s-slang spirit.

"Yeah, I'll be fine. I just need some company right now. Hey, remember mini golf? There's gotta be a place to play on the way down."

Friendship continues. Agape conquers all. Romance might be nice, but who needs it anyway?

THE END

Author's Afterword

Cracked! is set very firmly in 2013 Seattle and is full of middle-class geekery. As such, the iPhone is a 4S model, the man from the Ukraine isn't worried about rioting yet, and so on. Writers are often warned against being too contemporary. "Don't use slang!" advice columnists say. "You'll be dated if you go too deeply into certain details."

But when I read E.B. White's *Here Is New York* for the first time (in 2012), I realized you could do such a thing on purpose. White's essay was dated the second it came out, and it's a beautiful slice in the life and times of a writer at that exact period.

I think of *Cracked!* as a love letter to the Seattle I lived in during 2013.

If E.B. White can do it, so can I.

Author's Apologies

To the people who play Pathfinder at Wayward on Tuesday night: If any of you are named David, I am so, so sorry. I swear I started writing this novel before you started playing there.

To anyone who hates product placement: I didn't get paid for any of the name-dropping. It was all chosen in the name of setting and characterization.

To the anonymous gentleman who explained all about Seattle's cocaine-purchasing system: thank you for your expertise. I hope I got it right.

Also By Janine A. Southard

Novellas
These Convergent Stars (2013)

Short Stories
"Prophesy Murder" (2014)
"Maintaining a Free Mars" (2014)

The Hive Queen Saga
Queen & Commander – IPPY award silver medal winner for best Science Fiction, Fantasy, or Horror eBook (2013)
Hive & Heist (2014)
"The Robot Who Stole Herself" (2014)

Book Group Discussion Questions

1. *Cracked! A Magic iPhone Story* is supposed to be a love letter to Seattle. Does it succeed? If you were going to tell people about your home town, what would you mention?

2. This novel is firmly set in 2013. It was dated before it even went on sale. What are some of the big changes that have occurred between 2013 and now? Do you think the author should update the book yearly to allow for these changes?

3. Early on, Morena believes that getting married will guarantee an end to loneliness. Clearly, she changes her mind. Do you agree with her at either extreme? Would you want to give up on romance if it guaranteed you the chance to live permanently with your best friend?

4. The first epilogue has a happy, potentially-romantic ending. The second epilogue, with Magic Guy 150 years in the future, is more bittersweet. Why do you

think the author wrote the second epilogue? Do you like it? Would *you* have ended the story at the first one?

5. Morena's mother is starting a business, even though she may already be at retirement age. Is there ever a "too late" to start a business? Can you think of a business you would want to start if you had the time and money?

6. This novel was made possible with crowdfunding (via Kickstarter). In Morena's 2013 Seattle, Kickstarter was very popular, first for games and then for everything else. What do you think of crowdfunding books?

About the Author

Janine A. Southard is the IPPY-award-winning author of *Queen & Commander* (and other books in The Hive Queen Saga). She lives in Seattle, WA, where she writes speculative fiction and reads it aloud to her cat. She's story gamed a few times and hopes to someday make a tie-in game for this novel, but first she needs to finish writing all the other books on her list.

To get a free short story and stay up-to-date with her releases, sales, and appearances, join her mailing list.
http://bit.ly/janinenews

Visit her on the Web: http://www.janinesouthard.com
Interact on Twitter: http://www.twitter.com/jani_s